"Sonya Lalli's charming novel explores how our relationships define us. Through honesty, humor, and vulnerability, Serena Singh reminds us that new, fulfilling connections are possible at any age. This equal parts relatable and entertaining story is a delight from start to finish!"
—Saumya Dave, author of *Well-Behaved Indian Women*

"Heartfelt and forthright, Lalli's culturally rich work of women's fiction is exceptional." —*Booklist* (starred)

"From yoga studios to finding oneself in trips abroad to online dating, Lalli gives readers a wonderful novel about love and belonging and meaning of happiness and home."
—Soniah Kamal, award-winning author of *Unmarriageable: Pride and Prejudice in Pakistan*

"Author Lalli's prose is deft, her characters are delightful and her book is the just-right holiday romance." —*USA Today*

"Anu's struggle to find herself is wrought with obstacles, and [is] sometimes frustrating, but the resolution of her story is both satisfying and realistic. A moving look at one woman's journey between her family and her desire for independence." —*Kirkus Reviews*

"Sonya Lalli offers up a tale of familial pressures, cultural traditions, and self-discovery that is equal turns heartbreaking and hilarious. . . . Lalli tears down stereotypes with humor and warmth."
—*Entertainment Weekly*

"An engaging love story that delivers on the promise of true love forever. . . . *The Matchmaker's List* comes through in spades (and hearts)."
—NPR

"Lalli's sharp-eyed tale of cross-cultural dating, family heartbreak, the strictures of culture, and the exuberance of love is both universal and timeless." —*Publishers Weekly* (starred review)

## Titles by Sonya Lalli

# Jasmine
# and Jake
# Rock
# the Boat

∿∿

# SONYA LALLI

BERKLEY ROMANCE
New York

BERKLEY ROMANCE
Published by Berkley
An imprint of Penguin Random House LLC
penguinrandomhouse.com

Library of Congress Cataloging-in-Publication Data

Names: Lalli, Sonya, author.
Title: Jasmine and Jake rock the boat / Sonya Lalli.
Description: First Edition. | New York: Berkley Romance, 2023.
Identifiers: LCCN 2022045382 (print) | LCCN 2022045383 (ebook) |
ISBN 9780593440650 (trade paperback) | ISBN 9780593440667 (ebook)
Subjects: LCGFT: Novels.
Classification: LCC PR6112.A483 J37 2023 (print) | LCC PR6112.A483 (ebook) |
DDC 823/.92—dc23/eng/20220926
LC record available at https://lccn.loc.gov/2022045382
LC ebook record available at https://lccn.loc.gov/2022045383

First Edition: April 2023

Printed in the United States of America
1st Printing

BOOK DESIGN BY KATY RIEGEL

*For*

*Anju, Georgia,*

*Heather, Annie,*

*and Jane*

# Jasmine and Jake
# Rock the Boat

# Chapter 1

~~~~~~

MY EYES WERE playing tricks on me, because there was absolutely no way I actually saw what I just witnessed through
the peephole.

I rested my back against the front door, steadying my breath.
I must have been hallucinating. It was 6:19 in the morning and I
hadn't had any coffee yet. It was a caffeine- and sleep-deprived
dream. *Yes*. I still hadn't woken up.

I made a move for Amber's high-end DeLonghi espresso machine, but then stopped short when I heard murmurs in the hallway. My heartbeat quickened. Pressing my hand over my mouth,
I shuffled backward and squinted through the peephole.

Oh god. I hadn't imagined it.

"You are *amazing*," a mystery woman murmured, as she made
out with my ex-boyfriend, Brian, with the vigor of someone sending their man off to war. "I could go again, you know."

I dry heaved as he grunted a response and cupped her ass. I
knew I should retreat, but I couldn't tear my eyes away from them.
The door to his condo—which, until three weeks ago, had been

*our* condo—was halfway open, and the way she was pushing him against the frame made me wonder if they were going to "go again" right there in the hall.

My mind started racing as I watched them smooch like their lives depended on it, a million conflicting emotions sucker punching me in the gut.

*Is this just a hookup or a new girlfriend?*

*I don't care.*

*I obviously care.*

*He's such a douchebag for moving on so quickly.*

*But he was* my *douchebag.*

*I'm going to go out there and tell him off.*

*I am way too classy to go out there and tell him off—*

"I better get ready for work," I heard Brian say, as he pulled away from Mystery Woman and cut off the chorus of voices in my head. She unlatched her lips from his, and for first time in three weeks, I looked at him. I'd had my fair share of post-breakup run-ins over the years, and awkward small talk with an ex in the produce section, or at a mutual friend's birthday party, always got easier. But the first time cut like a freshly sharpened knife.

Brian looked good, unfortunately, so the hex Amber and I had (jokingly?) cast on him last Friday had failed in its magic. He had blond hair, sharp features, and piercing blue eyes that could have claimed their own Instagram filter. He looked handsome in a suit, which he wore eighty-five percent of the time, and was even better looking in his natural element at home, when he dressed like a jock. Basketball shorts, baseball hats, football jerseys. This morning, he was sporting all three.

"Aw, really?" Mystery Woman, who was facing away from me, cocked her perfectly curvaceous hip to the side. "Isn't there an Egg-scelent just around the corner? Should we grab an early breakfast?"

*Excuse* me? I cracked my neck and rolled out my shoulders, preparing myself to go out there if he said yes. Eggscelent was *our* brunch spot. Thank god Amber was well paid and chose me over Brian in the breakup. I might just need her to bail me out of jail.

"I think it opens at six thirty." She glanced at her watch. "Maybe—"

"Sorry," Brian said limply. "I should really get going . . ."

Mystery Woman pressed her hands into Brian's chest, sighing. "I suppose I gotta go get ready for work, too." She paused. "When will I see you again?"

Brian crossed his arms so Mystery Woman had to withdraw her hand, and a smirk crept onto my lips. Was he trying to blow her off? Brian had fixed his gaze on the floor, disinterest and exhaustion plain as day on his face. Mystery Woman and I bided our time through what was becoming a long, and painful, moment of silence.

"Of course," Brian mumbled eventually, although it wasn't an answer to her question. "Sure, sure. But I have this big project this week . . ."

"Oh yeah? Which one?"

"You don't know it." Brian glanced at the Apple Watch on his left wrist, and even though I was mad at him for moving on so quickly, I suddenly wanted to hit him. God, he could be such a douchebag. Mystery Woman clearly liked him, and he was emotionally kicking her to the curb.

"Then I'll see you around sometime?" she continued, achingly oblivious.

"Totally," Brian said listlessly. "I'll give you a call."

"Awesome." Mystery Woman flipped her hair and then gave him one more long, agonizing (for me) kiss. "Give Mango a hug goodbye for me, would you?"

Finally, the woman turned to leave and I saw her face. I sighed out in relief to see that she was at least in her late twenties, because even though Brian was a giant turd, at least he wasn't a mid-thirties creep who went after much younger women. Brian watched her saunter down the hall, and as soon as she pressed the elevator button, without another word, he went back inside.

To *our* former home.

To wake up *our* goldendoodle, Mango.

I was livid, and irritated, and caffeine deficient, and not in my right mind—not thinking at all, actually—because the moment Brian closed his door, I flung open the one in front of me and raced down the hall.

Mystery Woman, who was acting all cool and collected and very unlike me, gracefully held open the elevator door as I hurled my body through the closing doors. I nodded in thanks. She was pretty. Like, extremely pretty. With no makeup. Under *fluorescent* lighting!

"Morning," she greeted me, when she caught me staring. Her lips curled upward into a genuine smile.

Oh great. She made small talk with strangers. She was nice, too.

"Morning," I said breezily.

She blinked, studying my face. Did she recognize me? No. We'd never met before, and even if Mystery Woman knew about my existence and followed Brian on Instagram, there was no way for her to connect the dots. Brian only posted pictures of crowds of Seahawks fans at Lumen Field, dumbbells at the gym, or blurry shots of Mango at the dog park. He had the same affinity for social media as his seventy-year-old mother.

"You live in the building?" Mystery Woman asked perkily.

"Just across the hall from Brian," I said, which I probably

shouldn't have, judging by the look of horror that flashed across her face. "Sorry." I grimaced. "I saw you two together in the hall."

She played nervously with her hands. "Oh. Shoot. Sorry about that."

"No worries." I hesitated. "Have you—uh—been together long?"

Mystery Woman studied me carefully, assessing my intentions, which was fair, because I wasn't sure if they were good or not. Her eyes tracked up and down, taking note of my monochromatic outfit composed of wide-legged Everlane trousers, a crop top and blazer from Reformation, and combat boots. My medium-length straight hair, the owl-rimmed glasses I only wore to work, and my "effortless" makeup, which actually took me a full twenty minutes and required nine of the fifteen Sephora products I had in rotation. I looked good. And until I caught Brian in the hall with another woman, I felt good.

Now, I was leaning hard into jealous ex-girlfriend stereotypes and trying to figure out if Brian had been a cheating douchebag.

Now, I felt about two inches tall.

"We're not together," she said quietly. "We're coworkers. Well, we work for the same company. He's downtown at HQ, and I'm at the customer service center out in the boonies."

"I see—"

"I met him at the Christmas party last year," she continued rambling. "And then yesterday there was this work drinks thing. I wasn't sure he'd be there, but I've been, well . . ."

She trailed off, embarrassed, and I wasn't sure how to feel. I was relieved that this was new and Brian hadn't cheated, but also angry that she'd just spent the night in the bedroom I decorated, on the memory foam mattress I picked out, with the man *I* had called my partner for over four years.

Curiously, I also felt bad for her.

"Anyway," she mumbled. "You're his neighbor, then?"

When the elevator pinged and the door slid open, I launched into a brisk walk, but she stayed in step with me as I marched toward the front entrance.

"We've both lived in the building for a few years," I said, which was technically true.

"What's your name?"

*Jasmine Randhawa. Your crush's ex-girlfriend.*

"*Oh.* Are you Amber? His neighbor across the hall?"

"Yes," I wheezed, grateful for the prompt. "That's me!"

"Brian mentioned you." She beamed. "You both bought condos in the building around the same time. And your girlfriend's name is Danica. You two are long-distance, right?"

"You have a good memory," I said blandly. And she had been *clearly* thirsting after my man for a while, although I didn't say that part out loud. Brian was no longer "my man."

We reached the revolving door. Mystery Woman went first, and when I jostled through, she was on the other side waiting for me, chewing her lip. It was my turn to be friendly. At the very least, I could smile and ask her *her* name. But I supposed I didn't really want to know. If she told me, I would waste my entire Friday stalking her on social media.

"I don't mean to be weird," she said, playing with the tassel on her purse. We walked in step to the sidewalk. "But can I ask you a question?"

I held my breath.

"What do you think about Brian?" She paused. "He's nice, right?"

If she was asking me if he was "nice," then she already her doubts.

*Brian was nice but emotionally unavailable.*

*No, tell her he's emotionally* disturbed . . .

The early-morning sun shone brightly down on us through scattered clouds, and just then, I noticed that Mystery Woman was more than just pretty. She was real. She was developing wrinkles, like all women our age. Her shoulders were stiff with discomfort. And she had a clear-eyed, totally lovestruck gaze, which told me she didn't just deserve a guy who was nice enough to call her back, but a guy who would be enthusiastic about doing so.

She deserved a man who fit in with her friends and took an interest in and respected her career; someone who made best efforts to change his juvenile, macho behavior he'd never bothered to grow out of; a lover who, after a few years together, wouldn't treat her like a roommate or grow to find her quirks annoying instead of cute; a boyfriend who wouldn't be on his phone all through dinner, but then complain if she spent more than five minutes on Instagram; a partner who noticed when she got a haircut or dressed up for a date, and didn't make condescending jokes about her family, and constantly made her feel bad about *everything*, and—

"You deserve better," I said suddenly, deciding to go with honesty. Mystery Woman's mouth gaped, and blood rushed to my head as I turned on my heels and walked away. It was 6:25 in the morning, and she'd just hooked up with a guy she really liked, and yes, it was cruel, but my words weren't coming from a place of jealousy, or pain, or meanness, but of sisterhood.

She did deserve better than Brian. And as I started to throw myself a pity party about why nobody had cautioned me, a sharp pain shot through my chest at the possibility that maybe I *had* been warned. I'd just never bothered to listen.

# Chapter 2

*Five months earlier*

I T'S STILL RAINING," I declared, tossing my keys on the counter.
Absorbed in his latest video game purchase, Brian didn't
answer, but Mango trotted over to say hello. I bent down, kissed
her, petted her, rubbed her belly, but when I tried to pick her up,
she decided that was enough. Yawning, she rolled her way back
to her doggy bed by the balcony door.

"Earth to Brian," I said lazily, peeling off my raincoat. "I'm
*hooome.*"

"Oh, hey." His eyes darted my way and then landed back on
the television. "How were drinks?"

I shrugged, stashing my coat in the closet. "All the new mar-
keting hires are so *young*. They're still out."

"What time is it?"

I glanced at the microwave clock and frowned. It was only
eight p.m. Even for a Tuesday, I supposed it wasn't that late.

I changed into my pajamas, pulled on some dry socks, and
then shuffled back out to the living room with a new thriller

Amber had lent me. I settled into the other side of the sectional, curling my feet up as I fired up TikTok. I'd scrolled through nearly a dozen videos before I remembered I'd pledged to cut down on screen time in the evening. I tucked my phone under a pillow and opened the book.

"Have you read this yet?" I asked Brian, showing him the cover. He didn't answer as his thumb furiously battled the Xbox controller, and various angry men, dragons, and other monsters on screen shot one another's faces off. The Sonos sound bar boomed as a grenade went off somewhere. I winced.

"Would you mind turning it down?"

"One minute."

Sighing, I relaxed back into the couch. I hadn't read more than a page, when another bomb exploded.

"Seriously, Brian. Can you use headphones or something?"

"You weren't home." There was a long pause as his thumbs shot down an aircraft. I scoffed, but before I could say anything more, Brian threw his hands up in the air.

"Jesus. Give me a fucking minute, all right?"

My jaw clenched as I looked up to study him. One of us biting the other's head off within three minutes of arriving home was par for the course. Some couples go ballroom dancing or play tennis after work. The game Brian and I had been playing these days was far more exhausting.

My nose ran inexplicably as I wondered if this time I was in the wrong, or if he was. But did it even matter? Even after those rare fights that had a resolution, where Brian or I admitted we'd made a mistake and apologized for it, why did it still always feel like I lost?

"I'm going to go for a run," I said quietly. Wiping my nose with my sleeve, I stood up from the couch, but Brian caught my hand. I closed my eyes, my fingers interlacing with his as he gently pulled me back down beside him.

"Are you pissed now?" he grunted.

"No." I turned to face him, breathing hard. "I've just been sitting in a chair all day. I'm feeling antsy."

"It's dark outside."

I gestured out the window to the Seattle skyline. "It's always dark here in January."

"Well. I don't think she wants to go," Brian said. "Look at her. She was at day care today. She's tired."

Ignoring Brian, I went over to Mango and squatted down. As soon as I started petting her chin, she opened one eye and made a noise that by now we knew meant, *I want to sleep, so if you don't mind, human, please fuck right off.*

"See?" Brian smiled.

I nodded in defeat. "All right."

My plan to exercise abandoned, I fetched two bottles of Stella from the fridge, handed one to Brian, and slumped back into the couch.

"Have you eaten?"

He shook his head. "I'm beat. I don't feel like cooking."

"Me, neither."

I scrolled through our recent orders on Uber Eats as Brian resumed his Xbox game on silent.

"Pizza?"

Brian didn't answer, so I kept scrolling.

"That Malaysian place last week was pretty good. But the noodles could have been spicier."

Still no response. Machine gun fire erupted on some mythical world.

"Oh!" I smiled, typing in the app's search bar. "I know. Amber told me about this Jamaican restaurant that delivers—"

"Jesus," Brian snapped. "Do you ever stop talking? Just pick!"

I was throwing my phone at Brian's head before I fully realized what I was doing. Luckily, it missed, sideswiping his shoulder and flying straight into the wall. I grimaced.

"Nice," he said, tossing his controller on the seat next to him. "You could have hit Mango."

I ignored him. "You can't talk to me like that. I don't care if the stock market tanked, or the gym was busy, or whatever the hell happened today to put you in that mood."

"OK," he said, "OK."

"I was trying to order us dinner."

"I don't care what we eat," Brian mumbled, tossing his controller on the coffee table. "I was in the middle of a game. Just pick something."

"Last time I 'just picked,' you complained it stank up the condo."

"Well," he said testily, "that's because Indian food *stinks*."

I clenched my jaw, resisting the urge to throw something else heavy at his torso. Like a lamp. Or that TV Brian never turned off.

"Speaking of Indian food," I said icily, as I got up to retrieve my phone from the floor. (There were no cracks. Phew.) "We're having dinner at my parents' house on Friday. Mom's cooking chicken curry, so be sure to wear a garbage bag you can throw out after."

"What?" Brian cried, ignoring my snide comment. "Why didn't you get us out of it?"

"I don't want to . . ." I slumped back into the couch, took a swig of my beer. "Sam is visiting Niki this weekend."

"So," he said slowly, "your sister's boyfriend comes to town, and everyone has to drop what they're doing? It's a waste of a Friday night."

"Firstly," I said, impatience turning to rage in my belly, "I want to see Sam. Secondly—" I glared at Brian. "When was the last time *you* had plans on a Friday night?"

Brian met me with a death stare of his own. I knew it was a low blow, but he was being a douchebag and deserved it. Brian was a few years older that I was, and all of his closest "bros" either had a new baby, a new spouse, or a new special someone they'd rather hang out with. And by all of his bros, I meant *every* single one of them. Unfortunately for Brian, he hadn't had to make new friends since his first year at the uppity private school he'd attended. He didn't know how to make them.

We didn't talk for a few minutes, choosing to angrily drink our beer instead. Eventually, my stomach started growling so loud that I caved and punched in our go-to banh mi order on Uber Eats and handed my phone to Brian. He nodded, clicked "place order," and then tossed it back to me.

"We're in a rut," I said to the wall, a few minutes later. Brian was still just sitting there, his video game on pause.

"I know."

My chest tightened. I'd expected him to ignore me, like he usually did when I threw out similar conversation starters that he called "attempts to provoke him."

"What do you want to do about it?" I asked hesitantly.

"There's nothing to do."

"Yeah. Winter here is brutal sometimes." I paused, suddenly worried he'd suggest a last-minute getaway, somewhere hot and expensive and unaffordable, but he didn't.

"It's not just the weather, Jasmine," he said, staring at his hands. "It's . . . everything."

Was he *finally* talking to me about "us"? After how many months of poking and prodding? I held my breath.

"What do you mean?" I whispered.

"What are we even doing anymore?"

I shrugged, my gut twisting with uncertainty. Brian crossed his left leg over his right and sighed.

"Maybe we should go to couples therapy." I laughed dismissively, even though I was serious. Two weeks earlier, I'd even researched counselors.

"Why would we do that?"

"I dunno . . . to fix our *problems*?"

"Jasmine," he said, still refusing to look at me, "I don't think we can fix us."

"How do you know? We haven't tried."

"I . . . don't . . ."

Brian finally met my gaze, and suddenly, I understood. All the times he didn't want to talk. All the evenings he spent sulky and withdrawn, and chose work, the gym, video games, or even doing laundry over having to speak to me. All the times he said no to sex, or date night, or anything even a little spontaneous. All the bickering and fights he cut short, rather than battling through to a resolution.

All the times he didn't say out loud what he'd been trying to tell me all along.

*I don't want to try.*

To Brian, our relationship was already over. He was just too fucking lazy to tell me.

"It's not like we were planning on getting married," Brian said eventually.

My hands trembling, I sipped from my beer bottle and fought the urge to cry. The day before I moved in with Brian, Mom had yelled at me for over two hours about how shameful and inappropriate it was to live with a man before marriage, especially a "no good one" like Brian. Her views were backward, so I'd ignored her disapproval and threats of disownment and gone ahead with the move.

"We don't have fun anymore," Brian added a minute later, and I thought back to what Niki had asked me, as we unpacked my clothes and hung them in Brian's closet.

*Are you sure this is what you want?*

*Do Brian and you want the same things?*

Yes, I'd told her, because at the time we both wanted to have fun. We didn't take life too seriously and were always up for an adventure, a good time, or a laugh. It's what made our relationship feel so good, seemingly worth the family drama.

But maybe there were other things we never talked about—that we *still* didn't talk about—more than four years later. How we felt about all our friends and relatives getting engaged and married, and whether we might follow suit with a wedding of our own. If we pictured ourselves as parents.

If we pictured a future together at all.

"You're right," I said stiffly. "You never wanted to marry me."

"Jasmine . . ." Brian reached for me, but I shook him off and checked on our Uber Eats order. Our banh mi was due to arrive in fifteen minutes, and I promised myself this breakup would be over by the time our delivery driver knocked on the door.

And that I wouldn't waste another second on a man I should never have been serious about in the first place.

# Chapter 3

～～～

Rowan: Jasmine! HR asked me to bug you
again about using your vacation days.
Apparently you still have two weeks unused
from last year?? How about you take it this
month? Let's discuss tomorrow.

I SWITCHED OFF MY computer, feeling a little smug that it was
only three o'clock and I got to leave early. I worked in the animation department of a trendy mixed-media company in downtown Seattle, and because the higher-ups were deathly afraid of
driving out millennial and Gen-X talent, they allowed for "flexi-
ble hours." While most of my colleagues took advantage by showing up hungover at eleven and working late, these days I arrived
at the crack of dawn and peaced out before half of them ordered
lunch.

I'd been paranoid about getting a 3D character just right for
an ongoing campaign and impressing my manager Rowan, so I
barely had time to think about Brian and his Mystery Woman

until my walk home. Brian and I were currently three weeks into our third attempt to break up, and each time we ended things, I moved into Amber's spare bedroom across the hall because half my stuff was still in his place. Because we had Mango to care for. Because he wasn't *always* such a douchebag and could be really sweet when he put in the effort. Because most of the time I secretly enjoyed the comforts of being in a serious relationship. Because...

I let out a squeal of frustration, startling the woman speed walking next me. There were so many reasons I tried to make it work with Brian for so long, but they were no longer good enough.

At the end of the day, Brian didn't want to marry me or have children together. It had felt like a crushing blow, but lately I'd been wondering if he'd more so bruised my ego than my heart. Did I even want to marry *him*? I massaged my stiff left shoulder as I weaved through other pedestrians and concluded that literally *anyone* else would be a better match. When I stopped at a pedestrian light, I noticed the silver fox waiting next to me and gave him the up and down. Brian had moved on; maybe I needed to move on, too. At the very least, I needed a *rebound*, preferably a smoke show who was partial to getting frisky in the condo building's communal spaces right under Brian's dumb nose.

I bit my lip, hoping the foxy gentleman would make eye contact. He had Henry Golding vibes, and looked not that much older than me. I flicked my eyes at his left hand. OK, maybe not him. Maybe he was a little married.

I scanned the four corners of the intersection, my eyes stopping at the guy in head-to-toe Lycra standing next to his bicycle across the street. It was hard to tell from this distance, but he was pretty cute. Maybe a little young. I straightened my shoulders and thought about how I might initiate a rendezvous, but then the walk light went green and he stepped in the road. The soles of his sneakers flashed neon blue and purple.

Ugh. Maybe not him, either.

Back at Amber's condo, I slipped into my Lululemon high-rise tights and New Balance running shoes and then picked up Mango from Brian's. She was so excited to see me that she un-learned her obedience training and jumped up to hug me, knocking me back against the door, and I was so excited to see her that I didn't scold her when she licked me all over my face.

Back when the relationship was still OK—not great, but it hadn't gotten bad yet, either—I'd been the one to float the idea of getting a dog. A few weeks later, Brian came home with Mango, a two-year-old full-size goldendoodle whose former owner, Brian's distant cousin, was about to move in with a boyfriend who was deathly afraid of dogs. We couldn't believe our luck. Mango was gentle, and sweet, and cuddly, and took to both of us right away. But what we didn't know was that goldendoodles were expensive, high energy, and hard work. And Brian and I weren't used to putting anyone or anything ahead of what we wanted, not even each other.

Getting a dog may have been the catalyst to us ending our relationship, but it made both of us a lot happier, too. No matter how much Brian and I fought or bickered or ignored each other, at least we had Mango. Most of the time, the only thing Brian and I agreed on was how much we loved her.

We took the elevator down to the lobby, and then Mango and I started running toward Myrtle Edwards Park. It had become our afternoon routine three or four times a week, while Brian was still at work and I could spend time with her without risk of bumping into him. I tried to focus on my breathing, the sun on my face, my perfect dog, the fact that I was about to see my little sister, Niki, after several months. But my mind was going faster than my legs, and I spent the next four miles ruminating about Mystery Woman; if my living situation with Amber was sustainable; how just the thought of cannonballing back into the dating pool scared the crap out of me; if the 3D character I'd just created was up to snuff; about my bank account balance; about how, these days, I just couldn't help but feel like a total waste of space.

Drenched in sweat, I found myself back near the condo building, panting on the sidewalk as Mango lapped up water from the doggy water fountain by the postbox.

I smiled, watching her. She was so happy after a run. It made me feel happy.

Well, it made me *want* to feel happy.

I took an artsy picture of Mango, posted it on Instagram, and then reluctantly left her at Brian's. After I showered, I packed a weekend bag, ordered Amber a surprise pizza to be sent to her office, and then hopped into my Lexus. I had less than an eighth of a tank of gas, but absent major traffic jams other than the usual rush hour hell, I'd just make it to my parents' house.

Mom and Dad still lived in the same house I'd grown up in, about a half hour away in the suburbs. On the drive out there, I blared my favorite pop radio station and psyched myself up for forty-eight hours under the same roof. I barely went home to visit, even less so now that Niki—who had recently moved to LA to be with her now fiancé, Sam—wasn't around to mediate. The front door was unlocked, and I tossed my bag on the floor, announcing my arrival as if I were holding court. Nobody answered. I could hear them talking in the living room. I peered around the corner.

"Good evening," I said in my most offensive British accent.

My eyes landed on Niki. "Jasmine Kaur Randhawa. Thirty-three. Fabulous. Glamorous. And at your *service*."

I curtsied, and by the time I was standing upright, Niki had launched herself across the room and was squeezing the oxygen out of my lungs with a bear hug.

"Good to see you, too," I laughed, wrapping my arms around her. "How was your flight?"

"Fine," she breathed into my hair. "How are *you* doing?"

I stiffened at the pity in her voice.

"Jasmine?" she whispered.

"Fabulous!" I pulled away, smiling so hard for her my cheeks hurt. Niki had clearly flown back to Seattle just to check on how I was coping with the latest breakup, but she could have hidden it a little better.

"Glamorous," I added. "Just like I said!"

She eyed me. "Really?"

"Jasmine, come sit," Dad interrupted excitedly. "Niki was telling us her good news!"

I followed Niki to the couch, mumbling my hellos to Mom and Dad, who smiled and nodded at me the same way they might greet the person who delivered their mail or groceries. Or a summons. Their eyes quickly returned to Niki and lit up like a Christmas tree as she filled me in on how she'd just scored a new client who was flying her out to New York. I squeezed her hand, unwilling to let the fact that she was the favorite child taint how proud I was of her. After she had been laid off two years earlier, Niki had started her own data analytics consultancy, and had been a million times happier ever since. (I'm sure it also helped that, around the same time, she'd met the love of her life.)

"You are *killing* it." I grinned after Niki told us all about the client, who was *kinda* a big deal in the sporting goods sector. "You *bawse*, you!"

"I am a bawse, aren't I?" Niki flipped her hair in jest. "Now I'm just like you, Jasmine."

I laughed. "Come on."

"*You* come on." Niki punched me lightly on the shoulder. "You know how I've always looked up to you . . ."

I gave her a big smile. Niki, who was much more thoughtful and practical, had always idolized my artsy career path. I majored in visual art—against the extremely vocal wishes of my parents—and miraculously parlayed an internship in animation to gainful employment. But nobody, not even Niki, needed to know that I'd thrown a Hail Mary and scored a career touchdown against all odds. I was lucky to get my job. And I was *very* lucky to have a patient manager. I screwed up royally on the regular, and instead of firing me—which Rowan could have by now—she gave me diligent feedback. She spent hours upon hours of her precious time training me. She gave me more chances than I deserved.

"What are you working on these days?" Niki grinned. "Or is it 'top secret,' like the time you couldn't tell us about that bridal commercial—"

"Oh, that reminds me!" Mom stood up suddenly. "Niki, before I forget, I must show you the tablecloth samples for your engagement party. There are seven different shades of gold to choose from. Can you *imagine*?"

Niki turned her gaze to Mom and then back to me. My mouth was still open, because before Mom interrupted, I was about to remind Niki that the only reason I couldn't tell her about that particular campaign was because there was an A-list celebrity attached and we'd all signed NDAs. I was about to talk about *my* work, which was often *pretty* cool, but which my mother did not give a shit about.

"Go ahead," I whispered to Niki, winking. "God forbid you choose the wrong tablecloth!"

I squeezed Niki's hand and then left my parents to plan their favorite daughter's engagement party. As I trudged to the kitchen to get started on happy hour, I briefly wondered if someone would ask for my opinion on which shade of gold would work best for the end-of-summer banquet they had planned, but my art degree was no good here. (Just my bartending skills.) I half listened to Mom natter away about "mustard gold" and "Tuscan sun gold" while I concocted four stiff lychee martinis, which had an alcohol content that guaranteed my time with the parentals would pass a little more quickly. I zoned out of their conversation, and by the time I returned to the living room with a tray of cocktails and big bowl of salt and vinegar chips, they were no longer talking about the party.

"Are you sure you cannot join?" Mom cooed. She had moved to the other couch and was sitting next to Niki, their thighs flush.

"Who wants a drink?" I called out, just as Niki mumbled, "Sorry, we can't."

"Count me in," Mom said to me. "These are not too strong, Jasmine, *hah*?"

"No," I lied. I handed everyone a glass and then placed the chip bowl in the center of the coffee table. "What are you guys talking about?"

No one answered. There was a weird tension in the air, which was even weirder because I wasn't the source of it. I sat down cross-legged on the floor with my cocktail, eyeing Niki. "What's going on?"

"Um . . ."

"What did Mom just ask you?" I prompted.

"We were talking about our trip to Alaska," Dad answered instead. He stretched out his legs in front of him and started cycling in the air. It was his idea of exercise. "The cruise line has extra cabins and they are selling at a discount. We found out this morning only."

"OK . . ." My parents left for a ten-day cruise with a bunch of their friends from the South Asian community the following week, but I didn't understand why . . .

"Hold the *phone*." I sat up straight as something sharp niggled in my chest. "Did you just invite Niki and Sam to tag along on your cruise?"

"*Hah*," Dad answered again. "The discount is very deep, Jasmine. It's a bargain!"

"Were you planning on inviting *me*?"

My cheeks flushed when nobody spoke up. It wasn't like I wanted to go, but I was still going to force my parents to spell out their favoritism.

"We did not think a cruise would interest you," Mom said finally. She took a sip of the drink, scrunched up her nose, and then set the glass on the coffee table.

"You like more adventurous holidays," Dad said. "Do you not?"

"They have a point." Niki, resuming her post as family mediator, shrugged in agreement. "When was the last time you went on vacation that didn't involve skydiving or camping through a blizzard or trekking a mountain pass with a bunch of Aussies you just met?"

"They could have at least asked," I said, more hurt in my voice than I'd intended.

"You are more than welcome to come, *beti*," Dad said slowly.

Mom nodded stiffly. "Of course. Would you like to join us?"

I blinked, my eyes darting between my parents. Their invitation was not genuine. There was no way they wanted me on that cruise. Funnily enough, it kind of made me want to say yes.

"My manager did just tell me I have to take two weeks off *this* month," I said, taunting them. I waited for their faces to show their bluff, but they didn't budge.

"So, come," Mom said, holding my gaze.

"*You* want *me* to join you on a cruise with your friends," I said slowly, leaving plenty of room for her to read between the lines. "With all the aunties and uncles."

"Not just *our* friends," Dad chimed in, oblivious to subtext. "We hear there will be lots of kids joining."

"He means the young people from your generation," Mom clarified. "You know, the boys and girls you grew up with. You haven't seen them in so long." She cleared her throat. "If you came, I suppose you could reconnect."

I stuffed a handful of chips into my mouth and thought seriously about which was the sadder of two scenarios: (a) Going on a cruise where I'd have to socialize with the Punjabi community who had made my adolescence a living hell, or (b) sitting on Amber's couch for two weeks of forced vacation. Going with option (a), at least I'd have my old crew growing up for company. Option (b), I'd have Mango.

Crunching loudly, I passed the bowl to Niki so she could take a scoop. Instead, she disappeared, grabbed napkins from the kitchen, and then offered the chips to my parents first.

"Thank you, *beti*," Mom purred. She reached out and lightly gripped Niki's chin with her thumb and pointer finger. Smacking her lips together, she double kissed the air. It was Mom's signature gesture of love and attention and good humor. My stomach squirmed, the liquor burning a hole in my mostly empty stomach. I couldn't remember the last time Mom had touched me like that. Now that I thought about it, I couldn't remember the last time I felt like I was really a welcome part of this family.

It was no secret that I was their problem child. They loved us the same because it was basically the law, but it made total sense they *liked* Niki more, and wanted *her* to crash their holiday. She was sweet and kind and the type of good Indian girl who remembered the napkins and to offer food to our elders first. She had a stable profession. She was even marrying a good Indian boy. I, on the other hand, had been raising hell, flouting rules, and defying community norms since my early teens. Everyone thought I was immature, impulsive, selfish, unreliable, and defensive, not to mention the shame of the family. I wasn't even exaggerating. Those were the exact words Mom used to hurl at me constantly.

My parents turned their attention back to Niki and her engagement party, to the capacity limits on the venue, how many appetizers to serve. My pulse was racing, heat prickling on the back of neck, and when I opened my mouth . . .

"I think I'll come," I said suddenly, surprising everyone in the room. Including me.

"Come where?" Mom asked.

"On your cruise," I said calmly. "To *Alaska*."

"Really?" Dad said.

"Yeah." I nodded, narrowing my gaze at Mom. "Is that OK?"

"Why of course," she said breezily.

*Bullshit.*

*Call my bluff, Mom. Just like I'm calling yours.*

*Admit that you wanted Niki there. Your good Indian daughter. Not me.*

"The cruise departs next Wednesday," Mom continued. "You're free?"

"As a bird."

Our words were civil but our eyes were at war.

"I'll tell my manager I'm taking two weeks off," I simpered, doubling down.

Mom pursed her lips and stood up from the couch. Smiling, she beckoned for me to follow. "First let's call the cruise line, *hah*? I'll give you the discount code."

Mom left the room, and a beat later, she hollered out for Dad because she couldn't remember where they'd left their travel documents. When I felt drool pooling at the corners of my lips, I realized my mouth was hanging open. I closed it.

Wait . . . what?

*What?*

"Jasmine," I heard Niki say, her voice low and hoarse. "Are you sure you want to go on a cruise with them?"

No, I wasn't *sure*.

I did not want to go on vacation with my *parents*, two people I barely had a relationship with these days, who never had and never would respect any of my choices. I did *not* want to be trapped with a literal boatload of judgmental South Asian aunties and uncles who had ostracized me from the community when I was fifteen years old because if you weren't a good Indian girl, then by default, you were a *bad* one.

"Yes, I'm sure," I lied, ruffling Niki's hair. She was still gawking at me, but I chose to ignore it and followed my parents into the other room.

And, if I was being totally truthful, I also didn't want to go on a cruise because I couldn't exactly afford to. Just like I couldn't afford the Venti Starbucks I'd picked up that morning on the way to the office, or the fashionable outfit I was currently wearing and for which I'd paid full price, or the fair market rent I insisted on paying Amber for letting me crash in her spare room.

Nobody knew. But guess what?

I was broke.

# Chapter 4

〜〜〜

Dad: Would you like ride to the cruise ship terminal?

Jasmine: amber offered to drive me . . . but if it's on your way, sure?

Mom: You are staying with Amber . . . again?

Mom: Please ignore my earlier text. It is not my business.

ALTHOUGH AMBER WAS sitting upright on one of the stools at her kitchen island, she wasn't really awake. I topped off our cappuccinos with a sliver of milk chocolate and held one of the mugs beneath her nose until she opened her eyes.

"Any exciting plans while I'm gone?" I asked Amber, sliding onto the stool next to her. Her eyes flitted to the front door, where my suitcase was waiting for me.

"Yup." She nodded. "I'm having a house party on Friday, then a weekend wine tour in Napa, *then* booked a mani-pedi with my sisters." She paused. "After that, Danica and I are going to fucking Florence and I'm going to propose!"

I blinked at her. She blinked in response.

"So, you'll be working the whole time?"

"No shit, Sherlock."

"Oh, darling," I purred. "Does someone need her coffee?"

"Does someone wanna make me one?"

"It's right in front of you."

"Oh." Amber's chin slumped forward. "Thanks."

I was usually at the office by the time Amber was getting ready for work, praise the *lord*. She was a delight on evenings and weekends, but those who caught her when she was psyching herself up for her usual fourteen-hour workday didn't always make it out alive.

"When can you quit working like a feudal serf?" I asked, hoping the question wouldn't result in decapitation.

"I'll find out this summer if I get the promotion." Amber sipped her coffee. "I better fucking get that promotion."

"You will."

She cleared her throat. "And if I don't?"

"Then you'll *quit*?" I offered. "Storm out and tell them where to stick it? Go work for their competitor?"

"I have a noncompete in my employment contract," Amber said flatly. "So, I'll probably just have to try again next year."

"That's the spirit!"

Amber and I drank our coffees in a comfortable silence, while she stalled going to the office and I waited for Mom and Dad to pick me up.

I know, I *know*. Agreeing to go on a family vacation to spite your parents, when you really couldn't afford to go in the first place, wasn't a great idea. It was a terrible idea. One of my worst, actually, and that was saying something. My college bestie and I once hitchhiked our way down to Joshua Tree National Park, covering several hundred of those miles with a trucker who was a dead ringer for someone I'd seen in a rerun of *America's Most Wanted*. The fact that our bodies weren't currently decomposing in the desert continued to blow our minds.

After I booked my cruise ticket on one of my credit cards, I spent the rest of the weekend sitting quietly watching Niki plan the engagement party with my parents, or sitting quietly next to Niki while we binged all three Bridget Jones movies. She gently tried to talk to me about my breakup a few times, but I didn't feel like getting into it. Besides, the state of my finances was affecting the neurons in my brain. On Sunday night, back at Amber's condo, I'd forced myself to take a good look at my finances and finally open the budgeting app I once downloaded aspirationally. There was a reason I hadn't used my vacation days from last year. My credit card debt had gotten out of control, and I didn't have the cash flow to travel like I used to.

It had taken four hours to input my expenses into the app. There were the big ones like rent and my share of utility bills. (To Brian, and now to Amber.) Student loan payments. Car payments and fuel. (Why oh why did my bougie self demand a brand-new Lexus?) Groceries, which I *thought* I usually picked up from Trader Joe's or Safeway. My credit card statements, however, were claiming that at least twice a week, I could spend up to eighty bucks just on produce at Whole Foods.

I earned decent money, and my salary was enough to cover those big, predictable expenses. But the thing that had really gotten me in the red was what the budget app unhelpfully called "nonessentials." My half of Mango's vet bills, obedience classes, and doggy day care, for the days Brian and I were both slammed at work. Streaming service subscriptions to Netflix, Prime, and Hulu. Clothing. (I preferred to buy from brands that ethically sourced their textiles, but they were hella expensive. Damn you, morality!) Seasonal ski pass to Mount Baker. My morning coffee runs. Sushi lunches with the animation team. Happy hours and trendy dinners out with my friends. My book of the month club. My wine of the month club. *My coffee* of the month club.

I was a team player, all right? I liked clubs!

I wanted to bitch-slap myself back to college when I saw everything laid out like that. My messy financial situation was all my fault, and had I been responsible with my money, I wouldn't be here. Maybe I'd be debt-free and have more than two hundred dollars in my savings account. Maybe, by now, I'd even have been able to afford a down payment on my own condo.

*In* today's *economy? Maybe not . . .*

The good thing was, I could afford the cruise because I'd gotten paid the week before, and the "bargain" Dad had proselytized about really was a good deal. The cruise called itself all-inclusive, and my ticket would supposedly cover everything except alcohol, which I would undoubtedly need to stomach ten days at sea with my parents' friends. But being the budget-minded, sensible woman I was blossoming into, I'd tucked a bottle of gin at the bottom of my suitcase right next to my winter parka. Take that, budgeting app! I hadn't even bought top-shelf gin, which was my usual MO. I'd picked it up at Costco.

"I better get ready for work," I heard Amber say limply. I checked the microwave clock. My parents weren't due to arrive for twenty minutes.

"Do you want another coffee?"

"Would you mind?"

"No." I stood up from the stool and sauntered around the counter. "You want breakfast? I meal-prepped you overnight oats for the rest of the week."

"You're the best roommate ever, you know that?" Amber sighed. "The coffee. The breakfast." Her voice was singsong, which meant she was still half asleep. "The surprise pizzas. I wish you could stay forever."

"Maybe I can." I paused. "I mean, until Danica's done her master's and moves back to Seattle."

"You *can*," Amber said slowly. "I would honestly love to be roommates with you. But would it be a good idea?"

I chewed my lip and pressed the on switch to the coffee grinder as Mom's passive-aggressive texts from last night popped into my head.

*You are staying with Amber . . . again?*

"I think it's a great idea," I insisted. "It means Brian and I can both keep Mango."

"That's not what I meant."

I knew that wasn't what she meant, but I widened my eyes and played dumb to Amber's look of pity. The same face Niki had worn her entire weekend in Seattle. The same subtext of judgment in my mother's text.

Did everyone and their dog think I couldn't handle living in such close proximity to Brian? That I was weak and stupid and would wind up taking him back for the fourth time?

No. I could handle it. I had finally accepted that we weren't a good match. The era of Jasmine and Brian was officially over.

Amber and I slammed our coffees, and after she hopped into

the shower, I grabbed my suitcase and went down to wait for my parents. Unexpectedly, I smiled as the fresh air hit my face, my nerves tingling in anticipation. There were a million reasons to dread going on the cruise, but I hadn't traveled in over a year and, who knew, maybe it wouldn't be so bad. Cruise ships were huge, and if I was careful, I could easily find myself a secret rebound to keep me occupied. Maybe I'd suck face with some auntie's handsome son on an iceberg, or zip-line into the arms of a single DILF, or get frisky with the sexy staffer handing out towels at the pool. I wasn't a big planner. I just liked to send good vibes out into the universe and let the magic happen!

And even if there were no good prospects, at least the "kids" I grew up with were going. I hadn't seen most of them since I was fifteen and stopped going to community events, but we were close at the time. Daljit knew how to sneak in alcohol without getting caught. Sweetie was a karaoke queen who I'd heard made it to the Showcase Round on *American Idol*. And Krisha? I definitely hoped *she* was coming. She and I used to be the life of every party.

I was so busy imagining myself having cabin ragers with the old gang that I didn't notice Brian and Mango on the grassy patch just ahead by the sidewalk. Mango was in the middle of a poop, and Brian was hovering over her with a compostable doggy bag, ready to pounce. He was wearing a gray pin-striped suit, the same one he'd worn to his brother's wedding in Whistler three years earlier. He looked good, even picking up dog shit.

Boy. Did he still look *good*.

I thought seriously about hiding behind a tree, but Mango saw me, and as soon as she finished her business, she tugged Brian in my direction. I delayed the inevitable by bending down to hug her, breathing in her scent. I still saw her every day, slipping in and out when Brian wasn't around, but I missed her. I missed having a *home*.

"Hey, Jas," I heard Brian grunt. Reluctantly, I unwrapped my-self from Mango and flashed him my most fabulous, I-don't-miss-you-at-*all* smile.

"Brian." I sprung up to standing. "Hey!"

"How've you been?"

I nodded, stalling. Since the most recent breakup, we hadn't yet communicated other than by text message, and only about logistics. Such as who was picking up Mango from day care. Or that I was going to be out of town and had hired a dog sitter to take Mango for a walk weekday afternoons. I wasn't sure yet how to answer these sorts of broad, impersonally personal questions. What was I supposed to say?

*I'm broke and your new squeeze is beautiful!*

*You wasted four years of my life, which is currently a hot mess!*

"I'm . . . great," I said finally. "Excellent. Swell. You?"

Brian shrugged, studying me. One of the things that first drew me to him was that I never knew what he was thinking. That mys-teriousness got old pretty quickly.

"I never asked," he said, ignoring my question. "Where are you going?"

"Alaska."

"Sweet." Brian nodded. "My buddy and I went ice climbing there in college. You flying into Anchorage?"

Now it was my turn to avoid the question. Brian would smirk if he knew I was going on a cruise, which I'd once heard him call *tacky armchair traveling for children and the elderly.* We were both adventurous vacationers—one of the reasons we were so compatible in the beginning—but Brian was a bit of a snob about it. In fact, he was a bit of a snob about everything.

"I planned the trip pretty last-minute," I said instead. "This dog sitter I hired to help you is supposed to be good, by the way. She watches Amber's sister's dog all the time."

"It's fine." He smiled. "Thanks for organizing that."

Brian and I went quiet while Mango sat down between us and looked from him, to me, and then back to him. Having a dog, one we both loved beyond measure, had complicated the breakup. And neither of us had the heart to address the big unknown that still hung between us: Who would get Mango? Which one of us would have to say goodbye to her?

I opened my mouth to speak, to at least acknowledge the issue. I wanted to be responsible, and not only with my finances. But what would I say?

*I'm takin' the dog . . . dumbass! (To quote* Legally Blonde.*)*

*Maybe I'll just live across the hall forever so neither of us have to give her up. You, Mystery Woman, and I can co-parent!*

*But it was my idea to get a dog! Damnit. She's mine . . .*

"Isn't that your dad's car?"

Brian's question snapped me out of my cerebral moment, and I glanced across the street. Indeed, there was a gray Volkswagen Tiguan with Dad's familiar giant #FarmersProtest bumper sticker on the windshield.

"Is this a family vacation?" Brian laughed.

I grimaced at his tone. Another thing that Brian and I bonded over was that neither of us were close to our parents, except when he was trying to extract money from his trust fund. It never bothered me before, but for some reason, it did right now.

"They're driving me to the airport."

"That's sweet."

"Isn't it?" I hiked my purse higher on my shoulder, unsure why I couldn't be honest with him, why I still cared what he thought about me, why I even respected the opinion of a man I had grown to viscerally disrespect.

What was wrong with me? Four years ago, how did I not see him for what he truly was? Most of my friends dated guys like Brian—cocky *jerks*—in college, in their early to mid-twenties. I had been nearly thirty when we met. I had known better.

I was about to spiral, say every nasty word to Brian I'd held back, but then Dad swung open the car door, and I knew the only thing worse than having a meltdown in front of my ex-boyfriend was having a meltdown in front of my father and my ex-boyfriend that my father despised. So as quickly as I could, I gave Mango another hug, attempted a breezy *see-ya-later!* with Brian, and then beelined to the car.

# Chapter 5

〰️〰️

Jasmine: morning! just thought i'd check to
see if you'd had a chance to review the
character i uploaded? let me know if you
have any feedback you'd like me to
incorporate before sign-off.

Rowan: You knocked this one out of the park.
I see real growth. Go have some fun!!! And
don't you dare contact me during your
vacation!

S THAT *BRIAN*?"

I slid into the back seat of the car, having safely stowed my
suitcase in the trunk, and found Uma Auntie gawking at Brian
through the window.

"That's him." I put on my seat belt. "Hi, Mom, hi, Dad." I cleared
my throat. "Hi, Uma Auntie."

"Hello, sweetie," Uma Auntie said, finally turning to me. "You know, he looks different than I remember."

"Oh?"

"Was he not Mexican-American? This man is very blond!"

"You are thinking of one of Jasmine's other ex-boyfriends," Mom said quietly, as Dad veered into the street and we drove past Brian, who waved at us lazily from the sidewalk. "It was the IT specialist she brought to your housewarming. This one was business development something or other."

I bit my tongue.

*One of Jasmine's other ex-boyfriends.*

"Your parents mentioned you and Brian broke up recently," Uma Auntie continued. "I am *so* sorry, my dear. How are you coping?"

"I'm OK, Auntie. Thank you for asking." I looked pointedly at my parents. They hadn't asked me how I was doing. Not once. When Niki convinced me to finally tell them about the breakup, all Mom did was send four heart emojis to the group chat.

"I'm so glad to hear it," Uma Auntie continued. "We'll have some nice girl talk on the cruise, *nah*? Have you heard we are roommates?"

*Roommates?*

My jaw dropped, but I quickly covered with an excited smile as I tried not to look as shocked as I felt.

"Really!" My voice was shrill and high and annoyingly similar to the one I used when I was trying to coax Mango into her crate. "How . . . exciting!"

"Very." Uma Auntie lowered her voice. "We are both single, *nah*? And ready to mingle!"

I tried to ignore the sinking feeling in my stomach as we

drove to the cruise ship terminal and Mom and Uma Auntie chatted away about some work drama that apparently mirrored a plotline in their favorite Pakistani soap opera. If I'd found out that I was bunking with any other auntie, and I mean *any* other auntie, I would have flung myself out of the moving car and happily forgone the nonrefundable cruise ticket. Most aunties tucked backhanded compliments in the folds of their saris, and were fluent in Hindi, proficient in English, and a Rhodes freaking scholar in *Nasty*. But I supposed if I were to force myself to think on the bright side, rooming with Uma Auntie wasn't the end of the world. She wasn't your typical auntie.

Uma Auntie was warm and progressive, and ironically, Mom's best friend. I'd always found their dynamic strange. Mom was uptight and agonizingly conventional, and Uma Auntie was a free spirit, had two ex-husbands, and had never wanted children. They'd worked with and known each other for years, and when I still lived at home, finding Uma Auntie and Mom gossiping over coffee in the kitchen was a common occurrence. I'd long ago blacklisted myself from all community events, but Uma Auntie I'd kept in touch with over the years. Apparently, I'd even brought my ex-boyfriend Daniel to her housewarming? That relationship was so long ago, I'd totally forgotten about him. Hmm. I surreptitiously checked Instagram on my phone. I wondered what ever happened to Daniel . . .

We reached the terminal in good time, and with the fresh knowledge that Daniel and his pregnant partner, Ella, were happily shacked up in Spokane, I was determined to make the most of my days at sea. There was a long line for security—apparently we were among three thousand passengers boarding this morning—and afterward, cruise ship staff directed us to a banquet hall on an upper deck to rendezvous with our group. With every step, my legs increasingly turned to jelly, but I put on a brave face and told myself that I didn't care what a platoon of aunties and uncles said or thought about me, because I was Jasmine Randhawa.

And I did not give a—

"Holy shit," I muttered, as we turned the final corner into the banquet room. My stomach clenched; I flicked my gaze from the massive crowd to my father. He looked equally stunned.

"I didn't realize the group would be so *large*," Dad whispered. "I thought it was our community only."

"I heard there are more than two hundred in our group now, from all over the US and Canada," Uma Auntie said from behind us. "Someone posted the discount code on Facebook!"

I was going to have to play emotional tactical warfare with *two* hundred aunties and uncles? This wasn't just a platoon. I was about to face off with a freaking brigade.

These aunties and uncles were armed and ready for battle, their uniforms an intimidating mix of saris, polyester pantsuits, and Palm Springs–branded puffer vests. I scanned the crowd, searching desperately for my allies. Daljit, or Sweetie, or Krisha, *anyone* from my youth, but they hadn't arrived yet. And were my eyes playing tricks on me, or were a handful of these aunties and uncles *staring* at me? I locked eyes with an uncle I vaguely recognized. I bared my teeth and gave him a wave. He cleared his throat and looked away.

"Are you OK, *beti*?" I heard Dad ask.

*I'll be OK when my friends arrive and I can avoid these people.*

"Yes, I'm fine, Dad."

"Good—ah! Yes. Bishan is here." He patted me awkwardly on the back, relieved that I was clearly lying. "*She* will know what is going on."

I took a deep breath, turning my gaze to the entrance. Turn

down the lights. Cue the Beyoncé music. And all the single ladies, please do not put your hands up, because Queen Bishan—or Queen B, as Niki and I had called her—was the worst of them all. She was the monarch pulling the strings behind this military operation.

Childhood memories faded, but Bishan Auntie I remembered clearly. Always with her nose in other people's business. (Cough. *Mine.*) Always something rude or condescending at the tip of her tongue. Always, *always* in charge. She'd been the president of our Sikh *gurdwara* since the mid-2000s because, according to Niki, everyone had been too afraid to oust her once her term ended.

Bishan glided through the banquet room and then stood up on a chair at the front. Her jet-black hair was pulled into a low ponytail, and even though I always remembered her in traditional clothing, today she was sporting skinny jeans, a flattering black raincoat cinched around her waist, and an oversize scarf. As much as I wanted to hurl my purse at her like a grenade, I had to admire her panache. The monarch was keeping up with the times. She'd started dressing like Kate Middleton.

"Welcome, welcome!" the queen exclaimed, as if she had a microphone in front of her. She smiled through tight lips, waiting for everyone to pay heed.

"May I have your attention, please?" She paused. "May I have your attention, *please*?"

Laughing, I mumbled, "*Will the real Slim Shady please stand up?*"

Dad looked at me quizzically, and I shrugged. Damnit. Where was my old crew? *They* would have known the queen had just inadvertently rapped the first two lines of Eminem's hit song.

Eventually, the room quieted and Queen B commenced her speech. The first five minutes were purely thanks and welcomes and "isn't this exciting?" and finally, she moved on to logistics, announcing that she would be handing out room keys, wristbands, and itineraries. Each "couple"—I supposed Uma Auntie was my couple—also would get a pamphlet outlining the excursions and activities on offer for an additional fee, as well as the amenities, such as the disco, multiple restaurants and buffets, pools, gym, and various theme nights and shows.

My head was spinning with all the information, and I kept glancing at the door as stragglers came in, waiting for my friends. I checked my watch, my palms dampening. In less than twenty minutes, boarding would be closed.

"Ah-ha, Jasmine!" Queen B exclaimed, after she finished her speech and spotted me in the crowd. "Our last-minute addition! How many years has it been?" She didn't wait for me to answer. "Come, come. I'll take care of you first!"

I *bet* she'd take care of me. She'd take care to throw me overboard. At least sharks were less vicious.

After an obligatory hug, I held my breath and followed her fog of Chanel No. 5 to the front table, which had stacks of pamphlets, papers, and wristbands, one of which she fastened tightly around my left wrist. Then she held my hand up, sighing at the sight of my empty ring finger.

"I was so sorry to hear about Brian," she whispered, as if it were a secret. "I told your parents so many times—I would help them plan the wedding. Your mother didn't think you would ever marry, but I was convinced. *I* was convinced you and Brian would get married."

I withdrew my hand, smiling icily. Mom didn't think I'd marry Brian? And although she'd never talked to *me* about the breakup, she'd happily discussed it with Uma Auntie as well as the biggest gossip in the state of Washington?

"Marriage isn't for everyone," I managed.

"But he was *so* handsome, *nah*?"

"He was, yes," I deadpanned. "Until the surgery, at least."

The queen's eye twitched, and I tried my best to keep a straight face. Finally, she cleared her throat and moved on.

"Breakups are very hard, I am hearing. You are feeling well, Jasmine?" Auntie smiled at me sweetly. Too sweetly. "Are you sick? You are very gaunt."

"Thank you," I said perkily.

"Come by my cabin sometime, OK? I am in the same corridor." She lowered her voice, ignoring me. "You are thirty-three, am I right? It is high time you use antiaging skin care products."

My gut twisted.

"Especially now that once again you are sing—"

"So, where is everybody?" I interrupted loudly, even though it was rude. I was hungry, my neck was stiff, and I wasn't sure how much more of this I could tolerate sober. Besides, I started using retinols, serums, toners, and all that other crap the day I turned thirty. I had the Glossier receipts to prove it. "When does everyone else get here?"

"Everyone else?" She laughed. "Look around you. Our group has two hundred nineteen people!"

"Well," I said, my heart racing. "Not everyone is *here*—"

"That's true. My elder brother—your Ranjit Uncle—just texted. There are a few stragglers with them by security."

"Just . . . just a *few* are missing?"

"Yes. Why do you ask?"

"Well," I stammered, trying to process what I was hearing. "Where are all the kids?"

"The kids?"

"Yes, I mean." I took a breath. "Like the people my age. Where are Daljit, and Sweetie, and Krisha—"

"Oh, honey. *They* are not coming."

Bile rose in my throat and I started seeing spots.

"That's why I was so surprised you decided to join."

"I . . ." I didn't know what to say. "I . . ."

"Jasmine," Queen Bishan said, pinching the flesh of my cheek. "This is a *seniors'* cruise."

# Chapter 6

≈≈≈

Jasmine: sos sos sos sos sos

Niki: ????

Jasmine: 33yo fallen single woman trapped on seniors' cruise. send help.

Niki: WHAT?

Niki: You're not answering your phone. Call me back?

Jasmine: if I speak right now i have no idea what's going to come out of my mouth. i'll text you later.

UM, MAY I please speak with you for a moment?"
My parents were deep in conversation with another couple, and everyone stopped talking to look at me.

"Jasmine," Mom said, placing her hand on the woman's shoulder. "This is—"

"Hi, Auntie," I said quickly, pressing my hands together in front of my chest. "Hi, Uncle. Lovely to meet you. I'm so sorry, but may I borrow my parents for a moment?"

Mom laughed sheepishly. "*Jasmine . . .*"

"*Please.* It's urgent."

Mom's cheeks reddened, but when I grabbed her and Dad by the hand, they followed me over to an empty corner of the banquet room.

"That was your father's cousin-in-law from San Francisco," Mom grumbled. "Did you have to—"

"We just got here," I snapped. "Am I embarrassing you *already*?"

I challenged her with my gaze, pressing her to clap back. I was furious at her for being tricked onto the cruise, and in that moment, I wanted her to lose it on me. I wanted her to yell and scream the way she used to; pass judgment on every single thing I did and didn't do; compare me to perfect little Niki. I wanted her to remind everyone within earshot that the only thing she cared about was what the community, her friends, or the *granthi* thought about me, and not what I—her own daughter—thought about myself.

"You said it was urgent?" she responded calmly, after a moment had passed. My shoulders slumped.

But Mom didn't fight me anymore, no matter what I did. No matter how much I provoked her. She didn't get mad anymore, because the simple truth of it was, she no longer cared about me the same way.

"Very urgent." My voice felt small and I crossed my arms. "Bishan Auntie just told me this was a seniors' cruise."

I watched my parents' faces as I handed them a pamphlet and pointed out the fine print that the queen had just highlighted for me.

Journey to Alaska and beyond with Kensington Cruises'
premier sailing, perfect for the adventurous 50+ traveler.

Dad frowned while reading and then handed the pamphlet to Mom. She cleared her throat.

"Jasmine," she said softly. "We did not know."

"You told me there would be people my age."

"That is what we heard, yes," Dad insisted. "Everything was planned so removed from us. It's a simple mistake."

"It's a simple *mistake* that is going to kill me," I exclaimed. "Do you know Bishan Auntie looked at my ring finger, sighed, and then told me I looked *old*? I've been on this boat for ten minutes. How am I going to get through ten *days* of these people commenting on my weight, my marital status, my dark skin, my bathing suit, my . . . my . . ."

*My reputation.*

I thought it. But I couldn't stomach saying it out loud.

"You are not here for the people only," Dad interrupted. "You are here to experience Alaska, *hah*? You will have *excellent* time . . ."

Dad prattled on about the cruise and, as usual, ignored the root of the problem. Fleetingly, I thought Mom might intervene, say something even a little empathetic that acknowledged how hard this cruise was going to be for me. But she didn't. She wouldn't even look at me.

Eventually, I excused myself and dropped off my and Uma Auntie's suitcases in our cabin. There was a brief moment when I thought about making a run for it, but when I asked a cruise staffer if there was still time to disembark, he said there was no turning back. The ramps had detached.

I. Was. Stuck.

Blasting my PMS playlist through my AirPods, I started wandering the cruise ship, mulling over the ways I could play this.

My first option was to be the spokesperson—nay, mascot—for fallen Indian girls everywhere and stick it to the metaphorical man. Despite the cold weather on the way, I could wear skimpy clothing and swim attire, drink heavily, and seek out the good sports among the cruise staffers. It wasn't like my reputation could get any worse. At least I'd have some fun.

Option two. Abandon ship the moment we got to our first port of call, wherever that was. I hadn't had time to do any research. I could hitchhike my way back to Seattle like the good old days, or alternatively, stay in Alaska forever. I was outdoorsy. I had Timberland boots and could build a campfire without matches. I was basically the brown Steve Irwin of the Pacific Northwest.

Finally, there was option three, the most reasonable course of action and the one Niki would likely force me to follow when I eventually called her back.

Lay. Low.

Maybe I really was getting older, because acting out didn't seem as appealing as it used to be. I just needed to get this cruise over with. Picking up my pace, I wandered through the passenger decks, the casino, past two of the seven buffets, toured the viewing deck, all the while wondering how the hell I was going to cope.

I was angrier at my mother, who'd barely said two words to me, than I was at Queen B, who had emotionally disemboweled me in front of two hundred seventeen witnesses. But most of all,

I was pissed off at myself. Jasmine. The Creator of Her Own Suffering. Why the hell had I volunteered myself for a vacation with my parents when they didn't want me here? When *I* didn't even want to be here? Just because they had invited their perfect Niki, and not me? What kind of spiteful adolescent crap was that?

When I spotted Uma Auntie and a few others in line at the poolside bar, I did a one-eighty and darted through the closest door. I couldn't face anyone right now, not even Uma Auntie. I found myself in a coffee shop that was trying to pass itself off as Starbucks. I avoided eye contact with the bored barista, selected a table at the back, and decided to wait the aunties out.

I'd only been aggressively scrolling TikTok for a minute when I felt a tap on my shoulder. I looked to the side, expecting to find the barista, but it was a waiter I hadn't noticed when I stormed in. I wasn't sure how. He was a major babe.

I tried not to lick my lips as I drank the guy in. He could have been anywhere from twenty-five to thirty-five, rich caramel skin and fudge-brown eyes that put me in the mood for dessert. My eyes skirted up his arms and across his chest. He was broad and built like a quarterback, his white polo hugging him in all the right places. I bit my lip, trying not to drool. I was ready to move on, and would need a distraction from the Auntie-Uncle Brigade. Was my luck about to change?

Casually, I tucked my hair behind my ears. Don't judge me: I may have also batted my eyelashes.

"Hi," I simpered.

"Hey . . ."

The waiter smiled at me, and I leaned back in my chair to get a better view, because he was standing extremely close. God, that mouth. So soft and kissable, when the rest of him was all sharp features and hard edges. I waited for him to speak, so we could quickly get over the part where he took my order, and could move on to the question of whether he was offering anything off menu.

"So," I said seductively, biting my bottom lip just so. The silence lingered. Seriously, dude, just take my order.

"I already had two double espressos today," I breathed. "So, like . . ."

*Offer me a sparkling water?*

*Better yet, offer me you?*

"Me, too," he laugh-coughed. "I drink *way* too much coffee."

"Uh-huh . . ."

"So, how have you been?" he asked me, still not asking me for my order. Instead, he pulled up the chair next to me and sat down. Oh dear. I'd worked in a dozen restaurants and bars over the years, and while flirting with customers was always condoned, sitting down with them was a big no-no. This waiter was not the brightest bulb on the ship, was he? Never mind. The plans I had for us wouldn't involve much brainpower.

"I've been great." I nodded. "Yeah. Super."

He palmed his jawline, sucking in his cheeks as if he were posing for a photo shoot. "Wow," he said slowly. "Girl, you look incredible."

I'd had my period for two decades and recently found a gray hair in my left armpit, and although I didn't appreciate being called a girl, I had ample appreciation for the way he was checking me out. The way his tongue darted seductively over his bottom lip. And the way his voice got all raspy when he complimented me?

"Do I?" I purred, glancing down at my outfit. It was just athleisure wear, but the pieces fit me like a glove. "*No*, I don't . . ."

"You do," he growled. "You look amazing."

Hmm. This guy was being forward, maybe a little *too* forward, but as someone who was celebrating the end of a four-year relationship on a seniors' cruise, I was going to let myself lower the bar. He placed his left elbow on the table, letting his head fall into his hand as his gaze dropped to my lips. Was he flexing? His bicep bulged against the seam of his polo. Yep. He was definitely flexing.

"You're not so bad yourself." I bit down on my thumb, my heart racing as I flicked my eyes toward the barista. I looked back at the waiter. "Um, are you going to get in trouble?"

"Do you want me to get in trouble?"

"No." I giggled. "So, why don't you just"—I tickled my fingertips on the inside of his wrist—"take my order, so you don't get *fired,* and then we can . . ."

I stopped talking when his face changed. Had I been out of the game that long and misread his signals?

"Excuse me?" he said crisply.

He was scowling at me, albeit sexily. I held my breath.

"Did you just ask me to take your *order*?"

Confused, I flicked my eyes down to his polo shirt. The same white polo shirt I'd seen on a dozen staffers since I boarded the ship. Squinting, I narrowed in on the Kensington Cruises logo on his left pec.

I blinked. It wasn't there. In its place was the creepy green crocodile trademarked by Lacoste.

"Shit!" I gasped, my cheeks heating up. "Are you not a waiter?"

"No," he said icily. "I am *not*. Do I look like a waiter?"

"What's *wrong* with being a waiter?" I snapped, my temper flaring up at his snobbish tone. "Do you work on this cruise?"

"No!"

"So, you're just some *rando* hitting on me?" I asked.

The guy didn't answer, looking me up and down like I was a piece of recycling he was about to discard, and suddenly, all his duck facing and flexing and smoldering didn't make me want to jump him. It made me want to *smack* him in the face.

"I wasn't hitting on you," he answered finally, his voice hollow and aloof.

Yes, he had been, but I had been flirting back, so I didn't want to belabor the point.

"Mhm . . ."

"You really don't know who I am?" he asked. "*Jasmine*?"

I frowned when he mentioned my name. This guy knew me? And I was supposed to know him?

"You don't remember me," he said gruffly. "Clearly."

"Should I?"

"It's Jake," he said, as if he were Madonna or Cher or Rihanna and didn't need a freaking last name.

"Jake," I repeated.

"Jake," he insisted. He looked annoyed, but I was starting to get *really* annoyed by his conceited attitude, so I crossed my arms and sat forward in my seat.

"*Jake*," I cooed. "Any chance you have a last name, bud?"

"Don't be condescending."

"If anyone is condescending, it's *you*. Don't assume just because you're handsome that I will remember who you are."

"You think I'm handsome?"

He winked, and I swear to god, I almost did smack him. Maybe I should have. Maybe the master-at-arms would have kicked me off the boat and I could have gone back to Amber's.

"My name is Jake *Dhillon*," he said finally. He leaned forward, his shoulders stiff, his biceps, yes, flexed.

I squinted at him, trying to place him. *Jake Dhillon. Jake Dhillon.*

He had an ethnically ambiguous look, but now that I knew his surname, I could see the Punjabi in him.

"So, you're part of the queen's—" I stopped. "You're here with the massive group of South Asians?" I asked him. "The one Bishan Auntie organized?"

He nodded, stiffly. So there *was* another "kid" who'd been duped into this mess. A kid I had no memory of.

"You really don't remember me?" he said quietly.

I *really* didn't remember him. Was I getting that old that I'd started to forget people's names and faces? Although I'd partied in my heyday, I rarely got out of control. Rarely . . .

"We didn't . . ." I pointed to his chest and then to mine. "Did we?"

"Are you kidding me?" Jake's face split into a grin. "You would have gone to prison. Jasmine, you were my *babysitter.*"

I didn't want to just smack Jake anymore. I wanted to attach weights to his limbs and chuck him over the side of the boat. He laughed heartily, and I, like a flustered fool, realized that I did know Jake Dhillon.

I'd failed to recognize him because we hadn't seen each other since he was *ten.*

"Some auntie asked me to watch you and your friends at the *gurdwara* for, like, ten minutes. One time!" I insisted, my face hot.

Jake grinned again, as if he was taking pleasure in my embarrassment.

"Seriously," I said. "It must have been . . . 2005? The adults were all right next to us decorating for Vaisakhi. It didn't count as babysitting!"

"Why does it matter if you were my babysitter?" Jake asked

calmly. "That would only be weird if you were into me." He bit down on his bottom lip. "*Are* you into me? When you thought I was the waiter, it kind of seemed like—"

"Keep dreaming," I scoffed. "Are you even old enough to drink?"

"I'm twenty-eight," Jake said. "How old are you? Clearly, old enough to be on a seniors' cruise."

My jaw dropped. Was he fucking with me, or just being a dick?

"You . . ." I stammered.

*You are irritatingly handsome.*

*You remind me exactly of Brian.*

". . . are such a douchebag," I said instead, and immediately, Jake's face dropped.

On some unreachable level, I knew I was letting my emotions get the better of me. I'd been told more than once I was hotheaded and always ready for a fight. And it seemed the tongue-lashing I'd wanted to give my mother earlier had been sprung upon Jake.

"So, that's what you think," he said after a moment.

It wasn't a question. Just a statement. His voice was so quiet I was almost tempted to apologize.

"You know me pretty well, huh?"

"Hey," I said softly. "You called me old!"

"I was kidding around."

"I . . ."

I had not been kidding. And Jake knew that. And even though he was the one who had been acting so full of himself with all that flexing, and had been *so* offended I'd mistaken him for a waiter, he now got to act like *I* had judged *him*?

Nope. Wasn't going to happen.

"So, tell me about yourself, Jake," I said suddenly, changing my tone.

He didn't answer me.

"Seriously, tell me something." I shrugged. "It's been—what—eighteen years since we saw each other? What's going on, *man*?"

Jake hesitated before speaking.

"I'm about to graduate from the University of Chicago Law School. It's one of the best in the country." He nodded. "Majored in poli sci at USC before that, went there on a swimming scholarship." He paused again, studying me. "And now I'm in the process of moving back to Seattle. I've got a job lined up at one of the top firms on the West Coast."

*"Really?"* I gawked.

"Yeah . . ." He trailed off, taking note of my expression. "Why are you making that face?"

I pointed to my mouth, which was still hanging open. "This one? Don't you want me to be impressed?"

Jake was several inches taller than me, and I stared up at him furiously.

"Well, guess what? I'm not impressed. Nor am I surprised. My friends and I created a litmus test on how to tell if a guy is full of himself or not. We ask them to tell us about themselves. Guess what kind of guy reads out their résumé?"

Jake and I stood there, eyes locked, breathing heavily as who knew what happened around us. I blinked, and for a moment, I could have mistaken him for my ex-boyfriend standing across from me. Smirking at everything that wasn't cool. Too good for anyone who wasn't as smart or successful or cultured as he was.

"Douchebags?" I heard Jake say.

*"Ding, ding, ding."* I swallowed hard. "You're *so* smart. You must have gone to a fancy law school."

Jake opened his mouth wide, a half smile as his jaw clicked. I steadied myself for him to clap back, to throw my own flaws in my face. But instead, he took a step backward. He shrugged. And a beat later, he walked away.

# Chapter 7

Jasmine: WHO IS JAKE DHILLON?

Niki: Oh, Jake! We grew up with him. He's a
couple of years younger than me. I think he's
in law school or something?

Jasmine: OR SOMETHING IS RIGHT. HE'S
HERE!!!

WHAT A . . . UGH! Douchebag did not even *begin* to describe
him. My high school English teachers failed me, because I
did not possess that sort of vocabulary!

And who did he think he was, walking away from me, letting
me have the last word? What was he trying to prove, that he was
not only better than me, but also *mature* or something? There were
a thousand put-downs he could have hurled my way, besides the
fact that I was a "senior." I could have written him a list.

When I returned to my cabin, Uma Auntie popped her head

out of the tiny bathroom to let me know that we were expected
at dinner at the Greek restaurant in thirty minutes. The queen
had created an itinerary I hadn't bothered to read. I collapsed in
the bed, annoyed, and checked my phone for the twentieth time.
Niki had replied.

> Niki: Why the all caps lol? I haven't seen him
> in a while, but he was always such a sweet
> guy. That's exciting you'll have someone to
> hang out with!!

> Jasmine: hang out with, or avoid?? he's a dud.
> i'll be steering clear.

I waited a minute before texting again.

> Jasmine: what's his deal though . . . is he
> single?

I almost expected Niki to reply with an eggplant emoji or a
suspicious "Why do you ask?" but she didn't.

> Niki: Can't tell from his IG. But he used to
> date my friend's little sister. They broke up
> last fall.

> Niki: Sorry to hear he's a dud. You could have
> had a spring fling ;)

I rolled my eyes, replying with a vomiting emoji. If Niki were
here in person, she would ask me why I was having such a visceral

reaction to Jake, but she wasn't. Ha! She was the intelligent sibling who had stayed on dry land.

But she followed Jake on Instagram . . . What an interesting piece of information, and purely because I had time to spare before dinner, I did a little creeping. I found him pretty easily. He used his real name; had his alma mater, grad years, and majors in his bio; and his profile was public.

I scrolled through his recent posts, my thumb pressing the screen so hard I suspected a bruise coming on. God, Jake really was a douchebag. Who ever said jumping to conclusions was a bad thing? It was an efficient way to live. Your intuition about a person was usually right.

Every single picture was a selfie, or clearly staged with a tripod, ring light, and some dumb filter that made him look airbrushed. Jake posing in the mirror, wearing a suit, tie, and sunglasses #style. Jake pretending to study from a clothbound textbook in the law library #thegrind. (As if. Who studied from real textbooks anymore?) Jake in a muscle tee, his arms around beautiful women at a musical festival. A bar. Another music festival. *Another* bar.

I stopped scrolling at a picture dated a few months earlier. It was different from the rest. He was seated at a dining room table with Queen B and another man. Was Bishan Auntie his mother? I squinted, trying to remember. No. She wasn't. The queen had two daughters who were much younger than us, and I only knew that because Niki used to babysit them.

I moved my eyes to the man, a handsome uncle I vaguely recognized from my childhood but hadn't seen in person in years. His resemblance to both Jake and Queen B was striking. So, this was Jake's father. And Queen B was . . . Jake's biological aunt? Before she dropped the news that we were on a seniors' cruise, I suddenly remembered her having said her brother and a few other stragglers were still by security. Now it made sense. Jake and his father were running late; that's why I hadn't seen them in the banquet hall earlier.

But why would Jake have voluntarily boarded a cruise designed for seniors? If his aunt planned the whole thing, then he would have known what he was getting in to. If only I'd known what I'd signed up for. I'd be at home on a staycation, drinking too much wine and coffee, reading books, and justifying my many "of the month" clubs.

Eventually, I changed out of my athleisure and into something an *Us Weekly* article the week before had called "cruise casual," which was basically Kate Spade loafers, vintage no-stretch mom jeans, and a white turtleneck I'd snuck out of Amber's closet. After, Uma Auntie, who was a devout Hindu and never skipped her morning puja, wanted to set up what she called her Mobile *Mandir* on the vanity before dinner. I had lots of Hindu friends and was familiar with many of the customs, but as I helped her, I was still surprised by the quantity of items required for Auntie's "mobile" setup. In addition to the marble statues of the deities to which she prayed, she had everything from rice, flower petals, and prayer beads to brass candleholders and matches.

We arrived right on time for dinner at seven p.m., which I took as my cue to commence Operation Lay Low. Unfortunately, at 7:31, my parents arrived and the forced mingling began. I was introduced to a Tamil couple from Portland, a Gujarati couple from Miami, and two Punjabi sisters from Toronto "taking a vacation from their husbands." But eventually, I had to say hello to the aunties and uncles I knew from Seattle—all of whom knew exactly who I was, my checkered past, and had "heard" all about Brian. All of whom were fascinated about why I had decided to come on the cruise.

I could tell they weren't just judging me anymore. They were practically laughing at me. A thirty-three-year-old single woman with nothing better to do than tag along on her parents' holiday? How sad. Gossip about girls with bad reputations traveled fast, didn't it? Jesus. I flicked my eyes to the other corner of the room, where Jake, his father, and the queen were also doing the rounds. I bet no one was giving him a hard time. Jake going on a cruise with his family made him look like freaking Son of the Year.

Finally, I followed my parents and Uma Auntie to a table in the far corner. Apparently, the queen had booked the entire restaurant for our group. I supposed, when you were responsible for selling several hundred tickets, they let you do what you wanted.

"Did you see the view, Jasmine?" I heard Mom ask me. She sounded nervous, but the fact that she didn't know how to talk to me anymore—even nicely—made me weirdly sad.

"Yeah, it's pretty." I pretended to search for something in my purse. A moment of silence passed before Dad chimed in.

"We live in such a beautiful part of the country. I am in *awe*."

I mumbled another agreement and then reluctantly followed their gaze. OK, fine. The view was pretty incredible. We were on open water, but still by the shoreline, the sky and water lit up magically by the sunset. I snapped a quick photo with my iPhone and uploaded it to my Instagram with no caption or filter. The windows were spotless. Anyone who saw it wouldn't be able to tell from where it was taken.

"Is this seat free?" I heard suddenly.

I lifted my chin. Déjà vu. Was I experiencing a glitch in the Matrix? It was Jake. *Do I look like a waiter?* Jake. Looking down his nose at me.

"Yes," I lied. "It's taken."

He placed his hand on the back of the empty chair next to me. "It looks pretty free to me."

Ignoring me, he sat down in the chair, and I tried not to scowl, or look at him too much. He was wearing a powder blue collared shirt and had left the top three buttons undone, having abandoned his tight white polo. God forbid that *snob* be confused for "the help." And what was that smell? Axe body spray? I took a big sniff. OK, fine. Maybe it wasn't. Maybe it was a cologne that smelled pretty good, now that I reconsidered. Cedarwood. Maybe rosemary? *Tobacco*? Ugh. Damnit. The cocktail was intoxicating.

"Jasmine, so good to see you!" a man's voice said. I looked across the table. Several aunties and uncles had just joined us, including the queen and Jake's father. I'd recognized him from Instagram, but in person—his tender smile, his thoughtful brows—a flood of memories came pouring back.

"*Ranjit* Uncle?" I said quietly.

"How you've grown! It's been so nice to see you after all these years."

"It's nice to see you, too," I said, and oddly, I wasn't lying. I tended to remember the community from my childhood in one big angry lump, but not everyone was so terrible. At least, not at first. Ranjit Uncle I definitely remembered. There were holes—I still couldn't remember any more details about this family—but *him* I now remembered. He was the uncle who always remembered your name at the *gurdwara* and never tattled when you stole an extra *jalebi* or *ladoo* from the community kitchen. He was an uncle who looked you in the eyes and praised the fact that your favorite subject at school was art, unlike the others, who tried convince you to like math instead. He was an uncle who always had a stash of bubble gum in his pocket, a compliment on his lips, his heart on his sleeve.

"You remember my son, *hah beti*?" He gestured to Jake. How the hell had this wonderful man fathered *him*? "It's been a long time."

"A *long* time." Baring my teeth, I flashed Jake a smile. "*Jake* Dhillon. Of course! How could I forget *you*!"

"Jasmine." He cleared his throat. "What are the odds?"

I regretted not having sampled from my suitcase gin before dinner. The waiter arrived and discreetly pointed out that the negroni I had my eye on wasn't part of the all-inclusive package and would cost me a whopping thirty-one dollars. My eyes nearly sprung from their sockets.

"Actually, I'll have a sparkling water," I said quietly to the waiter. Whether Jake heard the exchange or not, I wasn't sure, but then his eyes tracked my way.

"Thank you," I said to the waiter, raising my voice so Jake could definitely hear. "Thank you *so, so* much."

"No worries—"

"Seriously," I insisted. "*Thank you.*" I glowered at Jake. "I really appreciate your service."

The waiter cleared his throat. "Of course ..."

"I know not everyone appreciates you," I said even more loudly. "Some people think too highly of themselves, and might even be offended to be mistaken for a waiter, but I wouldn't be. I *value* you."

"Uhh ..." The waiter took a step backward. "I ..."

"You're making him uncomfortable," Jake interrupted, turning to him. "Sorry about her. She has a thing for waiters."

My cheeks burned red as the waiter chuckled and moved on to Queen B, who was seated on Jake's other side.

"Nice," I said to Jake in a harsh whisper. "By the way, you missed a few buttons on your shirt."

Before Jake could reply, I shifted my body away from him and toward the rest of the table.

"Mom. *Dad*." I made my voice go sticky-sweet. "Did you know our little Jake is about to graduate from *law* school?"

Mom's and Dad's eyes lit up as they turned to him. "Already?"

"How time flies!"

"*Beta*, we're so proud of you."

I faked an enthusiastic smile as everyone joined in on congratulating Jake.

"University of Chicago," I said loudly. "I heard that's one of the best law schools in the country. Isn't that right, Jake?"

I nodded vigorously, and to everyone at the table, everyone except Jake, I looked like I was gushing. I had been his babysitter, after all, right? I was his elder sister, his *didi*. I was *so* very proud.

"Do you know he had his choice in law schools?" Queen B chimed in. She had finished with our waiter. "How many offers did you get?"

"Um . . ." Jake hesitated.

"Seven." Ranjit Uncle nodded. "Or was it eight?"

Jake shifted in his chair, blushing. As if. He totally loved the attention.

"Seven."

"Yes. He was rejected from Harvard," Ranjit Uncle said. "It *should* have been eight."

Jake opened his mouth but then closed it again.

"And he will officially be lawyer soon, *hah*?" Queen B nodded, squeezing Jake's hand. "When will you receive your bar results?"

"Soon." Jake shrugged. "In the next couple of weeks."

"Are you nervous?" Uma Auntie asked. "My first ex-husband"—
she threw my mom a look that said there was a story there—"you
know, *he* was lawyer. He had to sit the bar twice. But he was not
so bright, Jake. I wouldn't worry."

"I . . ." Jake glanced at his father, his shoulders tightening. "I'm
not worried. It was super easy."

*Super easy.* The only exam I'd ever found "super easy" was the
pregnancy test I took two years ago after Brian and I got back
from Cabo. It was also the only exam I'd ever been thrilled to
fail.

"So, Jasmine," Jake continued. He leaned his elbows forward
on the table, shooting me daggers. "What about you? It's been,
what, eighteen years? Tell me about yourself."

My body stiffened at his word choice and how he'd thrown
my question back in my face.

"You work in animation," Ranjit Uncle offered, before I could
say anything. "Jake, you know this. I told you this so many times.
I told you how Jasmine is one of those rare people who was able
to turn her childhood passion for visual art into her career!"

I felt giddy at Ranjit Uncle's compliment. At the fact that Jake's
attempt to embarrass me further had been thwarted by his own
father. Who said blood was thicker than water?

"Thanks, Uncle." I beamed. "Yes, I've been an animator for
eight years now."

"That's great, *beti*," Ranjit Uncle said. "You followed your heart.
And speaking of the heart, where is . . ." He trailed off, just as my
stomach twisted into knots.

"I'm so sorry, dear," he whispered. "Bishan had shared the news,
but I forgot. I apologize."

"It's OK," I said awkwardly. "No worries. It only just happened."

"What just happened?" Jake asked.

I wasn't about to say it, and my parents—who hadn't contributed a word since the topic of conversation switched to me—were definitely not about to say it. Finally, Queen B stepped in.

What a hero.

"Jasmine and her boyfriend have ended their *cohabitating* relationship," she said, drawing out the words.

I chanced a look at Mom. She was staring at her hands.

"I see," Jake said stiffly. "Sorry."

She looked around the table, making sure every single person was listening. "Can you imagine what *our* parents would have thought about the kids these days?"

I bit the inside of my cheek. What they thought about all of us kids, or just women like *me*? I didn't see anyone asking Jake about his relationship status, or the roster of half-naked women he posed with on Instagram.

"You should move in with your parents for a while," the queen continued. "That would make them *so* happy. And it will ground you. Give you some clarity."

I was tempted to say that, in reality, my parents had not once extended me that invitation, and my disrupting the peace in their home would make them anything *but* happy, but I stayed quiet and let Queen B continue her roast.

It wasn't just her style and clothing that had evolved. Bishan Auntie's military tactics had, too. In 2005, slut shaming was directed behind the harlot's back, and the community steered clear of her like she carried an infectious disease. Evidently, now she was happy to do it to my face.

I'd taken a lot of shit over the years, but even this was getting a little much. I kept looking for an out. A pause. I threw Uma Auntie a pleading look, but she had struck up a side conversation with Ranjit Uncle and wasn't paying attention to the beatdown I was getting. I bit my tongue, unwilling to make a scene, disrespect an elder in public, but it was hard. Hard to hear the queen list off the names of the other women in our community who had had long-term boyfriends who didn't turn into husbands. The women who, like me, were childless and single in their thirties. The women who were considered failures.

"I was even starting to get worried about your sister, Niki," the queen pushed. "But then we heard about *Sameer*. We are *so* excited for the engagement party later this summer. Niki is *thirty* years old now?"

I nodded, my eyes on my hands.

"That's a good age to get married," she declared. "A few years ago, I would have said twenty-five, but I have updated my views in light of my new understanding that girls, too, like to have careers. My daughters have insisted I realize twenties are *too* young, *hah*? Thirty is the right age for marriage. Thirty, but *no* older, is the appropriate—"

"*Bhua*," Jake interrupted suddenly. "Do you know more than half of my class at law school were women?"

I looked up. Jake hadn't spoken in several minutes, but now he had his elbows on the table and was staring eagerly at his aunt.

"Really, *beta*!" she exclaimed.

"Really." He paused, his eyes so fixated on his aunt it as if he was trying not to look at me. "I took an advanced seminar on criminal justice and the rule of law in the developing world. And that one was eighty percent women. Anyway, the seminar was fascinating. It was taught by a brilliant professor who had clerked for Ruth Bader Ginsburg . . ."

The drinks arrived, and then our meals, and the rest of the dinner turned into Jake Dhillon 101, in which the queen and

Jake took turns educating us on his college accomplishments, swimming accolades, and general wonderfulness.

The food grew cold on my plate, and I sat there, picking at it, trying to hold myself together. Trying not to let the queen's hateful comments lodge too deeply in my throat. She was my elder. I couldn't have clapped back, but Mom and Dad could have stood up for me.

They had been right there, watching. Listening. And they hadn't said one word.

# Chapter 8

*Eighteen years ago*

JAKE."

He didn't answer.

"*Jake,*" I said again. "It's your turn."

"Huh?"

The kid was either really not paying attention, or not very good at Monopoly. His head was in the clouds, and his fingers—ugh! One of them was picking his nose. Why were kids so gross?

"It's your turn," I repeated, unable to hide the annoyance in my voice. I didn't know how I ended up with *this* job after I'd been volun-told to come help at the *gurdwara*. Niki was outside with Mom and some aunties stringing garlands, but she was much better at looking after children. I thought they talked too much, or too little, and were somehow always super sticky.

Jake rolled the dice, finally, knocking over half of my housing development on St. James Place through New York Avenue in the process. Sure, my adversaries were between the ages of seven and ten, but that didn't mean I had to go easy on them. Kids needed to learn how to lose. I heard that in tenth grade social studies. It was character building.

"I'm on Boardwalk!" Jake exclaimed, after he rolled his wheelbarrow down the game board. "*Yes*. Yes! I'll buy it."

"You're going to have to mortgage something," the kid next to him whined. "You don't have enough money!"

"I do, too."

"Nuh-uh."

I leaned back against the wall, determined to let the kids figure it out. We were playing downstairs in the *langar*, and I scanned the room, the various aunties, uncles, and their children who had been tasked with jobs to prep for the festival this weekend. I didn't even really know what Vaisakhi was, honestly. We hadn't been in years. Mom and Dad were usually too busy working for these kinds of events, but then last year they caught me smoking at the mall and decided I wasn't Indian enough. That I needed to be more "community minded" and good, like the other girls at *gurdwara*. As if. I bet all of them had tried smoking, too. They just hadn't gotten caught.

It was kind of fun watching them think of new ways to punish me, whenever I got detention or they found a beer bottle in the trash or a boy dared to call our landline. They couldn't take away my cell, because that was how I communicated with Niki. (We bused home together after school and god forbid their baby girl get lost.) They couldn't force me to do more chores, either, because—news flash—I already did most of them anyway. And they couldn't really ground me. Sure, in theory I was barred from leaving the house at night, and was supposed to be home by *five p.m.* on weekends, but who exactly was going to stop me? Dad was either working or sleeping, and Mom was in night school again this spring. Some weeks, the only time I saw her was when she was yelling at me for leaving her clothes in the washing machine.

"Jasmine..."

My ears perked up at the sound of my name. But it wasn't coming from the kids. They were still debating Jake's cash flow problems.

"Her, *yes*. Last night..." More murmurs. "The *elder* Randhawa girl."

OK, that I definitely heard. I sat forward, uncrossing my legs, which were getting numb from sitting on the floor. Who was talking to me? Or about me? I stood up, my pulse steadily rising. I flicked my eyes to the left. A group of aunties were staring at me and, a beat later, went totally silent.

I swallowed hard, feeling exposed. Had they just been talking about me? I took a hesitant step forward, offering them a smile. No one smiled back.

"Hello." I pressed my palms together in respect. "*Sat Sri Akaal*, Aunties." I paused. Still no one spoke. "Can I help with something?"

Crickets. A bead of sweat formed on my temple, and I brushed it away with my hand. What was going on? What did they think—

Oh.

Oh *shit*.

"Bishan," one of them said. "Shall we go upstairs?"

"*Hah*." Bishan Auntie pursed her lips and, her eyes not leaving me, ever so slightly shook her head. "Let's go, ladies. *Chalo*."

Ignoring me, the aunties went upstairs, and my ears burning, I went back to the Monopoly board. I let Jake win the game, and then we switched to Junior Scrabble, but my heart wasn't in it. I came in last.

The drive home later was quiet. Too quiet. I let Niki have the front seat, and I stared out the window, watching the rain splatter against the glass. At home, Dad was in the living room, working on his taxes. Her voice low, Mom said something to him in Punjabi. He frowned.

"Hi, Dad." I took off my coat and threw it in the closet. He didn't reply.

"Niki, will you give us a moment?" Mom said. "And, Jasmine, hang up your coat properly."

"But Jasmine promised we'd watch *The Princess Diaries*," Niki whined.

"Your sister is not watching any television today," Mom said. "You go ahead, *beti*."

Niki sighed, gave me the eyes, and then headed for the stairs. Mom stopped her on her way, softly gripping her chin with her thumb and pointer finger. My stomach squirmed.

"Do you have anything to say for yourself?" Mom said quietly after I'd hung up my coat and was sitting across from my parents in the living room. I decided to play dumb.

"About what?"

"You know about *what*." Mom winced. "Last night. At . . ."

At another community event they dragged Niki and me to, some uncle's retirement party, because they didn't trust me home alone.

"At the dinner party," Mom said finally. She was struggling for words, and by the looks of it, for air. She looked at Dad for help. I wasn't sure why. He never helped.

"Last night at the dinner party," Mom repeated. "Where were you?"

"Uh. Having *dinner*—"

"Don't be smart. You know what I am talking about."

I did know what she was talking about, what, apparently, *everyone* was talking about. My lungs burned.

"Do I?"

"What happened last night, Jasmine?"

Mom already knew, but as my parents waited for me to answer, it dawned on me that they wanted me to lie. They didn't want to believe the gossip.

I swallowed hard, screwing up my face, unsure if I wanted to yell at them or cry.

But why *should* I have to lie? I hadn't done anything wrong.

"I was bored. The kids downstairs were watching some dumb Pixar movie. So, I went into the backyard." I crossed my arms. "The Patels' nephew from Detroit was on the patio. Suresh. And we started talking and—"

Before I could finish my sentence, Dad stood up from the couch and started pacing the room, muttering to himself in Punjabi. Mom sank into the couch, her mouth open.

"So, it's true."

"Yes, so what?" I cried. "What's the big deal? I'm fifteen. All we did was *kiss*—"

And off she went.

*Don't you care about your reputation?*

*No good boy will ever marry a girl like you.*

*After all the sacrifices we made so you could be an American?*

*You are shaming us, Jasmine. You are shaming your father.*

I'd heard this shit before. But I'd never heard Mom yell it so loudly. I'd never heard her say it to me like she really truly meant it.

I wiped the tears from my face, waiting for her to stop. Wondering if she'd ever try and see my side. I was fifteen. I was an American. I was just a normal *teenager*.

Wasn't I?

"Do you know," I said, when she finally took a breath, "when Becky told her mom she was thinking about having *sex*—"

Mom gasped.

"—with her boyfriend," I continued, "her mom actually *talked* to her about it?"

"You disrespectful girl," Mom spat. "You speak in such way in front of me, in front of your *father*?"

"But Becky—"

"Becky is no longer allowed in this *house*, young lady. Is this why you are bringing such shame on the family? Because of *Becky*?"

Mom restarted her rant. She had not understood my point. She didn't want to hear about how Becky's mom, who was actually open to having an honest conversation with her daughter, had talked Becky out of having sex at the age of fourteen, when none of us virgins could. Mom didn't want to hear about how desperately I wished I could talk to her sometimes like that, about how restless I felt at school, or about how demoralized I'd been about my painting ever since failing to even place in the top ten in the competition I entered last winter, or how I'd lost five pounds last summer but then gained it all and then some back.

How, Suresh, the guy who kissed me last night, promised he'd message me this morning, but he never did.

Fuck Suresh. Fuck *everyone*.

There were two pairs of lips involved in that kiss last night, yet I was the only one getting blamed, being made to feel that biological human urges were something to be ashamed about. No one cared about his role in all of it. No one was going to say shit about Suresh, a *college* guy, who had been the one to kiss a fifteen-year-old in the first place.

I'd pulled away initially and glanced back at the house. He had told me no one could see. Now that I thought about it, I realized he hadn't even cared. Why should he? His whole life, he'd be able to do whatever he wanted, with whomever he wanted, and still be everyone's golden *boy*.

I couldn't even be a normal fifteen-year-old girl.

# Chapter 9

~~~~~~~~

Brian: Having a good trip . . . ?

W<small>E'D LOST CELL</small> service overnight, and Wi-Fi cost twenty-five dollars an hour, so my cute morning routine of doom scrolling under the covers was replaced by pretending to sleep under the covers while Uma Auntie meditated on the floor. I felt antsy being disconnected from my whole world back in Seattle. I wanted to see the comments on my new Instagram post, and find out if Rowan had e-mailed me about something work-related, and check in with Niki and Amber and my school friends.

I did not, however, feel any need to reply to Brian's text.

I swapped out my pajama bottoms for leggings, threw on some sneakers, and then told Uma Auntie I was skipping the "optional" morning pool party on our group's itinerary in favor of the gym. The last two times Brian and I broke up, it started like this. Brian sending out a vague, noncommittal text that had nothing to do with Mango or moving-out logistics. Brian, just a *teensy* bit curious about my life without him. If this was another attempt to get me back, then good riddance, sir. It was not going to work!

I stopped at a coffee kiosk, shot a double espresso, and then found a map that directed me to the gym. It was located on the top deck, had floor-to-ceiling windows, and was actually pretty swanky. I picked the treadmill in the far corner, blared Drake in my AirPods, and started jogging. It was misty outside and I couldn't see much, and in less than a half mile, I found myself obsessively checking my phone, as if cell service this far at sea would magically return.

Could I really get through the day without knowing what was going on? I was already in withdrawal. Someone needed to mainline me with 4G stat. Hell, I'd even accept 3G.

Instead, I picked up my pace and resisted temptation by asking the nice woman squatting nearby to hide my phone in her towel. After I hit five miles, I cranked the treadmill up to its highest speed and sprinted for another minute, endorphins rocking me like a shock wave as I slammed the "off" button and started my cooldown.

I was on my way over to stretch on the floor mats when I spotted Jake. I stopped dead in my tracks. He must have arrived while I was running. I took a hesitant step forward, hoping he wouldn't notice me as I inspected him from his head to his Air Jordan running shoes. He was sporting red basketball shorts and a tight black T-shirt and was lying facedown, as if he'd just collapsed after a set of push-ups.

Of course Jake would be at the gym. After all, he loved to flex.

I stalled by drinking from the water fountain, my eyes not leaving him. What was he doing lying there like a beached whale? Or perhaps a beached bodybuilder. Regardless, it had been nearly two—I glanced at my phone—*three* minutes, and he still had not moved from his resting position. What kind of workout was that?

I crept up to him, slowly, wondering if maybe he was ... *dead*? His gym shorts had ridden up a bit, exposing the bottoms of his thighs. Not that I was looking at his thighs. I couldn't have cared less about Jake's stupid thighs.

When I was just a few feet away, I stopped and squatted down, wondering whether I should leave the gym without saying hello. He had no idea I was here. Jake, too, had his AirPods in, and when I craned my neck, I saw that he watching something on his phone. Curious, I leaned farther forward, careful not to make a sound. Jake was on his belly, his forearms against the ground, watching something on the screen in his left hand. I traveled my feet forward to get a better look. Squinting, I realized I recognized the actors. And that setting ...

I clasped my hand over my mouth when it hit me. He was watching the TV adaptation of Diana Gabaldon's *Outlander*.

What a turn of events. Jake Dhillon. A douchebag, yes, but one who liked historical romances with strong female leads!

I got down on my knees, then on all fours, and lowered myself down. Slowly, I combat crawled forward. I was so close to him I could smell him—the same earthy cologne from the evening before—but he still didn't notice me. I inched forward, and then a little more, until my head was only just out of his line of sight.

"Hey, bud!"

Jake whipped his head toward me, and I burst out laughing at his shock of realizing I was lying right next to him. He pulled out his AirPods, stammering, and flipped over his phone—all while I was *dying* of laughter.

"Jesus, Jasmine, you scared me!" He looked pissed. He pushed himself up off the floor to a seated position. With great effort, I sat up, too. My stomach hurt from laughing so hard. Perfect. I could skip the five sit-ups I had planned.

"How long were you . . ." Jake trailed off, his eyes briefly dipping to my drenched T-shirt. "Did you already work out?"

I pointed at the bank of treadmills. "I was over there."

He nodded, uncomfortable.

"You were doing push-ups?"

"Yeah," he grunted. "This and that."

"Planks, too, I bet. Huh? Core strength is important," I said earnestly. "In your twenties, you do it for the bod. Wait until you hit your thirties—you'll be doing it to protect your lower back."

Jake's expression softened, the corners of his mouth turning upward.

"You know who has a *great* core?" I said dreamily. "Like, superhot abs?"

Jake blinked, waiting for me to answer.

"Sam Heughan," I deadpanned. "Do you know him? He plays Jamie Fraser on—"

"All right, all right," Jake said, just as I burst into another fit of giggles. "You caught me watching *Outlander*. Don't tell anyone, all right? I . . ." He paused. "I . . . My friend got me into it."

"Friend or girlfriend?" I winked. "Does she know you're watching without her? Are you Netflix cheating?"

Jake rolled his eyes. "No, I don't have a girlfriend."

"Too many to choose from, huh?"

"What is that supposed to mean?"

"Nothing. You're just a hot commodity, Jake." I leaned forward to stretch out my calves. "Here I thought you were just a stereotype, but you're not. You watch *Outlander*. You have complex emotional needs."

"Yeah, well *you* . . ." He trailed off, glaring at me.

"Say it."

"I have nothing to say."

"Of course you do!" I laughed. "So, go for it. I bet you can't find an insult that I haven't already heard a thousand times."

"Why do you want to fight with me?" Jake asked quietly.

"Why do *you* shut up just when the fight gets good?" I pushed. "You scared of me, Jake?"

Jake's eyes were smoldering again. On one hand, he looked as if he wanted to fire something back, go in for the kill, and on the other . . . No. Never mind. I'd better not dwell.

Neither of us spoke for a second, and I half expected him to shrug me off and disappear again, but he didn't. He pushed his left leg out in front of him, curled his right foot into that leg, and leaned forward in a stretch, too.

"You run a lot?" he asked. As *if* he was interested in someone other than himself.

"Occasionally . . ."

Jake scoffed. "Don't sound so suspicious. I'm just making friendly conversation."

"Oh. Is that what this is?"

Jake didn't say anything again, which made me feel bad, so I sighed. "I run after work, a few times a week. Four or five miles, usually."

"What's your time?"

I told him and he blew air through his teeth. He was impressed. I thought he would use this as a launching pad to tell me about *his* time, and how much faster and better he was than me, but he didn't. Jake asked me how long I'd been into the sport.

"I started running last year, after we got our dog, Mango," I answered, a pit growing in my stomach. I missed her already. "Her previous owner was a runner, and trained her. Brian's more of a CrossFit guy, so I thought, why not, I'll run with her."

"What breed?"

"A full-size goldendoodle. She's the best." I paused. "I'm also not sure she's going to be mine anymore."

Jake, who was still sitting close, knocked his knee against mine. The way we were sitting, it could have been an accident. It also could have been a gesture of comfort. I chanced a look over. He was staring at me but averted his gaze the moment our eyes locked. His hair was cut short above the ears and neck but long on top and drooped over his forehead in a way that was maybe a bit adorable. Had I written him off too quickly? Last night when he started blabbing about himself at the dinner table, was he just rescuing me from Queen B?

"So," Jake grunted, when the silence started getting awkward.

"So."

"What are you up to the rest of the day?"

"No idea." I sank farther into my stretch. "Avoiding the Auntie-Uncle Brigade."

"Is that what you call them?"

I shrugged. "I have other names for them, too."

"Like?"

"The Sith Empire."

He laughed. He must have seen *Star Wars*, too.

"Aging dementors—"

"Come on," he said. "They're not so bad."

I scoffed. "Oh really?"

"Aren't they kind of adorable? The uncles are *so* excited I'm here." He stretched his arms above his head, smiling. "They keep asking me to race them. And the aunties . . ." Jake trailed off, his eyes searching my face. "What is it?"

"Nothing."

"What is it?" he pressed. "Why do you look like that?"

"They're adorable if you're a *guy*," I said, after a moment had passed and I could manage the words. "But if you're a single woman over thirty . . ."

At some point, my lips had started trembling, so I sprouted up from the floor with excuses about requiring a shower. I bee-lined for the exit. Jake stayed hot on my trail.

"Listen, about what Bishan Auntie said to you last night—"

I waved him off as he caught up to me. So he *did* rescue me at dinner by diverting Queen B's attention back to him. Cool. *Awesome.* I wasn't just an unmarriageable hag these days. I was also a damsel in distress!

"I don't want to talk about that."

"She's my dad's sister. I know what she can be like—"

"Please. It's fine." I stopped short in front of the elliptical train-ers and gave Jake a reassuring squeeze on the forearm. It had the density of a lead pipe and, interestingly, the energy of Aladdin's magic lamp. It was as if the genie came out and zapped me back to life.

"Oh, I forgot to ask," I whispered excitedly. "What episode of *Outlander* are you on?"

"Jasmine, I—"

"Have Claire and Jamie banged yet?"

"If you insist on changing the subject, can you at least lay off about *Outlander*?" Jake sounded pained. "It's not a big deal—"

"If it's not a big deal, why can't I ask you about it?"

He frowned.

"There's nothing wrong with a man who likes romances, Jake," I said, louder than I needed to. A gray-haired woman getting her cardio on chimed in her agreement.

Jake waved at the lady pleasantly and then hooked his arm through mine and led me out of the gym. When we were through the doors, he stopped abruptly and I bumped up against him. It almost hurt. It was like running face-first into a brick wall.

He took a step backward. "I'm just trying to have a conversation with you. I'm trying to show you I'm not a douchebag. But you're being extremely adversarial."

"Adversarial? *OK*, Jake, thank you for mansplaining that to me."

Jake threw his hands up in the air.

"And I'm not being adversarial," I said quietly. "I thought we were just having a friendly—"

"Torturing me for watching chick flicks isn't exactly *friendly*."

"Chick flicks, huh?" I crossed my arms. I had just about run out of steam and had been willing to call it a draw, but now I was ready for round two. "What else is a chick flick?"

Jake blushed. "Sorry, you're right. That terminology is out of date. I didn't mean—"

"*Game of Thrones*?" I interrupted. "*Breaking Bad*? Does having a woman character make a show a 'chick flick'?" I asked sarcastically. "Because in that case, I think everything on TV is basically a—"

"I didn't mean it like that and you know it."

"What did you mean, then?" I spat out. "That's sexist. Romantic, dramatic, emotional shows like *Outlander* are for everyone. In our society, 'chicks' are usually just socialized to better acknowledge and explore those emotions."

Jake took another step away, shaking his head. "Earlier, you teased me about watching it, as if I *should* be embarrassed, and now you dump on me like that."

"I..."

"You may think I'm a douchebag, Jasmine, but do you know what *you* are?"

"Yes," I said dryly. "I do. But I'd love to hear you say it."

"You—" He pointed at me, wagging his big stupid finger around until it landed on the edge of my nose. "Are..."

"*Too* emotional?" I offered. When he didn't say anything, I continued. "Irresponsible? Defensive? Self-centered? Impulsive?"

*A shame on my family.*

"Trust me," I continued. "I've heard it all before. Nothing you can say will—"

"Irritating," Jake said finally.

# Chapter 10

～～～

Niki: Hey! You surviving?

Dad: We are near the excursion desk on deck 5 and making plans for tomorrow. Come find!

Niki: Not sure you're getting my texts, but FYI... my friends are planning to do a choreographed Bollywood dance at the engagement party. Diya is in charge. You remember her—the one in Mumbai? Anyway, she's wondering if you want to join them. No pressure. I know it's not really your thing...

Amber: Saw Brian in the hall. He asked me who you went to Alaska with but I didn't say shit because #TeamJasmine #BriansAButthead

ALTHOUGH I TRIED to avoid the Auntie-Uncle Brigade, I bumped into Uma Auntie in our cabin and she dragged me to lunch with some women she'd befriended at the pool party. I only agreed to go because they weren't from Seattle and didn't know about My Past.

Margarita Auntie was the best. (They didn't offer their first names when we met, so I gave them all nicknames in my head.) Like the drink she unabashedly ordered three of at the buffet, she was a little sweet, a little spicy: president of the board of directors at her mosque, and also dropped curse words like a sailor. Next to her was Hot Water with Lemon Auntie, who pointed out immediately that my meal choice of fried eggs and toast wasn't Ayurvedic, and didn't say much else other than to comment on how the hot water was lukewarm at best. And then there was Espresso Auntie. After having one tiny sip of coffee, she sounded like she'd popped some awful party drug.

We hit the badminton courts after lunch. (Jake was there playing his father, and I didn't want to *irritate* him, so I ignored him.) After, the aunties and I played card games in one of the multipurpose rooms until we met up with the group for dinner. When it looked like Jake was coming toward my table, I pulled a random auntie from Austin into the seat next to me and threw myself into conversation with her. Two hours of listening to her go over her various aches, pains, and medical appointments was worth not having to sit next to him again.

Overnight, the cruise called into the port of Ketchikan, which was our first stop and named after the Tlingit phrase for an eagle with its wings spread. Sans cell service, I'd read the cruise's many brochures cover to cover. The Indigenous peoples of Alaska had migrated to the area thousands and thousands of years ago, and were colonized by the Russians in the eighteenth and nineteenth centuries. Alaska was then "sold" to the United States. I was eager to learn more about the traditional peoples of Ketchikan—Tlingit Nation, Haida Nation, and Tsimshian Nation—so I wandered over to my parents' cabin to see if they wanted to join me on a visit to the Totem Heritage Center, which housed a collection of totems from the area. I felt mildly guilty for having avoided them the day before, although I wasn't sure why. At dinner, they'd barely even spoken to me.

Dad answered the door. He was already dressed, sporting his winter parka, sunglasses, and fanny pack.

"Where did you get that? You look so cool," I said admiringly. I, too, was wearing my travel fanny pack.

"A car dealership. It was free!"

"Free is always cool." I laughed. "Dad, you look like a hipster."

He stepped back so I could enter. "Well, if *you* think I am cool, then it is official. I've made it."

I smiled, encouraged by the positive interaction. "Where's Mom?"

"Here I am!" She popped her head out of the bathroom, pressing a lash curler against her left eye. "Good morning, *beti*."

"Morning." My eyes drifted to her lower body. "Mom, are those *yoga* pants?"

Mom spun around, showing off her outfit, and Dad admired her jokingly—although it wasn't really a joke. My parents were in love. Not "we've been married for thirty-five-plus years and our lives are in sync" love. But *actually* in love. Like, "if their bedroom door is closed, even in the middle of the day, do *not* go in there" sort of love.

"Hey, can I use that curler when you're done?" I asked Mom,

after Dad not so subtly smacked her on her bum. "I forgot to do my lashes this morning."

"Sure. It's new, and very strong. I have to press for three, four seconds only."

"I know . . . I gave that to you for Christmas." I paused. "I have the same one."

"Oh." Mom frowned nervously. "Right. Of course. I . . . I use it every day, Jasmine."

When Niki bought her a present, Mom posted about it on Facebook and showcased it on the mantel so guests, and even the Internet service guy, could see how wonderful it was. My chest tightened, but instead of running my mouth, I forced the corners of my lips upward.

It was only day three of the cruise. I still had well over a week to go.

KETCHIKAN WAS BEAUTIFUL, everything from the scenic landscape to the bright wooden buildings to the crowds of enthusiastic tourists taking it all in. My parents had signed up for a paid excursion organized by the cruise line, sea kayaking, so we went our separate ways once in town. They invited me to join them, but I was eager to check out the museum. Not to mention the fact that excursions were expensive. Even if I were to forgo food and shelter for the weeks following the cruise, until my next paycheck arrived, I literally could not afford to go.

After I did a solo tour of the Totem Heritage Center, which was *incredible* and briefly lifted my mood, I walked back to the main tourist area downtown, and slowly but surely, the melancholy I felt earlier returned. I wandered down Creek Street, popped in and out of shops, trying to decide what to do. Niki, Amber, and my other friends were all at work and too busy to text or call, so after I uploaded a few of my best shots to Instagram, I stuffed my phone into the bottom of my purse and tried to focus on my surroundings. The sun was out, and there was a cold, crisp breeze coming in off the ocean. I grabbed a ninety-nine-cent coffee and plopped myself down at the edge of a dock where there weren't too many people. I hung my legs over the edge, swinging back and forth as I sipped on the terrible brown liquid that I'd bought under false advertisement. I'd purchased it from a tourist shop that also sold green cotton candy and problematic cultural souvenirs. I should have known better.

I wished Niki were here. The way my parents always put her on a pedestal was exasperating, but her absence was even worse. There was a reason I avoided going to my parents' house alone ever since she moved to LA. My parents were afraid to have a real conversation with me. They were afraid they'd do or say something that would make me snap, and cause a typical Jasmine Tantrum that would shock or embarrass them.

Inching forward, I let my legs hang farther forward until the toes of my Adidas sneakers hovered just a hair about the water's edge, asking myself again why I had chosen to come on this damn cruise. Was I just being impulsive and spiteful because they hadn't invited me? Or was it more?

They didn't like me. They didn't respect me, or my choices, and in recent years they had withdrawn almost completely from my life. But they were still my parents. I still wanted them to . . . *care.*

Didn't I?

"Mind if I join you?"

I whipped my head around. Jake was standing right behind me, about ten feet back. He was wearing aviator sunglasses, an olive green Henley, and dark-washed jeans. He looked . . .

"Hi." I cleared my throat, knocking back the next thought. "Sure."

"I thought about scaring you in retaliation," Jake said, plopping himself next to me. "But I was worried you'd fall in the water."

"Oh, come on. You would have loved that."

"Of course," he said. "But then you could have sued me. Have you heard I'm a fancy lawyer?"

I grinned against my will.

"No excursion today?"

I shook my head. "You?"

"No. Dad wanted to save his energy for the big one tomorrow." He paused. "The Endicott Arm Fjord and Dawes Glacier. Sounds like it's going to be the highlight of the trip. You going?"

My gut twisted. "All-inclusive" vacation, my ass. Tomorrow, I would be alone in the cruise ship pool while the other 2,999 passengers had the times of their lives.

"Maybe," I said vaguely. "We'll see."

Jake cleared his throat. "Hey, have you been avoiding me?"

I breathed in the ocean air slowly through my nostrils. "Maybe," I repeated.

"And why is that?"

"I didn't want to *irritate* you again," I said pointedly. "We seem to rub each other the wrong way."

"We could try rubbing each other the right way."

I scrunched up my nose, turning to look at him.

"That wasn't a line." He grinned. "It was a joke, I swear."

"You sure about that? I can tell you have some good ones up your sleeve."

Jake's cheeks reddened. "What makes you say that?"

"Look at you," I laughed. "Look at your Instagram. I'm willing to bet a lot of money I don't have that you have a little black book just full of pickup lines, and they *work*."

"You checked out my Instagram?"

I copied his duck face and then flexed my muscles. "It was pure anthropological curiosity."

"Anthropological or . . ." He raised his left eyebrow. "Anatomical?"

I laughed. "Now, *that's* a line."

"I looked you up on Instagram, too," Jake said, ignoring my declaration. "You're very talented."

"I'm an *artiste*," I said sarcastically.

"Yeah. You are."

I turned to look at him. He wasn't smiling, or making a joke. He'd been serious.

"Oh." I cleared my throat, suddenly self-conscious. "Thanks."

"Has digital art always been your . . . medium . . . of choice? Sorry. I don't know the right terminology."

"You're doing fine." I smiled. "And no. When I was younger, I was really into painting—oil, acrylics, watercolor, anything. But after I saved up for my first MacBook, I never went back. I tend to live my life by trial and error, and I like to create content that way, too. Digital art is more forgiving."

"That makes sense." Jake scooted closer. "And what about photography?"

"What about it?"

"I loved that portrait of Niki you posted a few weeks ago. You have an incredible eye." He paused. "Did you ever think about photography as a career?"

I squirmed. Jake had had a close look at my feed. "Not really . . . I just take shots with my iPhone. Those are just for fun."

"Well, why don't you have any pictures of yourself? All your photographs are of other people, or . . . scenery."

I was about to say "because I'm not a douchebag" but then decided against it.

"I'm the one behind the camera." I shrugged. "Besides, I already know what I look like."

"Fair enough." He nodded. "So, you like camping, huh?"

I furrowed my brows, wondering how far back Jake had looked. I hadn't gone camping in over a year.

"I do, too," Jake continued. "I go with my older brothers every Labor Day weekend. This year, we're going to Cape Lookout in Oregon. Have you been?"

"A long time ago." I paused. "Who are your brothers? Are they my age?"

"Even older." Jake grinned. "You probably didn't know them. Sunny and Shaan?" When I shook my head, Jake continued. "They're twins, and they weren't around the *gurdwara* much when we were younger. They were both in competitive swimming, track, hockey, football—everything. They never had time. My dad ran them pretty hard."

"A family of athletes," I said.

"Two, at least. I was just trying to keep up."

I was trying to picture how anybody could be more "athletic" than Jake, who looked like he could bench my weight with his pinkie finger, when I remembered our encounter at the gym. He seemed to be thinking about yesterday, too, because he suddenly started mumbling about the emotional and domestic labor assigned to South Asian women. And then intergenerational trauma. And *then* the patriarchy...

"Uh, Jake?" I interrupted, after he used the words "ecofeminism" and "praxis" in the same sentence. "Do you mind speaking in English?"

"Sure. Yeah, yeah. What I'm *trying* to say—"

"Is that you took a gender studies class in college?"

Jake stiffened, his mouth curling up into a grin I could almost call silly.

"*That* . . ." He paused. "And I'm sorry for being obtuse yesterday. I'm aware our community treats boys very differently than girls."

He caught my gaze and held it. "You have every right to think they are a brigade of . . . Sith lords."

"Thank you."

I appreciated that Jake recognized the reality that men (and some women) found easier to ignore. I also didn't feel like getting into the fact that the community was particularly harsh on girls like me who didn't toe the line, so I decided to move the conversation along.

"I guess I'm sorry, too."

I didn't do apologies well. I interlaced my fingers and squeezed.

"You were right," I said slowly. "I shouldn't have teased you yesterday as if it was embarrassing for you to like *Outlander*. It's a great show . . ."

"Thank you. And yes, it is."

"But *you*," I said quickly, jabbing his chest with my pointer finger, "shouldn't have called it a chick flick."

"I know. I'm sorry about that, too."

"Thank you."

I paused. "So, you like chick flicks, then?"

"I thought we weren't supposed to call them that," Jake said.

"*You* aren't." I shrugged. "I'll do as I like."

Smiling, Jake set his hands against the dock, leaning back. I turned around to look at him.

"Do you like *The Mindy Project*?"

"Who doesn't?" he replied

I nodded my approval. "What's your favorite '90s/early 2000s rom-com?"

"My favorites of the *golden age* of rom-coms," he answered slowly, "are *She's the Man* and *10 Things I Hate About You*."

"Good choices. Although, being a fancy lawyer and all, I would have thought you'd pick *Legally Blonde*."

"Right—how could I forget my girl Reese?" Jake exclaimed. "OK, that's also in my top three. What are your top picks?"

"*Clueless, How Stella Got Her Groove Back*, and *Legally Blonde*."

"You didn't even hesitate. I'm clearly speaking with a connoisseur."

I smiled, thinking of Niki. We'd never had that much in common. Niki had been a straight A student, and after school, she practiced the piano or read novels. Meanwhile, I studied the bare minimum and spent all my free time painting or hanging out with my friends. Bingeing romantic comedies in the basement was where we'd found common ground.

"Niki and I watched a *lot* of rom-coms back in the day." I nodded. "I always pretended like I watched the movies for her, but really, I loved them just as much."

"I'll take your secret to my grave," Jake said quietly. "As long as you don't tell my dad what I was watching at the gym . . ."

Just then, a gust of wind came ashore, so strong that it tore through my puffer. Jake's teeth started chattering.

"Where's your jacket?" I asked him. He was only wearing the thin Henley. "You must be freezing."

"I . . ." He stopped. "It's colder than it looks, huh? With the sun out I figured it wouldn't be so bad."

"Did you not bring one ashore?"

Jake grimaced. "I didn't bring one at all."

"*What?*" I cried. "We're in Alaska!"

"Yeah, but it's summer..."

"It's early May, Jake. It's not summer. And like I said before, we're in *Alaska*." I rolled my eyes. "Here..."

I had an extra jacket folded up in my purse. It was a turquoise baggy rain shell I used as an outer layer, and although it wasn't as warm as the one I was wearing now, it was better than nothing. I pushed it toward Jake. Shivering, he handed it back.

"I'm good. I'm not that cold."

"You'll get hypothermia," I said testily. "Put it on."

"Don't tell me what to do," Jake challenged.

"You called me your babysitter." Our eyes locked. "And right now, you're acting like a baby. So put it on."

I shoved the jacket back at him, our hands brushing, and suddenly, I didn't feel cold in the slightest. I was hot all over.

What was this sorcery? Jake was a handsome, sure, hot, *fine*, but it's not like he was Jamie Foxx—the hall pass I had been sure to secure in writing at the start of all my previous relationships. It wasn't like I wasn't able to control myself.

"OK, I'll put on the jacket..." Jake's eyes flicked down to my lips. "Jasmine."

My name on his lips sounded good. *Too* good. Electricity pulsed where he was touching me, the pressure of our palms sending tingles up my arm. But no. No! I couldn't. Right?

*Stop it, Jasmine. No, you couldn't.*

Jake leaned forward, just an inch. His fingers hooked mine, and when he tugged, I leaned in, too, anticipating the fun ahead.

His lips parted, and I could hear his breath go raspy. I could feel how much he wanted to kiss me.

*Jasmine. Stop.*

But . . . But . . .

*Think about this! Do you really just want to have* fun?

I pressed my palms into the deck, steadying myself. It must have been a sign from the universe, because suddenly Jake's phone buzzed and he tore his eyes away from me, pulling it out of his pocket so quickly I thought he was going to drop it in the water. He looked at the screen blankly.

Brian was always secretly looking at his phone, too, never letting me see who it was—not that I would have asked. I was much too concerned pretending that I didn't care, that I trusted he was serious about me.

"Is that another woman?" I asked Jake.

"Why?" Jake mused, tucking the phone back into his pocket. "You jealous?"

"No," I said flatly.

He must have been expecting me to flirt back, because his face fell when I didn't. The wind had picked up again, and shivering, I stood up and brushed the dirt off my butt.

"I'm cold. I'm going to go."

"Sure." Jake hopped up, too. "Yeah. Want to grab some food? There's a diner—"

"I'm not hungry." I waved him off. "I'm heading back to the ship. I'll see you around."

I took two steps forward but stopped when I felt Jake gently take my hand. I turned around, jolting my arm away from him.

"What?" I snapped.

"I thought . . ." He paused, studying me. "I thought we were having a friendly conversation, but now you're mad at me again?"

"I'm not mad at you," I said quietly.

"You are, too."

"I am *not*," I huffed.

Jake was standing only a few inches away, and his shoulders—

*Jasmine. No.*

But his *eyes* . . .

*Jasmine. Shut. Up.*

"I'm not mad at you, Jake," I repeated, turning to leave. It was the truth. I wasn't mad at Jake, or Brian, or even my parents.

I was mad at myself for falling into my same old patterns.

# Chapter 11

≈≈≈

0034: Your monthly wireless statement is
now available. To pay your bill and avoid late
penalties, log in at http.// . . .

A FEW HOURS LATER, I found myself aimlessly scrolling through
my camera roll in the restaurant's bathroom, taking a break
from all the dinnertime small talk. I stopped on a selfie dated
over four years ago. It was the first picture Brian and I ever took
together.

I hadn't been out of a previous relationship very long when
my former roommates convinced me to redownload Bumble.
Brian and I matched a few days later, and we spent the next week
asking each other superficial questions, bragging about how adventurous we both were, trying to play it cool but interested. But
not *too* interested.

We skied black diamonds on our first date, and on our second—
at a casual taqueria—we ended up at a Steve Aoki concert and

danced until four a.m. The days flew by, and then the weeks, and all of a sudden I was thirty-three years old and willfully blind to the fact that all that damn fun we used to have made it easy for me to ignore that Brian and I had nothing else in common. That he was incapable of being a thoughtful, committed long-term partner.

Is that what I wanted, then? Someone to share a life with? Whenever Niki or my friends spoke in such a way, I pretended to dry heave into my purse, but maybe there was something to it. Maybe there could be more to relationships than just . . . *fun*.

I nearly dropped my phone when I suddenly heard Queen B's shrill voice just outside. I hopped off the edge of the sink, my heart racing, and moved closer to the wall.

"But the auditorium is *unoccupied*!"

Curious, I slipped my phone into my back pocket and took another step forward.

"The cruise itinerary has nothing listed for the second-to-last night of the trip," the queen insisted. "And the captain confirmed—"

"It's not the captain who makes those sorts of decisions," a woman's voice interrupted. "*I* am the activities director of this ship, and short-staffed as it is. I don't have enough people-power to throw a dancing competition at the very last minute!"

"We have more than two hundred in our group," Queen B snapped. "We are paying customers. The auditorium is empty. We simply want a chance to use an *empty* theater to put on a show, feature our heritage, our dancing, our *culture*! Are you really going to stop us?"

"You have two hundred people in the group?" the other woman said slowly. "Well, OK, then. Find me a few volunteers from *your* group to help me run the dang thing, and you've got yourself a deal. You can have the auditorium."

"We are on *vacation*, madam. We are not here to *work*—"

"Yes, but you're creating extra *work* for me, work I do not have time for—not on my salary. So, *Bee-shaan*, is it? Do we have a deal? I'll tell you what. For the volunteers, Kensington Cruises will even comp them a few excursions. They can have whatever they want, for free . . ."

The two of them moved away from the bathroom door, their voices fading. A minute later, I slipped out and returned to my table. I had a smile on my face for the first time in hours.

"*Attention*," Queen B called, a few minutes later. She had taken position in the middle of the restaurant where our group was eating, standing next to a woman I assumed to be the other one I'd overheard in the bathroom. "May I have your *attention*, please?" She paused, looking from table to table. "Yes. Ah. Thank you."

I sat up straighter in my chair.

"For those of you who have not yet been introduced to Tess"—Queen B shot her a look, and it wasn't friendly—"the activities coordinator—"

"Director," Tess interrupted.

"Director." Queen B threw another dagger. "Thank you, Tess. Well, she has *generously* offered us the use of the ship's state-of-the-art theater next Thursday. Where we will be able to throw a dancing festival!"

Crickets. Queen B looked uncomfortable as she searched for applause, and eventually, Margarita Auntie and a few others indulged.

"Thank you. Thank you. It will be just like old times, *hah*? Do you remember the dancing competitions we used to host?" More crickets. The queen pursed her lips. "Anyway, there is one *slight* hiccup. Tess requires help with the organization. Goodness me, I don't know—"

"I'll help," I interrupted, before anyone else could volunteer

and score the free excursions. I wanted to go see the Endicott Glacier tomorrow. It sounded spectacular, and what else was I going
to do all day?

Queen B, very slowly, pivoted to face me. In fact, the whole
room was looking at me now, every single colonel, sergeant, and
soldier in the brigade. The back of my neck prickled with heat.

"Thank you . . . Jasmine." The queen cleared her throat. "Right.
There we have it. Jasmine Randhawa will—"

"Bishan," Tess grumbled, "it's no walk in the park. Really, I
need two sets of hands, minimum."

"Then I'll help, too."

My heart jumped into my throat at the sound of Jake's voice
across the room. A beat later, he stood up.

"I volunteer as tribute!"

His mouth twitched as he caught my eye, and I squinted back
in a way that I hoped yelled, *Yes, Jake, I got the* Hunger Games
*reference, but no*, please, *you need to sit the heck down!*

"I'm good," I said coolly. "I can handle it, Jake. Besides, don't
you need a break before you start your *big* job?"

"Agreed." Queen Bishan pouted at her nephew. "You work *so*
hard. This is your vacation!"

"I don't mind, *Bhua*," Jake said brightly, his eyes not leaving
me. "I think Jasmine and I would work well together."

A few aunties seated near Jake started praising him so pro-
fusely it was like he really had just signed up to save his sister
from a dystopian fight to the death. Ugh. I couldn't do this. I
could *not* do this!

The only person more horrified than me was Queen Bishan,
who kept trying to get Jake out of it even after Tess pulled us
aside and started telling us about the free excursions I already
knew about. After she left, I invited Jake out into the corridor for

a "quick chat." The moment we were alone, my fake smile and the gloves came off.

"What are you doing?" I asked icily.

"Being helpful." Jake beamed.

"You're being . . ." I sighed, willing myself to hold my tongue. "You really don't have to do this, OK? Please. Back out."

"I don't want to back out," Jake said.

"Why do you have to impress them, huh? Come on. Everyone already worships you."

Jake scoffed. "Not everyone."

"Yes, they do. You're a guy." I smiled weakly. "If a guy goes to college, they're a genius. Any old job, and they're a breadwinner. Lift a single finger at home, or do something nice like run a danc- ing competition for your community? You're a freaking saint."

*Not to mention, sleep around, and you're still marriage material.*

"I understand that it's different for men and women. I do. And I'm not trying to impress—"

"Come on, Jake," I interrupted. "Just back out of this. Please?"

He inched closer, his face unreadable. "I'm tired. I don't want to fight."

"I don't want to fight, either."

I couldn't meet his gaze. He was standing too close.

"Please." My voice cracked. "Just back out—"

"We're doing this together," he said firmly. "Deal with it, or back out yourself."

"I can't."

"Why?"

*Because I'm selfish and wanted to see a glacier on vacation.*

*Because for a thirtysomething career woman, I'm embarrassingly broke.*

"Never mind," I sighed.

"Jasmine . . ."

Our eyes met, and a part of me wondered if he hadn't signed up to help to impress the aunties and uncles, and I hated that the scenario crossed my mind, that it sent a sick wave of pleasure down my spine.

So what if the physical attraction was mutual?

Maybe I didn't want to just have fun anymore, and throw myself at any man who turned me on and promised a good time. Maybe what I truly wanted was . . .

"Jake!"

We both turned to look at the voice. Queen B was twenty feet down the hallway, her eyebrows furrowed.

"Yes, *Bhua*?" he answered, folding his hands behind his back.

"*Aaja, beta.* Your food is getting cold!"

Jake nodded and then grunted a goodbye before disappearing into the restaurant. I needed a minute to pull myself together, alone, but Queen B lingered.

"Hi, Auntie." I grimaced. "I'll be right behind you. I just . . . have to . . . blow my nose!"

I pretended to dig around my purse for a tissue while she studied me.

"You and Jake will be required to spend a *lot* of time together this trip."

It wasn't a question, so I didn't reply.

"You know . . ." she said, playing with her bracelets. "At first, I thought perhaps it would be improper for both of you to volunteer, *hah*? It might not look so good for *you* to be spending so much close-close time with a boy."

"Really," I said dryly.

"Yes. I mean. Already, your reputation isn't . . ." She trailed off, and bile rose in my throat as my mind finished off the sentence.

*To quote Taylor Swift, my reputation's never been worse.*

*I was the friendly community slut.*

"But *then*," the queen continued, "I remembered you are so, *so* much older than our Jake, are you not?"

"Am I?" I said slowly.

"Five years at least." She nodded. "And with such a big age difference, no one will suspect anything. How do the young people say it? Jake is"—she narrowed her eyes—"out of your *league?*"

My nostrils flared as I held my tongue. She had immigrated to the US decades ago, and she knew damn well that wasn't what the phrase meant. She had also never brought up my reputation so brazenly to my face. The queen was on top of the throne for a reason; she was smart and, until now, had always been more subtle.

I interlaced my fingers, calculating my next move. What had she seen? What did she suspect?

"My nephew is very handsome," she purred. "Isn't he?"

I suppressed a grin as it hit me. She was trying to scare me, the cougar, from pouncing and getting too "close-close" with her nephew. But the fact that she was getting in my face right now meant she suspected Jake might be willing prey.

"You're quite right, Auntie," I said, with a burst of energy. "Jake is *extremely* handsome."

She smirked.

"So much younger than me. *So* innocent."

I blinked my lashes.

"*So* much to learn."

"*Jake* has so much to learn?" she said. "Well, not really. He is a very smart boy. And—"

"A lawyer. I know." I took Queen B's hand and lowered my voice. "What I mean is he has a lot to learn about the real world. About *women*."

Her eyes bugged out as I did my best to keep a straight face.

"Jake has been following me around like a puppy since we boarded." I shook my head. "He thinks us both being here is fate. Can you believe it, Auntie? He used the word 'kismet.'"

"I . . . You . . ." Queen B shuddered. "He . . ."

"Don't worry. I explained to him that I am just out of a serious relationship, and that he needs to focus on his career. That he needs to find a nice Indian girl his own age." I smiled and squeezed her hand. "I took care of him when we were young, and I'll take care of him now. Don't you worry, Bishan Auntie. I'll make sure our little Jakey falls out of love with me."

Queen B dropped my palm, her mouth pursed. Before she could step away, I linked my arms through hers, guiding us back toward the restaurant.

Whispering, I said, "You won't tell anyone, now would you, Auntie?"

She glared up at me.

"He would be so embarrassed."

"I won't tell a soul," she said stiffly.

I knew she wouldn't breathe a word. The fake news about Jake being in love with me would be embarrassing for his family. God forbid Jake end up with a woman not as perfect as him. I was the very last person they'd want him dating.

# Chapter 12

〜〜〜

Jasmine: amber, i don't know when you'll
receive this because I'M IN THE MIDDLE OF
THE OCEAN, but my current roommate
keeps bugging me to meditate with her every
morning and i'm running out of excuses. I
MISS YOU. I MISS YOUR BITCHY
MORNING FACE!

[Not delivered]

THERE'S NOTHING QUITE like messing with an authority figure, was there? My mood brightened, I crashed a ladies' night with Uma Auntie, Margarita Auntie, and Mom at the casino. Uma Auntie treated everyone to a "*Titanic*-sized" pitcher of sangria, and then Mom got tipsy and mistakenly put a fifty-dollar bill instead of a fiver into the change machine. On the plus side, the mishap gave us enough quarters to play the slots for the whole night—although the four of us gabbed more than we gambled.

Uma Auntie and Margarita Auntie proved to be an even more effective buffer than Niki usually was, because Mom and I actually had a great time together. No awkward silences or passive-aggressive remarks or rolling of eyes. It felt like I was hanging out with a bunch of girlfriends.

I'd also like to note for the record that I didn't think about Jake once. (Well, maybe once, but only when I spotted him walking past the casino.)

The following day was the excursion to Endicott Arm Fjord and Dawes Glacier. Although I was slightly seasick from the guilt of having scored the excursion dishonestly, the experience was worth it. We cruised past glimmering icebergs, a waterfall, and scores of wildlife, including a massive colony of seals. I'd never seen so many in one spot!

After, I followed my parents back to their cabin. Dad and I were in a heated debate about what species of whale we'd seen breach from a distance, when I realized Mom had crawled into bed.

"You all right?" I slumped down next to her on the bed. "Mom?"

"Long day," she whispered. "I just need to lie down."

Dad joined me by her side. "Chandni? *Tikh-hain?*"

"A rest, and I'll be A-OK."

"Are you sure?" My chest felt tight looking at her. "Mom, are you sick? Do you have—"

"It's just my hangover, Jasmine," Mom joked. "Although, not as bad as the one your father had early this morning. Did he tell you what the *uncles* got up to last night?"

Mom insisted it was just exhaustion, sangria, and the choppy waves we had had to endure on the catamaran. Unconvinced, I rummaged through my parents' toiletries bag. When I couldn't find any nausea medication, I grabbed my wallet, instructed Mom to drink a lot of water, and promised to have tracked down Dramamine by the time they woke up from their nap.

Despite Mom's attempt to make light of her condition, I couldn't shake this weird feeling as I headed up to the closest gift shop. It wasn't *that* long of a day. She'd only had two glasses of sangria. And the waves weren't all that rough . . . Or was that not true?

I was in my thirties. Despite all the memes and TikToks about how old millennials were, the truth was, I was relatively healthy and fit and young. It was my parents who were starting to get old.

I didn't like to think about it. Whenever Niki brought it up, I ignored her or changed the subject, told her flippantly that she needed to live in the present. But it was clear even to me that Dad's back was getting worse, and Niki mentioned that Mom's physician recently gave her a stern talking-to about getting her cholesterol under control.

My parents were on a seniors' cruise for a reason. They were senior citizens, and were finally doing all the things they never could afford or had time to do when they were younger. Like traveling with their friends, and trying sea kayaking for the first time, and drinking a little too much, and living out their golden years.

How much time would I have left with them? How much time had I missed spending with them already?

The gift shop was out of Dramamine, and instead of trekking to the one across the ship, I headed to the medical suite one deck below. The door was ajar when I arrived.

"Hello?" I knocked twice. "Anyone home?"

"No?" a man's voice called out.

"Oh really?" I called back.

When no one appeared, I tapped open the door with my fingers and scanned the room. There was a hospital bed, a few chairs, and various pieces of medical equipment I recognized from having binged the first nine seasons of *Grey's Anatomy*. I took another step into the room.

"Oh, it's you."

I spotted the man behind the voice. He was practically hidden in the far corner behind a stack of charts, three computer monitors, and a Taco Bell bag. He was in his late thirties or early forties, and had dark skin, a friendly smile, and an ink stain on the chest of his cardigan.

"I *heard* there were a few non-seniors aboard."

"Where did you hear that?" I asked.

"The staff all talk. You and the other guy stand out." He stood up from the desk, shaking crumbs off his pantlegs. "I'm Ethan, by the way. Can I help you with something?"

The doctor's suite didn't have medication for purchase, but Ethan offered me a packet of Dramamine from his briefcase. He wouldn't let me pay him, and instead asked me if I wanted to thank him by sticking around for coffee.

"Aren't you working?" I stalled.

He showed me one of his monitors. Where a *Spider-Man* movie was on pause.

"I'm off duty. And very bored." He moved over to the kitchenette. "Sorry, I didn't catch your name."

"Jasmine."

"Jasmine," he repeated. "How do you take your coffee?"

"With Kahlúa," I joked, but then a beat later he pulled out a bottle.

"You're prepared." I laughed. "Do you entertain a lot?"

"Of course. I'm the handsome cruise ship doctor." He paused

thoughtfully. "Although, usually I'm entertaining widows with made-up ailments desperate for a vacation fling."

"No," I gasped.

"Seniors are extremely sexually active, you know."

"I think I did know that." I nodded. "Do you let them down easy?"

"What makes you think I let them down?"

Ethan was joking, of course. He tossed the Taco Bell bag in the recycling and made room on his desk for our coffees and a box of Oreos he found on top of the fridge. I only meant to stay for a minute, but he had such a good sense of humor and was surprisingly easy to talk to. It felt like we'd known each other for a while. He must have felt that way, too, because at one point, he called me Princess Jasmine. I responded by throwing an Oreo at his head.

"Sorry! You must get that a lot."

"Do you know how many times guys have asked me if they can be my 'Aladdin'?"

"Ten times?"

"More."

Ethan popped another Oreo in his mouth. "Twenty?"

"I don't even know." I laughed. "Probably. And before you ask, my parents were not Disney enthusiasts or anything. The animated movie came out after I was born."

"Really?" I could see Ethan doing the math in his head.

"I'm thirty-three. And according to one of my aunties, I need a better antiaging regimen."

"Nah. You look great, Jasmine."

"Thank you! I was about to ask for a scrip for something stronger." I paused. "Do you know, I refused to wear sunscreen growing up? I'm surprised I have any skin left."

"Really? Why?"

"Call it an overcorrection for all the times the aunties told me and my little sister we were too dark."

"I may be biased, but dark skin is beautiful." Ethan, who was Black, grinned at me. It was a nice smile. And even though he was giving me a compliment, and we were joking around, I could tell the banter was strictly platonic.

"Tell me, Doctor," I continued, demurely, "why is it that men don't get told to stay out of the sun? And while we're on the subject, why don't *men* have billion-dollar skin care regimens forced down their throats?"

"Oh, it's coming. You heard it here first."

"You think?"

Ethan nodded. "I don't think beauty standards are going to change for women. There's too much money at stake. My bet is the standards rise for *men*. Higher expectation. Higher profits."

"Men's skin care and beauty are emerging markets. Untapped, even."

"Don't ask me how much I've spent on Rogaine and protein powder, and here I am still bald and with precisely one ab."

I snorted.

"Pretty soon, I'll be forking out money for the bags under my eyes, too."

"Don't forget the lip fillers."

He pointed at his forehead. "And Botox."

"But you're a *doctor*," I proclaimed. "Don't you get that for free?"

Although I'd enjoyed casino night and the glacier excursion, it felt good to hang out with someone who wasn't my parents, or an auntie, or *Jake*. Ethan must have enjoyed my company, too, because he ended up giving me a play-by-play of his adult life and how he ended up working for Kensington Cruises. He and his ex-wife were both family doctors in a small town just east of Seattle, and after they split up, Ethan said he needed to "get away." The week-off, week-on arrangement with the cruise line was perfect, because Ethan had a ten-year-old son, Landon, and had joint custody. Landon lived with his mother when Ethan was at sea, and with Ethan the rest of the time.

"I'm sorry for talking too much," he said, forty minutes and several Oreos later. "You're a good listener."

"Don't mention it." I shrugged. "I'm glad I met you. I needed a friend."

"What about the other young guy?" Ethan asked. "How did you both end up on a seniors' cruise, by the way?"

"I don't know about the *other* guy, but I had no idea what I'd signed myself up for."

I told Ethan a brief version of the story about how I ended up here. Understandably, he looked confused during the part when I agreed to go on a cruise with parents I didn't get along with. With a community that didn't really accept me. I was still making sense of that myself.

"So. You and this Jake guy," Ethan said, trying to fill some of the holes I'd left in the story. "You both signed up to plan a dancing competition together. But you're not friends."

"No." I scowled. "He's my enemy."

"That's a strong reaction to have to someone you haven't seen in nearly two decades."

"Well . . ." I paused, my stomach flip-flopping.

"Unless." Ethan leaned forward, studying me. "Are you into Jake?"

I scoffed.

"You are!"

"No!" My cheeks heated. "No way. He's such a douchebag."

"I sometimes act like a douchebag. Ask my ex." Ethan shrugged. "And here *we* are. Becoming the best of friends."

I laughed.

"So what if he's full of himself? Just be friends with the guy. I can't hang out with you all the time. I actually have to work."

"I can't be friends with Jake . . ." I was starting to feel flustered. "No. No way."

"Seriously, Jasmine," Ethan pressed. "I don't see what the problem is—"

"The problem is me," I exclaimed. "The problem is he's a cocky little shit, which is exactly my type, and if I'm anything less than *rude* to Jake, I will probably screw him, get caught red-handed, and make my parents even more ashamed of me than they already are!"

I closed my mouth, feeling suddenly awkward and overwhelmed by my outburst. Ethan avoided eye contact as I caught my breath. Finally, I summoned the strength to speak.

"Sorry about that . . ."

"No, I'm sorry," Ethan said. "I shouldn't have pushed. It's your business."

"You were just trying to help."

A few times, my best friends had pointed out that I tended to share more with drunk girls in bar bathrooms, with strangers like Ethan, than I did with the people closest to me. I had denied it, but fleetingly, I wondered if it was true. I also wondered why.

"The ex used to go off the rails when I tried to fix everything, instead of just listening," Ethan continued. "But can I say one more thing?"

I nodded.

"Do you really believe you're incapable of being around a guy you find attractive . . . without hooking up?"

"Yes," I said immediately. "Is that sad to you?"

"No. No judgment here." Ethan turned away, his eyes falling on the floor. "Most of the time, I don't have any faith in myself, either."

# Chapter 13

〰〰〰

AN HOUR LATER, I was perched on the windowsill in my parents' cabin while they got ready for dinner, Ethan's comment still ringing in my ears.

Of course I didn't have any faith in myself. Everyone had a little voice in their head, nitpicking, critiquing, judging, doubting. It was loud. It was painful. And in my case, it belonged to my mother.

*You're so selfish, Jasmine.*

I spent money without thinking about its value. I took my parents for granted. I always did whatever I wanted, whenever I wanted, and with whom I wanted—regardless of the consequences for other people. The embarrassment it would cause my family.

*You're too impulsive, Jasmine.*

What kind of person went on a cruise she couldn't afford to spite her parents? Someone who acted before she thought, judged before she considered, yelled before she had all the facts. Someone who spent all her money on the shiniest object or experience.

Jumped into relationships without a second thought about what she truly wanted.

*Why are you being so defensive, Jasmine?*

I chose a hill, and then I set up camp and died on it. I refused to budge or share the space or consider a different viewpoint. My parents had despised Brian, nearly disowned me when I moved in with him, yet that only made me want him more. In retrospect, even Niki and my friends had tried to hint at Brian's red flags. How could I have ignored everyone who loved me the most?

There was no denying anymore that I had a pattern. A *type*. The Brians and the Jakes of this world who turned me on and my good judgment off. Compatibility, trust, respect, values. I'd never been bothered by all of those things we were supposed to figure out after the first date, because I'd never been bothered by anything. I was Jasmine. I was the free spirit.

My brand was *not* to care.

So how could I then trust myself around Jake, a total player, who was blatantly attracted to me, too?

If I didn't keep my distance, we'd end up hooking up, and inevitably we'd be found out and it would be *my* reputation on the line all over again. My family—not Jake's—would suffer the consequences.

"Should I put on a skirt?" Mom asked, when she came out of the bathroom. The nap and Dramamine had helped, but she still looked worn-out.

"I'm not changing." I leaned against the windowsill and showed off my legs. I was still in the jeans I'd worn during our excursion earlier.

"Yes, well, you are young, *beti*." Mom smiled. "You always look fresh."

It was odd how one version of my mother lived inside of me, even when a totally different one was standing before my eyes. She hadn't yelled or directly passed judgment on me in years, yet the distance between us had never been greater.

My eyes burned as I watched her sink into the bed, her tired eyes drifting to the floor. What kind of mother sent four heart emojis to the family group text after her daughter got out of a long-term relationship, but otherwise didn't acknowledge the breakup? Didn't even ask her how she's doing?

But did that mean she didn't care about me? Or was her willingness to brush all our problems under the rug her way of making an effort with me? All this time, was Mom's silence an attempt to restart our relationship?

"I have an idea . . ." I said suddenly, remembering the time Niki pretended to be too sick to go on a planned family hike, just because Dad's back had flared up and he hadn't wanted to admit it. "Let's skip the group dinner tonight."

Their eyes widened.

"Skip?" Dad repeated.

"Yeah. Let's get room service."

"Room service?" Mom echoed. "Is that an option?"

I nodded. "Totally. It's part of the all-inclusive. We can order whatever we want from the main buffet." I walked over to the bedside table, grabbing a menu from where it had been stashed behind the lamp. "What do you say? Pizza or burgers . . ." I nodded at the television. "And a bad movie?"

"What about this tagine you've been telling us about?" Dad asked. "You were so looking forward to the Moroccan restaurant tonight."

"I'm kind of in the mood for pizza," I lied. "But I'm easy. We can go to the restaurant—"

"No," Mom interrupted, as she crawled back into bed. "It's a great idea. Room service sounds idyllic, *beti*. I could really use a break."

We ordered dinner, and I curled up at the foot of their bed as we gorged on pepperoni pizza and watched the second half of *Die Hard 2*, the only thing on TV we could agree on.

"I am going to take part in the dancing competition," I heard Mom say during a commercial break. "Do you remember the *gidha* I performed at the folk festival two years ago? Most of the ladies are here. We already know the steps."

I nodded enthusiastically, even though I had no idea what festival or which ladies she was talking about.

"I am looking forward." Mom nodded, catching my eye. "The dancing competition will be very fun." She paused. "Jasmine, it was very thoughtful of you to volunteer."

My throat closed up, and then tears threatened to spill when Dad reached down and ruffled my hair.

It occurred to me, rather suddenly, that I wanted my parents back in my life. I wanted to be in theirs, too, but maybe that meant I needed to be more like Niki. A daughter who was mindful of the needs of her aging parents and would encourage them to have a low-key night so they could conserve their energy. A daughter who they believed was about to selflessly assist with a community event, even if her motivations were dishonest. A daughter who wouldn't embarrass them in front of their friends.

A daughter they could have faith in again.

I let my legs curl up on the bed, until my feet were touching Mom's. When she didn't move away, my heart sang.

I was thirty-three. I was supposed to have lived and learned and been all the wiser for it. So what if my parents and I didn't used to get along? So what if I was attracted to Jake?

I didn't need to make a mess where there was none. I didn't need to lose control of my tongue and my impulses.

And maybe, just maybe, I didn't have to be the old Jasmine, either.

MOM INSISTED SHE felt well and refreshed enough for the salmon fishing excursion the following day in Juneau. I made her (and Dad) promise me they'd take it easy, and then I swallowed my guilt and cashed in my next free excursion. A guided mountain biking trip just outside the city.

The brochure wasn't lying when it called the trip "strenuous." But the mountainous uphill battles were worth the effort. The view from the lookout point was breathtaking, and as a bonus, I got some incredible photos in the afternoon light and posted them on Instagram.

As I boarded the ship later that afternoon, I caught sight of my parents talking to Jake and Ranjit Uncle, who'd gone on the same excursion. I sidled up to join their conversation and flashed Jake a big smile. It was a new day, and I was going to be a brand-new Jasmine!

"Hey, Jake."

He pretended not to hear me.

"Jake!" I called in a louder voice, so the whole group could hear. Finally, he looked up from his phone.

"Uh. Hey."

"So, how was it?" I asked brightly. "How many fish did you catch?"

His face was stone, so I threw him a "let's call it a truce" smile that I was hoping he could decipher.

"Five?" I pushed. "Five *thousand*?"

Jake blushed. "Not quite."

"None," Ranjit Uncle interjected, slapping him on the back, hard. "Not this time, right?"

"Next time, Dad."

"Maybe you should have practiced your technique before the cruise." Ranjit Uncle paused, glancing at Dad. "You'd think Jake would be good at all sports, but it was only swimming that came naturally to him . . ."

I leaned toward Jake, about to quietly tease that his fishing technique was probably better suited for women than salmon, but before I could, I saw Tess waving her clipboard at us.

"Oh." I sighed, pointed at her. "Jake, I think we have to go . . . help."

"We?" He sounded surprised.

"Yes, the Royal We."

"That's not what that means, but sure." Jake glanced at his father, who was deep in conversation with my parents about the time one of Jake's brothers caught a ten-foot tuna. "Dad?" he said quietly. "Dad, we . . ."

His shoulders slumped.

"Let's just go," he muttered to me quietly. "We'll find them later at the opera."

"Oh right!" I'd forgotten I'd read in the itinerary that the queen had organized for our group to attend this evening. "Do you like the opera?"

Jake didn't answer, and as we followed Tess to her office, he seemed dead set on ignoring my attempts to engage in lively conversation and a blossoming friendship. Oh well. I'd work on him after the meeting.

"So, do you think you can bhangra?" Tess asked, the moment we were all seated in her office. Jake and I looked at each other.

"No?" I volunteered.

"Well, that's what that Bishan woman wants to call the dance competition, but I explained to her that if we were gonna do the thing, then we had to open it up to all guests. All types of dancing."

"Of course." Jake nodded.

"We could call it *So You Think You Can Boogie*?" I joked, but then Tess's eyes brightened.

"Great idea. Yes. *Yes*." She wrote furiously on her clipboard. "One thing sorted. Now!" She grabbed a key from her pocket and tossed it in a clay bowl on her desk. "This is to get backstage. I'll keep it there. Come by anytime, whenever you need access, and someone here will give it to you. You look trustworthy. But don't tell the captain, you hear me? If something goes missing from the prop room that won't be covered by insurance—" She laughed. "Then again, insurance won't cover my therapy bills if I have to keep fighting with that *Bishan* character—"

Tess closed her mouth, eyes widened. I pressed my palm over my mouth to keep from smiling.

"Shoot," she said. "That's your aunt, Jake, isn't it?"

"Don't worry." Jake smiled. "Half my family has gone to therapy, and the other half should seriously consider it."

"You have a modern family," Tess declared. "Oh, I'm just remembering. Jake, *you* dance, don't you? Your aunt told me you're quite the Romeo. Can we count on you to make an appearance?"

"You dance?" I exclaimed.

Jake shook his head. "She must have been mistaken."

"I don't think so." Tess squinted. "Bishan specifically said you used to perform bhangra, ballet, hip-hop, tap—"

"Tess, I think Jasmine and I should be the masters of ceremonies that evening," Jake said quickly, clearly trying to change the subject. (Although I made a mental note to ask him about his dancing later.)

"Another excellent idea." Tess licked her lips and picked up the clipboard. "You two would be perfect hosts. Our very own Ryan Seacrest and . . ." She narrowed her brows at me. "Blake Shelton."

*Blake Shelton?*

*Come on, Tess. At least give me Paula Abdul. Give me Adam Levine!*

Tess gave us a tour of the auditorium, where the stagehands for the opera were busily prepping. Back in her office, she proceeded to explain that Jake and I would be responsible for finding performers, securing their props and music, the dress rehearsal, and, thanks to Jake's big mouth, being the masters of ceremonies. The staff would handle everything else.

I read once that the average person in the US spoke one hundred fifty words per minute. I guessed that Tess could clear a thousand. I tried not to think about how close Jake and I were sitting and instead focused on taking diligent notes on my phone. There was a lot of information, and I wasn't sure what would be important later. Most years, my manager Rowan flagged my listening and organizational skills in the "room for improvement" section of my performance review.

A full hour passed, and then another. I was starting to get antsy. My parents would be wondering where I was, and we had the opera to get ready for. I didn't suspect it was the type of thing I could show up to in my hot pink Adidas joggers.

At six twenty, I stopped taking notes and was using one of Tess's pens to raise my hand, hoping she'd notice that I was trying to get a word in. But she didn't. She was reading us, word for word, the staff's code of conduct.

"Uh . . . Tess?" I ventured. I closed my mouth and threw a pleading look at Jake.

"What?" he mouthed.

"The opera," I whispered back.

Jake nodded stiffly, and then he just stood up and Tess immediately stopped talking. Damnit. I should have thought of that.

"Tess, we have to go." Jake shrugged. "We have tickets to the opera tonight."

"The opera!" Tess exclaimed, glancing at her watch. "Well, I've kept you *way* too long. You both skedaddle, all right? It's rush seating. You don't want to be late."

Tess ushered us out the door, reminding us to eat and use the washroom beforehand because, although the show was supposed to be two and a half hours with no intermission, the show's star—a former big name who took this gig reluctantly—was self-indulgent and tended to run over.

"So, how was your day?" I asked Jake, as he speed walked toward the elevator and I chased after him.

"You already know," he grunted. "I didn't catch any fish."

"I . . ." My face flushed, as I fell back and watched him carry on without me. "So, you're ignoring me now?" I hollered after him.

He stopped but didn't turn around. "So, you're *talking* to me now?"

I approached, my tail between my legs. He let me catch up.

"Jake . . ."

My voice was small, and for the first time all day, he looked me in the eye.

"You made it very clear you want to be nowhere near me. I'm

trying to respect that. We'll do the dance competition, we'll say the bare minimum to each other, and in one week you'll never have to see me again."

*Ouch.*

I deserved that.

"But . . ." I started. "I . . ."

*I find you extremely attractive, against my better judgment.*

*I'm afraid of what you might do to me.*

*I'm afraid of myself.*

"I was hoping we could sit together at the opera," I said instead. "It's going to be a snooze fest. We could play hangman?"

Jake crossed his arms.

"We could . . . rub each other the right way."

Jake's mouth twitched. I grinned and shook him by the shoulders.

"Come on. You were right. Let's be friends." I sighed. "So, can we go back to when we were having a friendly conversation? I can be friendly."

"Can you?"

I pouted. "Sometimes."

"When you feel like it, right?"

I deserved that jab, too. I'd been hot and cold with Jake from the beginning. I flirted heavily and then tore into him the first day we met at the coffee shop. I joked around with him at the gym and then got in his face a beat later. We had a pleasant chat on the docks in Ketchikan, and then I bailed without any warning.

Jake stared down at me. That first day in the café, he'd been slick and cocky and *so* offended that I mistook him for the waiter, but I'd since discovered that arrogance wasn't his only quality. He may have been flawed, but so was I. I'd behaved badly with him, too.

"I'm sorry," I said, taking a step back. "I may or may not have projected some of my own shit onto you yesterday."

I paused.

"*And* the day before that."

Jake cleared his throat.

"*And* the day before that one, too."

Jake pressed the elevator button. It arrived immediately, and I thought he was going to take off, but he held the door open for me.

"What floor?"

"Seven."

He nodded. He'd already pressed the button.

Another group joined us on the ride up, but it was just us again by the time we got out on our floor. I felt weirdly shy and exposed while we both lingered, not looking at each other. Finally, I couldn't take the silence.

"I just gave a pretty epic apology speech," I said slowly. "And I don't really have any experience in this department, but I'm pretty sure this is the part where you forgive me."

A bemused Jake looked up from the ground. I batted my eyelashes.

"And maybe, like, give me a thousand dollars?"

Jake laughed, his face coming to life in a grin that I hadn't realized I'd missed. OK. Big deal. He was hot. He was . . . something else. But who cared? Not me. Not *this* Jasmine.

"I forgive you," Jake said finally. "I'm not always easy, either."

"What are you talking about, Jake?" I joked. "You're perfect."

Jake ran his hands through his hair, his mouth still curved. Having been outside all day, he was just as grimy as I was, but it looked good on him. That windswept hair, that musky mountain scent . . .

"So!" I cleared my throat, because friends didn't objectify their friends. "Truce?"

I extended my hand and firmly shook Jake's hand. Electricity pulsed through his fingertips, his eyes searing.

"OK, Jasmine," he said with a warm smile. "Truce."

# Chapter 14

〰〰〰

Diya: Jasmine!!! It's been so long. I can't WAIT
to party with you at Niki's engagement. She
might have mentioned already, but I am
organizing a group Bollywood dance with all
her friends. I am choreographing the routine
to be quite simple. Are you up for it?

Jasmine: hey, diya. nice to hear from you!
thanks for asking, but i think i'll sit this
one out.

RETURNED TO MY cabin and found a note from Uma Auntie,
Mom, and Dad saying they'd gone ahead for dinner without
me. As quickly as I could, I showered, threw on some mascara
and lip gloss, and pulled out one of the more formal outfits I'd
brought, a rose gold cocktail dress with a forgiving waistline and
three-quarter-length sleeves.

The auditorium was mostly full by the time I arrived at seven minutes to seven. I spotted my parents in the middle section with a cohort of their friends and quickly explained where I'd been while I stole a few of their snacks. (I hadn't had time to eat dinner, and my stomach was growling.)

There weren't any free seats nearby, so I grabbed one at the very back. I scanned the crowd, finding myself looking for Jake. He was sitting with his dad and other uncles, two rows ahead of me. He'd changed into a suit. His hair was still wet, and he looked . . .

"Jasmine?"

I turned at the sound of my name being called. Ethan was at the end of the row, waving at me.

"Jasmine!" he whispered more loudly.

He ushered for me to follow him, and instinctively, I glanced around to see if anyone had picked up on the fact I was being singled out by a man. Luckily, all the aunties and uncles were sitting ahead of me.

When Ethan hollered my name a third time, I awkwardly slipped through the row toward him and then followed him into the foyer.

"I've been looking for you everywhere," he said, just outside the main door. "You don't really like the opera, do you?"

"I don't know." I shrugged, extremely confused. "I don't re-ally have an opinion—"

"Perfect. Follow me."

"What? *Why?*"

Ethan beamed. "It's a surprise."

"Impressionable young women are not supposed to follow strange men, you know."

"Not even to a . . ." Ethan lowered his voice. "*Party?*"

"A party?" I squealed.

"Keep it down! It's top secret." Ethan smiled suspiciously. "During opera night, the majority of passengers on board are behind those doors. And the staff get a few hours to themselves."

I high-fived Ethan. Yes. A *party*. With people my own age!

"Hold on a second," I said quietly, remembering Jake. "Do I get a plus-one?"

"But you're my plus-one."

"Then are you allowed to bring a plus-two?"

Two minutes before curtain call, Ethan raced into the theater, returning with a very confused-looking Jake.

"This doesn't seem like an emergency," Jake said, his eyes darting between Ethan and me.

"It is. I'm rescuing you." I beamed. "We're going to a party."

WE STOPPED BY my cabin so I could pick up the Costco-sized bottle of gin from the bottom of my suitcase, and then Ethan explained the three ground rules to us on the way down to the party. We were not to tell any senior staff members, such as Tess, who was off duty for the evening and would fire everyone if she found out. We were not to get too drunk. The staff quarters had a balcony, and the year before, someone had somersaulted out of a keg stand and nearly gone overboard. Finally, it was millennial throwback night, and Ethan had been charged with creating the playlist; dancing at the party was not just encouraged, but a condition of entry.

"The Middle" by Jimmy Eat World was blaring when we entered, and I nodded my approval at Ethan as he handed Jake and me beers from the cooler. The party was already in full swing, and Ethan introduced us to several of his friends. Miguel from public relations. Denise from hospitality. Simu, who I recognized as the barista from the coffee shop. Lola, the other doctor aboard the cruise. They all knew us already. Jake and I were infamous below deck as the two "juniors" aboard the cruise.

I was hungry and drank my beer too quickly while we chatted. Before I knew it, I was nearly done with my second, lightheaded and unable keep my eyes off Jake. He was chatting to Denise, and I could tell they were hitting it off. She was about his age, lively, and a total babe, so when the others left to kick-start the dance floor, I excused myself to the bathroom. I needed Jake to hook up with Denise so I could be done with the temptation. He looked like freaking James Bond in that suit, and he was even acting like a gentleman. Unhelpfully, he hadn't bragged about himself once all evening.

When I returned to the party ten minutes later, the dance floor had swelled from three people to half the party. Denise had joined Ethan and the others at the very center, and I expected Jake to be right there with her, but he was still in the kitchen. Annoyingly, I was relieved.

"Where did you get that?" I asked, pointing at the sandwich he was in the process of eating.

"Over there . . ." Jake trailed off as he pointed to an empty tray. "That was fast. They're already gone."

"No worries." I grinned, noticing the mustard on his lips.

"What?"

"Nothing." I tightened my lips. "Sorry."

"Come on . . ."

"You have a little mustard . . ." I tickled my lips. "Mustache situation going on."

"Oh yeah?" Jake made a face and then licked his lips in an exaggerated fashion. After, he smiled at me. He had such a nice smile.

"Am I all good?"

"You're perfect." I squeezed his cheeks. "Our *perfect* little Jakey."

He raised one eyebrow at me and moved in close. I thought he was going to hug me, or *worse*, but instead he handed me his sandwich.

"Take it. I'm not that hungry."

"You must be." He hadn't had time to eat dinner, either.

"Not as hungry as you." Jake pushed the sandwich into my hand. "It's yours."

Could he tell I was tipsy just by looking at me? Yeesh. I hadn't gone out in a while; my tolerance must have been even lower than I thought.

"Thank you," I said, munching on the sandwich. I wiped my lips. "That's very . . . thoughtful of you."

Jake bobbed his head to "No Diggity" playing in the background. "Why do you sound so surprised?"

Three years ago, I'd had too much to drink at Brian's friend's birthday party. It was a cottage weekend with eight other couples at a lakeside mansion. I'd gone out to the patio to get fresh air and texted him where I was going, asked if he could bring me a glass of water. I fell asleep, outside, wearing a minidress, and had no blanket. He hadn't bothered looking for me until the next morning.

I sighed loudly, shaking my head, and reminded myself that Jake was not Brian. And even if they had some of the same qualities, why did that even matter? It only mattered if I kept up with my pattern with men. If I knowingly, blindingly repeated my mistakes.

"You're right." I smiled sheepishly. "Thank you for the sandwich. And for coming tonight."

Jake handed me another beer and then knocked his against mine. "Thank you for inviting me."

"It's what friends do." I paused. "Right?"

Jake grinned. "Right."

"What else do friends do?"

Oh god. Was I flirting?

"Go to the gym together?" I said quickly. "Maybe watch *Outlander*?"

"Maybe." Jake nodded. "Or they play beer pong."

He grabbed a stack of red plastic cups, positioned six plastic cups in a triangle on the other side of the counter, and then six more just in front of me.

"I don't think we have the pong part of the game . . ."

A beat later, Jake pulled a table tennis ball out of his suit pocket. I rolled my eyes.

"Do you always carry a table tennis ball around when you go to the opera?"

"Just in case of an emergency. You never know when you're going to be rescued."

I laughed, pushing Jake away from me. The way he was leaning, I got a fistful of his hair as I playfully shoved him back toward his side of the counter. He smelled good, and that slim-cut suit did wonders for his body, but I let the thought float by me and put on my game face.

"You any good?" I pretended to stretch in preparation. Jake grabbed another beer and split it six ways in the cups. "I've made grown men cry, you know."

"I believe it." Jake smirked, tossing the empty can in the recycling. "And yes, I . . ." He looked up. "I was going to say that I was law school champion, but that would make me sound like a douchebag, wouldn't it?"

"Maybe. But *that* kind of bragging I can get behind." I winked. "Show me what you got."

Jake went first. Our cups were set up much closer together than a standard beer pong game, so it was no surprise his first shot was clean. It didn't even hit the rim. I fished the ball out, downed the beer, and then lined up my shot.

Rim.

It circled the drain for a few seconds, making my heart stop, but finally it went in, too.

I did the robot in celebration, one of the only dance moves I knew. Jake called me a boomer. I called him a toddler.

Jake and I both missed the next few rounds, but we followed up with our strongest showing yet. Two clean shots in a row.

Later, by the time we both had only one cup left, the shit talk had escalated. But I showed my good sportsmanship when Jake made his final shot and I chugged the last cup of beer. If I didn't score now, then he would win. I couldn't let him.

"You can stop, you know," Jake taunted, as I breathed deeply and took aim. "I won't judge you if you're scared."

"Yes, you would. And I'm not scared."

I angled my hips to the left, lined up my arm.

*You got this! Come on, girl, show 'em—*

"Are you sure you're not scared?" Jake asked, interrupting my pep talk. Annoyed, I flicked my gaze his way. He had his arms up, his palms casually cupping the back of his head. His collared shirt tugged across his broad chest, the suit jacket stretching perfectly around his broad shoulders and biceps.

My eyes widened. He looked . . .

"Are you flexing?"

"Pardon me?" he asked innocently.

I grinned. "You're trying to distract me."

I lowered my arm, scowling at him. Jake proceeded to take off his suit jacket, slowly, and then rolled up his sleeves. He didn't break eye contact.

"You're a cheater."

"It's only cheating if it's working."

My eyes lingered on his forearms, which were toned but not so sculpted he looked like Popeye. And on his left side, he had a tattoo—something etched in black ink—but I couldn't make it out.

"You can give up now, you know," I heard Jake say.

I forced my gaze upward, challenging him. "This may have worked for you at *law school*, but it's not working now."

"Prove it."

Oh, I was going to. I took a sip of liquid courage from my beer and moved back into position, breathing deeply to calm my nerves. *Let's do this.*

The shot went in clean. I knew it was going in the second the ball left my fingertips. A few people near us in the kitchen were watching, and they cheered as I celebrated my win.

Well, actually, it was a tie. But not losing felt like a win enough for me.

Across the room, the dance floor—which had grown in size—erupted into cheers when "Oops!...I Did It Again" came on the sound system. Honestly, I screamed a little, too—it's a great song—and before I knew it, Jake had grabbed my hand and was leading me toward the crowd.

The music got louder, and more and more people swarmed in around us. Jake and I were standing a few inches apart, face-to-face, which was much too close—but that's all the room we were afforded. Every time I stepped back or to the side, I bumped against someone else.

I told myself friends danced with each other all the time. I couldn't really hold a beat, but I was a millennial who grew up on Britney Spears and Blink-182, so I didn't embarrass myself. My friends in middle school had showed me how to hold my own, how to knock my hips from side to side, shoulders loose, hands in the air. But that was the extent of my ability to dance.

I was self-conscious and mostly looking at the floor, but I glanced up when I heard Jake's voice over the music. He'd started rapping along to the lyrics of "In Da Club," this earnest, dorky, adorable look on his face as he pretended he was an MC, shaking his hand back and forth as if he were hard-core. My cheeks hurt from smiling, and when the chorus turned into the bridge, and Jake started to *dance*, my jaw dropped to the floor.

He was good. Like, *really* good. His moves were halfway between hip-hop and street dance, and his hips—oh god. Could they *move*.

Jake had denied in front of Tess he was a dancer, but he'd lied. His moves were literally good enough to compete on *So You Think You Can Dance.*

I cheered Jake on from the side, watching him bust a move. He kept trying to bring me into the dance—reaching for my hands—but every time I shook him off because I knew I wouldn't be able to keep up.

"Come on," he said, as the song changed and the room briefly went quiet. "Aren't we friends?"

"Yes," I said. "But I can't dance."

"Everyone can dance."

"Not me."

He pouted at me, shimmying closer and closer, and finally I laughed in defeat and let him twirl me. My head spun and the world turned until I'd gone three hundred sixty degrees and was facing him again. He pulled me by the hips gently, and instinctively, I put my arms around his neck.

"You're pretty good at this."

"Huh?"

I leaned in closer. "I said you're good at this!"

Jake leaned away, smiling. I wanted to ask him more about where he learned to dance like that, but the music was too loud, and I didn't want to get any closer. I could smell his soap, whispers of his cologne, and dancing with him already felt way too good. Someone knocked me hard from behind, and when I lurched forward, my stomach briefly pressed into Jake. My body tensed as I looked upward. Jake's lips were parted, his breath heavy, and the impulsive Jasmine inside me would have reached up and kissed him. She would have closed her eyes to the world, and every reason it was a bad idea, and planted her lips on Jake's. She would have run her hands through his hair and pulled him closer. She would have gasped against him until she couldn't deny him anymore.

Because that girl did what she wanted, when she wanted, with whom she wanted—without regard to consequences, or the feelings of others.

Without regard to her *own* feelings.

"Jasmine?"

My breath caught when he leaned in, his lips brushing my ear.

"Dancing isn't the only thing I'm good at."

Heat pooled in my core as his eyes dropped to my lips and I willed myself to step away. Jake's hands gripped my waist, gently, but still, I couldn't move.

"Like what?" I said instead.

He licked his lips as he grinned. "A gentleman doesn't say such things out loud."

"And you're a gentleman, are you?"

"Not if you don't want me to be."

My limbs felt heavy from the weight of his gaze. My body wanted him to be anything but gentlemanly, and I needed to look away. I wasn't imagining this tension between us. I barely knew Jake, but I knew that in this moment, he desperately wanted me, too.

The song changed then to "Despacito," the sexiest song ever made. Damnit. How was I going to resist Jake now? I dropped my hands from Jake's neck, ready to step away, but then he grabbed my palm and spun me halfway around. My arms crossed over my body, Jake interwove his fingers through mine on either side, softly pulling me closer until my back was flush with his chest. I could feel his hips move against me, swaying side to side as he led us in a dance.

A dance that was going to be the end of me.

Jake stepped forward with his right foot, nudging me to do the same, and then quickly he'd step back twice. I followed. I didn't step on his foot or fumble. I was secure.

I was dancing. I was really fucking dancing.

My hips rolled from side to side as Jake tugged me closer, and I felt him, hard, against me. I shivered.

"Our bodies move like they belong together, don't they?" Jake whispered.

His bottom lip grazed the top of my ear, and my mind went blank as my senses took over. I closed my eyes, breathing in his scent. This was by far the sexiest moment of my entire life. I'd heard friends say that with the right partner, dancing was the best foreplay, but I hadn't gotten it until right now.

"Doesn't this feel good?" he said into my ear.

I suppressed a moan as temptation swelled. His right hand

grazed my curves, my shoulder. He brushed the hair from the back of my neck.

Yes, this felt *good*. His body. The electricity. The anticipation. Tingling all over, I leaned my head back against his chest, and the world spun away from me as Jake breathed hard against my skin.

I smiled at the ceiling as we swayed. I felt him grinding against me as we danced. I felt sexy and hot and wet. I felt powerful, yet out of control. I felt . . .

My pulse raced as Jake dragged his bottom lip against my neck.

"Jasmine?" he gasped.

I felt too hot. *Too* good.

"I . . ."

Overwhelmed, I dropped Jake's hand and stepped away.

Once again, I felt totally and completely impulsive.

# Chapter 15

〰〰

I TOLD JAKE I needed some air, and he followed me out to the balcony. The cool wind was exactly what I needed to return to my senses. The moment I stepped outside, the flame went out. I felt under control.

The deck chairs were occupied, so we went to the far end of the patio, leaned our elbows against the railing. It was eight thirty, and this far north the sun was still hovering above the horizon, the sky and ocean a hazy pink. I glanced over at Jake. His eyelids were heavy. And it wasn't the sunset that he was admiring.

"Stop it," I whispered, tearing my gaze away. "We can't do this."

He stiffened. "We can't . . . have a good time?"

"No." I laughed. "I'm sorry, but no. This isn't a good idea."

"Sure. No problem." Jake gave me space on the railing. "Sorry if I was being forward. I just . . . kind of got the feeling back there you liked me, too—"

"You like the way I look, Jake. Not me." I shrugged. "You don't even know me."

He opened his mouth but then closed it and looked thoughtfully at the water. He knew I was right.

"How many times have you said that to a woman?" I asked a minute later.

"Said what?"

I smiled. "That 'our bodies move like they *belong* together'?"

"Christ." Jake squirmed. "You like embarrassing me, don't you?"

"You said it," I teased, "not me."

"Yeah, well." He flashed me a grin. "It seemed to work there for a minute."

"But then I came to my senses." I widened my eyes. "Because I'm thirty-*three*, and I know better."

*At least, I'm supposed to know better.*

"As an older, more experienced woman," I said slowly, "can I give you a piece of advice?"

"Have at it," he encouraged.

"You don't need the pickup lines, or the dance moves, or the flexing, or any of that crap." I lightly punched his shoulder. "You're already a catch, Jake. Just be you."

I briefly thought he was going to balk at the unsolicited advice, or go find Denise now that he knew I wasn't going to hook up, but he didn't. After an *extremely* awkward silence, Jake changed the subject and we started talking about the dancing competition and how best to recruit performers. Boring logistical details that squeezed the last drop of sexy out of the moment. Thank god.

"Have you ever been on a cruise before?" he asked me, after we decided to meet up the following afternoon to continue planning.

"Boats, yes. But not a cruise." I turned to him. "You?"

"In the Caribbean. I was twenty."

"Fun." I cocked my head to the side. "With a girlfriend? Friends?"

"Family." Jake nodded. "My entire extended family, actually. Even the ones still in India."

"Wow, that must have been something."

Jake grinned. "It felt like we took up half the ship. It was complete chaos at the time, but now I'm really glad we had that time together."

I nodded, turning back to the view. I supposed that was one way Brian and Jake were very different. Even from the beginning, I could sense Jake was family oriented by the simple fact that he was accompanying his father and *bhua* on a cruise. He had just finished law school, yet he'd chosen to celebrate with them.

"You guys are close," I said, remembering how I'd spent my summer after graduation backpacking solo through New Zealand. "Where's your mom, by the way? And your *bhua* is here alone, too, right? Did her husband come?"

"My uncle didn't want to take the time off work," Jake said, after a moment. "And my mom . . . Jasmine, she passed away."

I gasped, turning to him. "I'm sorry, Jake," I exclaimed. "I'm so sorry . . ."

"It's OK. You didn't know."

"When . . ." I trailed off. I was so stunned, and sad, I could barely think of any words to say.

"Five years ago."

I nodded, turning back to the sea. Clouds now covered the setting sun, and the world around us suddenly felt darker, more surreal.

I remembered Ranjit Uncle from my childhood, but I couldn't picture Jake's mother. As a child, it was easy not to learn the names of our aunties and uncles, which spouse belonged in which couple, and who their kids were. Gatherings and parties were big. The numbers at *gurdwara* and festivals were even bigger. Had I known her? Did my parents tell me that one of their friends had passed? Probably not. But they would have told Niki.

"I . . ." Shaking my head, I sighed. "I don't even know what to say, other than how sorry I am." I paused. "What happened?"

"I don't really like talking about her . . ."

"Of course." I nodded. "Sorry."

Neither Jake nor I spoke for a moment, and I was wondering whether I should change the subject, or suggest we go grab another beer, when I noticed a strange grin had appeared on his face. It was a different sort of smile than the one I'd seen on him before.

"Is something funny?" I asked quietly.

"Uh . . ."

"What is it?"

Jake breathed a laugh. "Well, usually this is the part where my dates don't know what to say." He paused. "And so they kiss me."

My jaw dropped. *"Jake!"*

"No, no." He shook his head, still smiling. "I swear. I don't use my dead mother to pick up women, OK? It's just . . . the last couple years, I've felt strong enough to date. And, you know, on a date one of the first things people ask about is your family."

Frowning, I nodded and waited for him to continue.

"And . . ." Jake shrugged. "I can't . . . I still can't talk about her. So I don't say anything, and then they feel really sorry for me and they, uh, kiss me."

"Wow." I shook my head. "Just. *Wow.*"

"I've literally never admitted that to anyone before," Jake said sheepishly.

"Then why did you?"

He shrugged. "I already made a fool out of myself in front of you."

I put my hand on his forearm. "No, you didn't."

Jake's muscle tensed, and when I looked down, I noticed I was touching him on the tattoo I'd seen a hint of earlier. With the tips of my fingers, I tugged his shirtsleeve up so I could get a better view. It was a name etched in black feathered calligraphy.

*Paulina*

"Paulina Auntie," I whispered slowly.

"You remember her?"

"Now I do." I smiled. "She had red hair, right?"

Jake nodded, and I briefly closed my eyes as a memory appeared from a long, long time ago. It was a dancing competition, the annual festival Bishan Auntie was trying to replicate here on the cruise. Paulina Auntie had stood out, and not only because there weren't too many women from other backgrounds who had married into the community. She was fresh-faced and beautiful with long hair, which, that day, she'd tied into a braid. Friendly, encouraging blue eyes smiling down from the stage. A traditional *salwar*. Blush pink. Or was it purple?

"Oh my god," I said, remembering her bhangra performance. "She was an incredible dancer. Did she teach you to dance like that?"

Jake's eyes widened, and I waved him off before he could speak.

"Sorry, I'll shut up," I mumbled. "You don't want to talk about her."

"It's fine," Jake said, his hands gripping the rail. "I . . . should. Plus, it's different. You're not some random person I met on Hinge. You knew her."

Jake turned around to lean against the railing, his eyes staring out into space. "It was cancer," he said after a moment. "She had three months left when they found it."

"Jake . . ." My eyes smarted. "Fuck."

"Fuck. Exactly." Jake ran his hands through his hair. "It felt way too fast at the time, but we were all so grateful she didn't have to live that way for too long. She didn't want to live like that."

I rested my hand on his forearm, lacking words to describe how sad I felt for him. "I can't imagine what that would have been like for you. For your whole family." I paused. "How is Ranjit Uncle doing?"

"Better now." Jake nodded. "But he was a mess for a long time." Jake rolled down his sleeves, slowly fastening the buttons. "She got sick during my final semester of college. Sunny and Shaan both work in San Francisco, so I deferred law school for a couple years and moved home to be with my father."

I put my hand back on his arm. I wasn't sure what to say.

"I got a boring office job. After work, I went home. And every night, Dad and I just watched *sports*." Jake laughed angrily. "We pretended like we weren't miserable."

"If you pretend something long enough," I said quietly, "maybe it comes true."

Jake's face changed, and when his eyes found mine, something strange passed between us. Nothing like the purely sexual, electric spark I'd felt with him earlier. It was different. Weirdly, it was more intense.

"That's enough talk about my mother," Jake said a minute or two later, raising his eyebrows. "But my former therapist, wherever he is, would be very pleased to know I just spoke about her in public."

I grinned. "You know, Jake, you're kind of a good guy when you want to be."

He clutched his heart. "How sweet of you."

"I'm serious." I knocked my hip against his. "You're all right, actually. When you're not trying to get in my pants . . ."

Jake laughed.

"I think we got off on the wrong foot."

"And why did we?"

"Well," I said slowly. "I . . ."

"You . . ." Jake prompted. He wasn't going to let me out of this one.

"I'd just had an almost-fight with my mother," I said finally. "I was already pissed off, and when you got offended I mistook you for a waiter, you really reminded me of my ex."

"Oh." Jake frowned. "*The* ex?"

I nodded. "As your *bhua* put it, the one I had a 'cohabitating relationship' with."

"I take it things didn't end well?"

"It ended fine." I crossed my arms. "But he wasn't a great guy. I shouldn't have stayed with him for so long. Come to think of it, I probably shouldn't have been with him at all. Most of the time, he acted like a complete douchebag."

"Similar to me?"

I winced.

Neither of us spoke for a long moment, and when I shifted my gaze, Jake was studying me. For some reason, I kept talking.

"You know, Brian's family was really rich," I said. "Like, *really* rich. And Brian was very entitled. He was too good for . . ." I paused. "Well, he thought he was too good for everyone.

"About a month after we moved in together," I continued, staring my hands, "Niki organized a dinner for all of us. She was the one to convince Mom and Dad to accept our 'cohabitating relationship.' They wouldn't listen to me . . ."

Jake nodded patiently as I struggled to find my next words.

"Anyway, Niki made a reservation for the five of us at the Cheesecake Factory downtown. And Brian and I showed up, and before even saying *hello* to my parents, he snorted and asked her why we were at the Cheesecake Factory." I laughed. "I love that place. It was the only restaurant my parents took us to when we were little kids because my mom used to work there."

Jake caught my eye, and I shrugged.

"She got the employee discount."

"Ah . . ." Jake tilted his head, studying me. "That's why you got so upset with me. But, Jasmine, I wasn't offended because I think I'm too good to wait tables. I was *bummed* you didn't remember me."

"Really," I said. It sounded like an excuse.

"Yeah." He nodded. "I knew that I was signing up for a seniors' cruise this week. But I thought, hey, I'll chill out, go somewhere I've never been, hang out with my dad. Have some down time. And then last week, I overheard my *bhua* telling Dad you were coming, too, and I was excited. I remembered you."

I laughed. "Uh-oh . . ."

"You were this older, insanely cool girl who didn't care what anybody thought about her. You had blond streaks in your hair for a while, too, right? I thought you looked like Beyoncé."

"That's the best compliment anyone has ever given me," I deadpanned.

"Well, I meant it." Jake poked my nose. "It's not a *line*."

My cheeks flushed, and suddenly, I felt out of sorts.

"I don't think I'm superior to you or your family or anyone who works in the service industry." Jake held my gaze. "OK?"

I nodded.

"And for the record, I used to wait tables, too. My parents made us get jobs as soon as we turned sixteen so we understood the value of money." He cleared his throat. "And guess where I worked . . ."

I hit him. *"No."*

"The Cheesecake Factory." Jake nodded proudly. "I bused tables for nearly three years."

"You lucky dog!" I gasped. "Your friends must have been so jealous."

"My whole high school was jealous. People used to show up asking for free cheesecake."

"Was it everything you imagined it to be?" I squirmed. "OK. Be honest. How many slices did you eat per shift?"

"One Oreo, one caramel, one strawberry," he said. "Plus two lemon if I had swim practice earlier."

"My favorite is their blueberry. I don't even like blueberries that much, but I'd literally kill for a piece of blueberry from the Cheesecake Factory."

"It was my dream job. I'm one of those people who peaked in high school, because I'll never be able to top that."

"What about the fancy law firm job?" I eyed him. "What kind of law will you be practicing?"

"General civil litigation. It sounds like I'll be doing everything from run-of-the-mill tort claims, malpractice, personal injury, maybe some antitrust—"

"Whoa," I laughed. "Slow down. You're not speaking English again."

Jake smiled. "Basically, I'll be going to court a lot—for anything but criminal cases."

"Cool! Although that sounds . . . challenging."

"It will be. But I'm looking forward to it. I think it will be a lot like swim competitions, which I loved."

"What do you mean?"

"Well, there's an adrenaline rush when everyone is watching. You've prepared all you can, and you either perform well or you don't." Jake scrunched up his face. "Weirdly, I like the pressure of being put on the spot. It's a thrill when it goes your way, and when it doesn't . . . well, it just makes you want to do better the next time."

"That's . . . amazing." I wasn't sure how else to put my thoughts into words. My passions had always been so singular. It was fascinating to see how they could translate so differently for Jake.

"I'm really happy for you," I added. "When's your first day?"

"In two weeks," he said. "My firm doesn't let new associates start until they've officially passed the bar."

"How did the exam go?" When Jake didn't immediately answer, I poked him teasingly in the chest. "You nervous or something?"

"No." A shadow crossed his face. "Not in the slightest."

There was an edge to his voice, a flicker of self-doubt I recognized all too well, and I was about to say so, but then I caught sight of Ethan and Denise coming our way with a tray of shots. I waved, smiling.

"I hope you don't mind," Ethan said, his speech slurred. "We used your gin. What's in this, Dee? Gin and . . ."

"Just gin," she laughed, flicking her gaze at Jake. "You want one?"

"Sure," he replied.

"Do you think you can handle it?"

My stomach somersaulted as I watched Denise move toward Jake.

"Probably not." He stepped forward, and just as I expected

him to flirt back with Denise, he wrapped his arm around my shoulders.

"But this one can."

I'd been holding my breath, and I smiled, gazing at the floor. Jake's weight felt good on top of me—but only because I was starting to get cold. Yes. That was absolutely the only reason. The four of us took a shot, and then the weaker two—Ethan and Jake—nearly wretched from the taste. Afterward, Denise lingered, suggesting we all go back to the dance floor. Her eyes were on Jake, his lips, his body, and a part of me hoped he'd follow her in there. But he didn't.

Jake took me by the hand, chastely, and then he challenged me to another round of beer pong.

# Chapter 16

~~~~~~

Jasmine: thanks for the invite last night! great party.

Ethan: Glad you and your "friend" made it ;)

Jasmine: shaddup. ok so when can we hang out again? free later today?

Ethan: Nope, duty calls. Come find me tomo?

Jasmine: deal.

SPENT THE MORNING with Mom and Dad in Skagway, our third port of call in Alaska. Drinking coffee from our to-go cups, we explored the historic gold rush town and visited a gallery featuring stunning metal, wood, and animal horn carvings by Tlingit artists. I'd studied Tlingit art in an Indigenous art class in college, and loved nerding out while touring the exhibition with my parents. They weren't really "art people"—most of the walls in their house were bare—but I appreciated that they joined me. It seemed like they enjoyed it.

After, at the tourist shops, Mom bought two heavy tote bags full of souvenirs to take back to her friends and colleagues, and because I was still nervous she would overexert herself again, I insisted on carrying them. Even though it felt uncomfortable at first, I found myself asking them about their health. I hadn't been able to shake my concern ever since Jake told me his mother had passed. But Dad told me his back was slowly improving, although he still didn't do his physio exercises as regularly as he should. Mom's cholesterol was under control, too, and the doctor had told her recently that she was otherwise in good health.

Although it was good news, the conversation made me feel a little melancholy. I regretted that we'd missed so much of each other's lives—the big things and the small ones—but were we making up for it now? All morning I'd been trying my very best to behave and be thoughtful and focus on the present rather than on our tumultuous past. And was I imagining it, or were my parents trying a little bit harder to connect with me, too?

Ten minutes before the opera had ended, Ethan turned off the music and everyone scrammed. I'd felt giddy running through the halls like a teenager with Jake, so we could make it back to the theater before the curtain went down and everyone realized we'd skipped out. Jake mentioned he would simply tell his father he'd gone to use the restroom and sat elsewhere afterward, and when I met up with my parents in the foyer, even though it made me uncomfortable, I let them assume I'd been watching the opera, too.

The cover story wasn't for us. It was to make sure the staff didn't get caught. If either of us were honest with Ranjit Uncle or my parents, Queen B was at risk of finding out—which meant with utter certainty it would get back to Tess or other senior cruise ship staff. But deep down, I was relieved not to have to tell my parents I'd spent the evening with Jake. I had nothing to hide. We'd had a few drinks, danced, and talked—that's it—but my parents were always ready to believe the worst in me. I didn't want to fight with them anymore, or try and make them understand my choices. I just wanted to be back in their life. Even if the version of me they got wasn't the real Jasmine.

The sky cleared in time for my parents' train tour of the valley. I dropped them off at the station in Skagway and then made my way back to the cruise. Although I'd been tempted to take Tess up on another free excursion, I was starting to feel too guilty about the whole thing and decided against it. Besides, Jake and I had a lot of work to do for the dancing competition. As scheduled, I met him at the buffet on board for a quick lunch, and then we spent most of the afternoon in planning mode. Tess lent me her computer so I could design a flyer requesting volunteer dance performers, and then after, Jake and I plastered them all over the ship. Afterward, we grabbed gelato and sat outside by the pool, and I showed him videos of Mango running. Mango rolling around in the mud. Mango sleeping. Even the one of Mango *eating* a mango.

Later on, Jake and I joined some of the group for an early dinner at the English pub–style restaurant. Mom and Dad's table was full, so I reluctantly followed Jake over to where his dad, *bhua*, and a few other aunties were sitting. Wonderfully, Queen B had been avoiding me ever since I told her Jake was in love with me, and she did not look pleased to see me now—she was addressing her questions and comments about the dancing competition exclusively to Jake. Eventually, she changed the topic of conversation to Jake himself. His impending exam results and big-shot job. His general awesomeness. I flicked my eyes at Jake as she bragged. He was already looking at me, his mouth screwed up in a silly, annoyingly adorable way that made it hard to keep a straight face. It made me wonder if he didn't actually like showing off for the Auntie-Uncle Brigade. Maybe he was simply humoring them.

"Such a sweet, sensitive boy," Bishan Auntie purred. "And *so* athletic, too. Did you know he received scholarship to the university?"

Hot Water with Lemon Auntie and I nodded. Yes, we had heard several times before.

"You should have seen him swim when he was a boy," the queen continued. "*So* fast. Like a shark!"

"What kind of shark, Auntie?" I asked, and Jake snorted into his lager.

She looked at me for the first time all evening. "Pardon me?"

"I asked you what kind of species of shark? Is Jake like a reef shark? A tiger shark?" I flicked my eyes at Jake. "A knucklehead shark?"

"It's called a hammerhead, genius," Jake interrupted, his mouth unable to conceal a smirk. "And no. I'm a great white. I'm at the top of the food chain."

"As if." I grinned. "You're more like a whale shark. You may be big, but there's no bite."

Jake's eyes crinkled at me as I burst into a fit of giggles. Ranjit Uncle and some of the other aunties started laughing, too. The queen remained silent.

"I'm so happy you are here, Jasmine," Ranjit Uncle exclaimed. "You are such good company for my boy!"

"And your boy is very good company for me, too." I threw my hands up. "Not that I don't love hanging out with *you*, Uncle."

"Do you like sports? I saw you playing badminton the other day," Ranjit Uncle continued. "Jake and I are racket sports *enthusiasts*. I must say, we were almost late for the opera yesterday because we snuck in a quick game of Ping-Pong. You should join us next time."

"Count me in." I flicked my eyes toward Jake, shaking my head. So *that's* why he'd had a Ping-Pong ball in his pocket. "I think I'll give Jake a run for his money."

The waiter had started arriving with our food. Everyone had ordered the fish and chips, except Jake, who picked shepherd's pie. He didn't get any french fries, and the moment my dish was set in front of me, he leaned over and plucked a few from my plate. I swatted his hand away.

"I just had an idea!" the queen exclaimed, her eyes fixated on my and Jake's hands. She leaned forward, clutching Ranjit Uncle by the forearm. "Do you know Pavarti-ji's niece? The one from Atlanta?"

Hot Water with Lemon Auntie stiffened in her seat. "*My* niece?"

"*Yes.*" The queen raised her eyebrows. "I have been thinking about this. She and Jake would be a very good match, *hah*? We should invite her to visit Seattle."

I stuffed a few french fries into my mouth. The queen was flexing because she didn't like that I'd spent the day with her nephew. That we'd arrived at the restaurant together. That we were having fun together. I knew I shouldn't let it get to me, but irritatingly, the thought of Jake being set up with a perfect Indian woman suddenly sent my blood boiling.

"I am not so sure about this," Hot Water with Lemon Auntie said quietly. "I believe she has"—she lowered her voice—"*boyfriend*!"

"No, not her." The queen waved her off. "I'm thinking of your youngest niece. What is her name? Kanu? Would they not be *such* a perfect match! She is young. And *so* fair." Queen B's eyes narrowed as they landed on me. "Just like Jake."

Ranjit Uncle, who had been preoccupied with his fish and chips, set down his fork. "How young is this girl?"

"College aged," the queen replied. "Nineteen. Maybe twenty."

Uncle nodded, wiping his mouth with a cloth napkin. "And how fair?"

I almost choked on my food.

"Is she as fair as the color of my cod?" Uncle continued, pointing at his plate. Next, he gestured at the bleached linen tablecloth. "This fair, maybe?"

My lips curled upward as Ranjit Uncle pointed to a bowl of clam chowder at a nearby table. "Perhaps she is the shade of a bowl of creamy soup?"

"Ranjit," the queen whispered harshly, "I don't know *what* you are implying, but—"

"No, I don't know what *you* are implying, Bishan. Jake will not marry a girl simply because her skin lacks melanin. And he will *certainly* not marry a girl barely out of high school." His hand shaking, Ranjit Uncle shoveled a forkful of fish into his mouth. "Jake has an old soul. Just like his mother."

My breath caught, and I couldn't help but glance at Jake.

"He will not marry a girl. When *he* is ready, he will marry a woman." Uncle nodded. "End of discussion."

Ranjit Uncle and the queen didn't say much during the rest of dinner, nor did they acknowledge their spat, so the other aunties and I pretended we hadn't heard a word and carried on with our conversation as best we could. Jake, on the other hand, downed his pint of lager and drank at least four more in the space of an hour. I could tell that just the mention of his mother had thrown him off, and a few times, I was tempted to reach over and—I didn't even know. Hold his hand? Touch his arm? For some reason, I just wanted him to know that I was there for him.

After dinner, Uma Auntie rushed over and invited everyone to the casino. Apparently, a game show was about to start—one where the host plucked people out of the audience to participate in comedic games. I was pleased to see that my parents followed them on toward the fun, but I declined, and Jake ended up staying behind, too. After the Auntie-Uncle Brigade had left and it was just us, he ordered another beer. I sipped my sparkling water through a straw and awkwardly watched him.

"So, what should we do tonight?" Jake leaned his elbow on the table, twisting toward me. He'd chugged that final beer and was definitely drunk. "I still have that Ping-Pong ball. Do you want a rematch?"

The restaurant had quieted down, but there were still a few patrons at nearby tables eating their dinner. I pulled my chair closer to Jake and, tentatively, put my hand on his forearm.

"Look, Jake. I don't know what happened earlier between your dad and *bhua*." I paused. "Do you want to talk about it?"

He tilted his chin upward, but it felt like he looked straight past me. "What's there to talk about?"

My chest tightened.

"I'm here for a vacation," Jake scoffed, "not a therapy session."

I bit my bottom lip as Brian's stupid face flashed before my eyes and I thought about all the times I tried and failed to help him grow up. The energy I spent trying to improve a man, rather than myself.

Jake wasn't the same guy as Brian. I knew that now. But I also knew I would no longer repeat my old mistakes.

"You know exactly what there is to talk about," I said quietly, as I stood up from the table. "But I have better things to do than drag it out of you."

Jake's face went white.

"So, if you need a friend, I'm here. If not, enjoy your beer. I'm going to bed."

# Chapter 17

~~~~~

I'D ONLY MADE it twenty feet out of the restaurant when I heard Jake calling my name. I turned around, crossing my arms in front of my chest.

"You can call me a douchebag again if you want," he said sheepishly. He stopped short in front of me. "I'm sorry."

I tilted my chin, studying him. The facade he'd put up earlier at dinner was suddenly gone.

"I'll keep that in mind."

Jake rubbed his jaw, staring at me. "I kind of hate that you see through my shit, Jasmine."

Our eyes locked. My pulse was pounding; a weird sensation fluttered in my belly, threatening to escape.

"You don't hate it," I said, pushing it down.

"I don't?" he whispered.

I threw Jake a sassy look. "You love it."

"Is there a third option?"

"No." I linked up arms with him, pulling him forward so we started walking in step. "So, are you—uh—OK?"

"I'm drunk." He swallowed. "I'm more than OK."

"Excellent coping mechanism," I declared. "Should we go find a bar and get you even drunker?"

"No. No bar." He scanned the corridors as if he were searching for something. "Uh . . . let's just go for a walk."

We continued wandering down the hall, passing other groups on their way to and from dinner, or an evening enjoying one of the cruise amenities. Jake was struggling and I didn't want to push him. It took a few minutes for him to speak again.

"She's not always so bad, you know."

I looked up at him. "Bishan Auntie?"

Nodding, Jake continued. "Dad loses it whenever she tries to set me up. It's a sore subject, because their family didn't accept my mom right away. They weren't exactly thrilled he married a white woman he met at IHOP . . ."

"Wow . . ." I smiled. "*That's* romance."

"I know *Bhua* is a lot," Jake continued. "But the only reason she's so invested in everyone else's life is because she doesn't have one of her own. I actually feel really bad for her."

I flinched. "Really?"

"My grandparents married her off to my uncle when she was twenty," Jake said. "He's twice her age, and *such* a jerk. He's never home, and when he is, he barely speaks to her."

We'd come to the elevator bank at the end of the passage, and I stayed silent as I processed the new picture I was developing of the queen. An unhappily married woman was a far too tragic, and common, story in our community, and I was filled with a sudden surge of empathy for Bishan Auntie.

"But she's too much," Jake said softly. "Sometimes, when she's bragging about me, I just want to scream."

"She's proud of you," I offered.

"No, she's trying to be my mother." Jake cleared his throat, his eyes darting to the floor.

"Dad brags about my brothers, not me." He shrugged. "They're more like him. Masculine. Good at sports. The *important* things in life."

"That sucks," I said quietly, suddenly remembering how Jake had asked me not to tell his dad he'd been watching *Outlander*. How Ranjit Uncle had, now that I thought about it, acted embarrassed when Jake hadn't caught any fish during their excursion.

"I take it dancing isn't a sport to him?"

When Jake didn't answer, I spoke again.

"So, it was your mom who encouraged it."

"She signed me up for every kiddie class at her studio."

I smiled, remembering our conversation with Tess; that she'd heard from Bishan Auntie about Jake's talents.

"Did you really take ballet, too? That's so cool."

"I plead the Fifth."

"You . . . own a *gun*?"

"That's the Second Amendment." Jake laughed. "The Fifth is the right not to self-incriminate."

"Well, by pleading the Fifth, you've basically admitted guilt, otherwise why wouldn't you just deny it?" I patted myself on the back. "Well done, Jasmine. You should have been a lawyer."

He looked over at me, bemused.

"Are there any videos of you in a tutu?" Before he could answer, I pressed my palms against his mouth and closed my eyes. "Actually, don't tell me in case it's not true. I'm enjoying this mental image way too much."

Laughing, Jake grabbed my hand and gently pulled it down. My heart started racing, but luckily, an elevator arrived. Jake hit a button at random, and we ended up in a long passage full of shops, which were now closed for the evening. In silence, we walked past the kiosks selling everything from luxury goods like Chanel perfume and Clinique skin care to tacky souvenirs and postcards. Halfway down the hall, there was an empty seating area beneath a glass atrium, and Jake and I sank into one of the couches at the far end, the night sky above our heads. I leaned my head back, searching for stars, but it was too cloudy.

"My head is spinning."

I rolled my head over. Jake was sitting a few inches away, his head reclined back, too. He checked his phone and, his face unreadable, closed his eyes and hoisted his feet up on the coffee table.

"You're drunk," I giggled.

"*You're* drunk," he fired back, and I shook my head.

"I'm as sober as a judge."

Neither of us spoke for a few minutes. Every so often, staff members or other passengers shuffled by, laughing, or talking in low voices. Somewhere far down the corridor, I could just make out jazz music playing. My muscles were still sore from cycling, and I tucked them beneath my feet in a deep stretch, sinking further into the cushions. For the first time since I left Seattle, I felt relaxed.

"What about you?" Jake said suddenly.

"Hmm?"

"That first day on board," he said. "Your 'almost-fight' with your mom. What happened?"

I reached my arms back far over my head as I delayed answering, surprised Jake had remembered.

"Come on," he pushed. "I told you my family drama."

"And now it's my turn for a therapy session?"

Jake's mouth curled into a lazy grin. His eyes were still closed.

"Well, it was nothing," I said quickly. "Mom and I don't always get along. We used to yell. Now we just get silently pissed."

"What about your dad?"

"What about my dad?" I sniggered. "He plays dumb, or ignores me and lets Mom do the talking."

"OK," Jake pressed. "So, why were you pissed at them that day?"

I shrugged, hoping it would get Jake off the subject, but then he knocked his knee against mine, and then again, and then again . . .

"Stop," I whined.

"Then tell me what you were fighting about."

Laughing, I pressed my palm into Jake's knee, pushing him away, but the pressure of his leg was too much. Finally, I caved.

"Fine. *Fine.*" I stretched my neck from side to side, thinking about what to say. "On the surface . . . the fight was about them having invited me on a *seniors'* cruise."

Jake opened his eyes, his chin tilting toward me.

"But really, I suppose, it was about the same shit we've been fighting about my whole life."

Jake pressed his knee against me again, softly this time.

"My parents don't respect me," I said quietly. "And I make it pretty easy for them to maintain that disapproval."

"What do you mean?"

I shook out my ponytail, avoiding his gaze. "You know what I'm talking about."

"I don't."

"Jake," I said, lowering my voice to a whisper. "Come on. You know I have a bad reputation."

I wasn't sure why I opened up to Jake, when I'd barely said anything like this out loud to those closest to me. Maybe it was because he was drunk and shared something personal with me first. Maybe it was because I was on vacation and not feeling quite like myself. Or was it something else?

"You thought I was so cool, like Beyoncé, right?" I said to Jake, after telling him about how at the age of fifteen I got caught kissing a boy at an uncle's retirement party. "I didn't care what anyone else thought?" I swallowed hard. "You're partly right. I didn't care about the shit your *bhua* and others aunties used to say behind my back, or how they acted as if my 'sluttiness' was some sort of infectious disease. The reason I lost touch with all my old friends from the community was because their parents banned them from hanging out with me."

I took a deep breath, and a beat later, I felt Jake's strong hand on my shoulder.

"But I didn't care. I pretended not to, but all I cared about was what my *parents* thought about me." I paused, my words fully hitting me. "I . . . still care. I think that's the reason I'm here."

I caught Jake's eye, my eyes filling with tears I desperately didn't want to let spill over.

"Are you OK?"

I nodded.

"How have you been handling the cruise? It can't be easy being stuck on a boat with your parents and the community after so long."

"It's been . . ." I furrowed my brows. "Not as bad as I thought, actually. I mean, things have been better with Mom and Dad the last few days." I laughed. "We can carry on an actual conversation now."

Jake smiled. "That's a start."

"And as far as the community . . . a lot of the aunties and uncles here don't know me, or maybe don't remember what happened.

There are only a few from back then who really made my life hell..."

I felt Jake squirm. We both knew I was talking about his *bhua*, Queen B.

"The funny thing is," I continued, "I wasn't even that 'bad.' I drank beer, tried smoking, ditched school to go to the mall. I sometimes kissed boys, like the one at that retirement party." I laughed. "I was a normal teenager."

"And you were shamed for it," Jake said angrily. "I'm sorry. I know us boys got it a lot easier than the girls. It's bullshit."

"Thank you for saying that." I shrugged. "I agree. And I hated my parents for never standing up for me, for wanting me to be this good little Indian girl, like Niki was. Everything was so black-and-white to them. And because everyone already thought I was a slut and a rebel, I decided to be a *bad* girl. I went out of my way to piss them off."

Jake smiled. "That doesn't sound like you at *all*."

I rolled my eyes, shoving Jake in the chest. He caught my hand with his, but only for a moment. Just when my heart started to pound, he let go.

"What happened later?" he asked. "After you grew up?"

I rubbed my thighs, trying to bring my pulse back to normal. "Same thing. I did whatever I wanted, what *I* thought was right, so we fought all the time. They dumped on me for going to art school, for having bartending jobs, for moving in with friends, for traveling, for having *fun*. For... dating."

"Brian?" Jake asked.

"Any guy. *Every* guy. But Brian especially because we lived together and he was..."

Suddenly, my chest felt tight. I exhaled deeply.

"Well, I already told you about what he was like." I nodded. "But after I moved in with him, everything changed. Mom stopped fighting with me. They gave up on trying to force me to live the life they wanted."

My bottom lip trembled as I tried to find the rest of the words.

"They gave up on *me*."

I felt Jake take my hand, squeeze it. "They love you, Jasmine. You know that, right?"

"Yes, but they don't like me."

I had started tearing up. I didn't know when. Jake sat forward, and I felt the tips of his fingers brush my cheek.

"I'm trying . . ."

*I'm trying to be more like Niki.*

"But I'm worried I'll never be able to fix it," I said finally.

I curled my body into a tighter ball, resting the side of my head against the back of the couch.

Whispering, I said, "I'm worried I'll never be good enough."

Jake's fingers dropped, and he tilted my chin upward until I was looking him in the eye.

"You're good enough," Jake said, his voice serious and low. "You're more than good enough. But you have to believe that about yourself first, Jasmine."

I swallowed hard, suddenly conscious of how close Jake was sitting. The directness of his gaze, and insight. The way he seemed to see right through me.

"Jake . . ." I bit my lip, smiling. Struggling to make sense of the voice in my head. "Who *are* you?"

He cocked his head to the side, studying me. "What do you mean?"

I laughed, my cheeks heating up. "You're such a sweetheart. You're . . ."

I never held my tongue, but I didn't understand how I was feeling, or what might come out of my mouth, so I stayed quiet.

"Does that surprise you?" Jake asked.

"Yeah."

"Why?"

"Because the guy you're being right now is just so different than ..."

I trailed off as Jake frowned.

"Than ..." he prompted.

"The guy flexing on your social media."

Jake stiffened.

"The guy who uses pickup lines." I smiled wryly. "The guy who reads out his résumé to women he's trying to sleep with."

I could feel Jake shutting down, pulling away, perhaps torn between two versions of himself. I wanted to tell him that I understood, but what I didn't understand was why I cared so much.

"Do you really think I'm full of shit?" Jake asked finally.

I leaned forward, feeling bad. "I never said you were full of shit—"

"No, but you think I'm just an act. For the aunties. For women." He met my gaze. "You don't think I'm real."

I smiled softly and, with my pointer finger, poked him lightly on the nose.

"You feel pretty real to me."

His eyes dropped to my lips, just for a moment, before they flicked back upward. A shiver ran up my spine as he touched my nose in return, drew small circles with the tip of his finger.

"I like your nose," he said.

"I like my nose, too."

Jake laughed, and before I could breathe or speak or even think...

He kissed me.

My mind went silent. My heartbeat calmed. Nothing and no one else existed. It was just the two of us alone on the ocean, floating away.

"Is this OK?" he asked, his voice a whisper against my lips.

I nodded, sighing against his mouth. It was OK. It felt more than OK.

My body went limp as he threaded his fingers through my hair and tugged me closer, parting my lips with his tongue. I pressed my hands against his chest, firmly, wondering if I'd push him away.

But I didn't. I couldn't.

Kissing Jake felt different than how I'd imagined it would be last night, when we were skin to skin on the dance floor and our bodies were doing the talking. Kissing Jake—*this* Jake—felt way more intense. My lips burned from his touch, but it was a heat without pain. Desire without angst. A question that didn't demand an answer.

I could taste how much he wanted me, too. Gently, I bit down on his bottom lip, gasping against him, something primal inside of me taking charge. His right hand slid down to my lower back. I tensed, wondering if he'd go for my ass, or try and pull me on top of him, but he didn't. It made me want him even more. And it made me want to . . . *stop*.

Reluctantly, I pulled away from the kiss. My eyes were still closed, and a beat later, I felt Jake's lips brush my forehead as he squeezed me in a hug. I could hear his heart beating. It was racing, too.

"I . . ."

I was speechless. And so was Jake. He held me close as my gut twisted in confusion, and just when I couldn't bear the silence a moment longer, I heard footsteps pattering down the corridor.

Instinctively, I launched myself to the other side of the couch, and a few seconds later, a young woman in a Kensington Cruises uniform appeared. I recognized her from the staff party.

"Hello!" she said cheerfully, stopping in front of us. "Jasmine and . . . John?"

"Jake," he offered.

"Right. So, uh, I just wanted to let you guys know . . ." She trailed off and pointed up at the ceiling. "There are security cameras, like, everywhere."

I winced, and off to the side, I heard Jake laugh awkwardly.

"Sorry . . ." I managed, scrambling to get up.

"Oh, I don't mind." She beamed. "But the fellas watching upstairs thought you might want to know the game show in the casino just finished."

She winked as my cheeks heated up in embarrassment.

"The group you came with is on the move!"

# Chapter 18

W E PASSED THROUGH a storm overnight, and I woke up several times to the unsettling sounds of Uma Auntie retching in the bathroom. I brought her peppermint tea and kept her company, all the while trying to keep my own mild nausea at bay. But every time I closed my eyes, I could feel the world turning on its axis. My own mind spinning out of control.

Jake and I had kissed. I had succumbed to temptation. Well done, Jasmine. Way to practice self-control!

Despite her seasickness, Uma Auntie crawled down to the floor first thing in the morning to meditate. She was literally green, and had a speck of vomit on her eyebrow, and I was so impressed by her dedication that I decided to cave and join her. I'd never meditated, properly. (Whenever I went to yoga and the teacher forced the class to meditate, I always just sat there and admiringly window-shopped the other students' Lululemon outfits.) I was hoping that today meditation might finally click and I'd find some much-needed clarity. But when I closed my eyes and took a deep breath, my thoughts only cranked up in intensity.

On one hand, I was angry at myself for having kissed Jake,

even after I realized hookups weren't what I was looking for anymore.

On the other hand, I *had* controlled my impulses on the dance floor at the staff party, when the fun and heat were at an all-time high. It was only last night—when Jake and I were pouring our souls out to each other—that I'd gotten caught up in the moment. That kiss had felt different than fleeting romantic encounters I'd had in the past, hadn't it? That kiss had felt surreal. Inevitable. Like an extension of whatever had happened between us last night.

Everything felt even more muddled as Uma Auntie and I got ready for the day. She did her morning puja, and after the prayer, she declared she was ready to try solid food. We wandered down to the closest breakfast buffet and found Mom and Dad sitting in a corner table, shoulders slumped. They, too, had gotten a bit seasick the night before, but because they'd taken Dramamine, they said they hadn't felt all that ill.

The four of us didn't talk much as we picked at our plates, and although we were silent, it was a comfortable silence. I gazed over at my parents fondly, taking note of the way Mom refilled Dad's mug before he even had a chance to ask for more tea, or the way Dad offered the rest of us his fruit bowl, which he hadn't touched, not wanting to waste it.

Was Jake right—did *I* need to believe I was good enough, before they truly let me back in? But didn't I already think I *was* good enough?

I projected more self-confidence than many people in our society thought proper for a woman, yet . . . my stomach churned. How much of that was an act?

*Acknowledge the anxiety you feel every day when you walk to work, every time you drive home to your parents'.*

Jake was right. I didn't feel good enough. Not for my job. Not for the money I earned, and spent carelessly. Not to belong to my perfect, happy little family.

I watched Dad stroke my mother's cheek as he whispered something to her in Punjabi. I remembered the way my future brother-in-law, Sam, had flown across the world to profess his love for Niki. I thought about how Amber, a total workaholic, carved thirty minutes out of her workday—no matter her deadlines—to help Danica with her master's thesis. I leaned forward in my chair as something else occurred to me.

Maybe I'd never felt good enough to deserve a true, loving partner, either.

Jake didn't show up for breakfast, but when Ranjit Uncle arrived and told me he'd gone to the gym, I excused myself to go talk to him. I had no idea what I wanted to say, or what he might say, but I knew myself, and I wouldn't stop obsessing until I'd seen him.

Jake and I hadn't talked about the kiss when we'd parted ways. There was a lingering hug by the elevator. An awkward "see ya later" and "not if I see you first" when we split up to go to our respective cabins. Would he even remember the kiss? He'd been drinking, yet he'd been clearheaded enough for us to have talked the way we did—unless I was imagining all of it. I almost hoped I had been.

When I arrived at the gym, I spotted Jake immediately. He was doing press-ups on one of the weight machines, sporting the same red basketball shorts I'd seen him wear before. His AirPods were in, and he didn't see me until I was standing right in front of him.

"Hey..."

He nodded hello but continued with his set, his eyes focused ahead of him. I wrung my hands nervously as I waited, and a few seconds later, he let go of the weights and pulled out his left AirPod.

"What did you say?" he breathed heavily.

"Uh." My stomach tensed. "I just said hey."

"Hey..."

Jake leaned back in a shoulder stretch, and I took a deep breath, unexpectedly nervous. When he sat back upright, I put on a smile.

"Not too hungover?"

"I drank a lot of water."

"Ah." I nodded. I couldn't read his energy. "Any nausea this morning? The storm last night was—"

"I don't get seasick," he said quietly. "Are *you* OK?"

I wasn't sure what he meant by the question, so I nodded and told him I was.

Jake put his hands back on the press machine. "Good. *Good.*"

Was Jake... shrugging me off? No. He was just working out. I could understand that. I hated being interrupted when I was jogging. There was nothing more irritating than bumping into someone you knew and having to stop for small talk when you were in the middle of a great run.

Still, my bottom lip trembled as I scanned his face, forehead to chin. That hard shell had returned overnight.

"Last night..." I managed to say.

Slowly, Jake pulled his hands back down, started rubbing them together. He wouldn't look at me.

"You're busy," I said, my voice shaky. "Maybe we should talk about that later, then."

"Yeah," he grunted. "Sure..."

My stomach clenched.

"But, Jasmine, I..."

Jake still wouldn't look me in the eye or say what was on his mind, but he didn't have to. It was written all over his face, blatant in his body language. He didn't want to talk about that kiss now *or* later. And I was a thirty-three-year-old woman who didn't need to be hinted at twice that she was being blown off.

"Actually, don't worry about it," I said, taking a step backward. "We're good."

Fleetingly, he met my gaze, and I *saw* him, the other Jake, and then once again he disappeared.

"Today's not a good day," he said quietly.

"That's fine." I breathed out deeply. "I said we're good."

# Chapter 19

≈≈≈

I TRACKED DOWN MY parents on the observation deck. We were cruising through Glacier Bay, a UNESCO World Heritage Site, and a guide was on the speaker system discussing the geological history of the region and the effects of ice melt on the world's climate. The fog was starting to burn off, and I put on my aviators as even the sun made an appearance. It was a beautiful day, and I was determined to make the most of this cruise, of time with my parents.

I would not let Jake ruin this for me. There were two versions of him, and I refused to be hurt by either of them. I couldn't care less about the cocky, vain man I'd met six days ago who set my blood boiling. And the other Jake? The sweet, thoughtful, silly, saw-into-my-*soul* Jake?

He wasn't real.

After I convinced my parents to treat themselves to a couples massage at the spa—neither of them had ever had one before—I wandered over to Tess's office and got to work on today's tasks we had planned for the dancing competition. Jake and I were supposed to meet up and work together, but I didn't want to be anywhere near him.

"Knock, knock."

A few hours had passed in a blink of an eye. Squinting, I looked up from where I'd parked myself in Tess's office. It was Ethan.

"I heard you were in here." He scanned the room, frowning. "Where's Jake?"

"I'm not sure." I glanced back at the computer. "Just one sec."

Quickly, I typed out the final names of the performers from the sign-up sheet, saved the file, and then logged out. "OK, I'm done."

I stood up, and as I reached my arms up in a stretch, a yawn slipped out.

"Tess has you working pretty hard, huh?"

"There's really not that much to do." I shrugged.

Ethan shifted his weight on his heels, studying me, as if he was unsure what he wanted to say. Finally, he just walked out the door and gestured for me to follow.

We ended up in the same coffee shop I'd gone on the first day, when I confused Jake for the waiter. Ethan and I grabbed lattes and a few pastries, and after we sat down, he started telling me about the masquerade ball that evening in the "discotheque." It was apparently the only night of the cruise the bar wasn't dead.

"Denise is on the roster," Ethan said, nodding. "She'll be bartending."

"Cool . . ." I stuffed my mouth with croissant. "Well, hopefully, Jake will be there and they can pick up where they left off."

Ethan didn't speak, and when I looked up, his eyes were throwing shade.

"*What?*"

"What was that supposed to mean?" he laughed.

"Wasn't she into him, at the staff party?" I asked innocently.

"Denise is in a happy open relationship with her dream guy back home," Ethan said. "Even if she fleetingly had her eye on Jake, trust me, she's not torn up about him having spent the whole night staring at you."

"Well, please tell her I didn't mean to cockblock," I said stiffly. "Despite what it may have looked like at the party, there is *nothing* going on with Jake and me."

"Oh yeah?" Calmly, Ethan picked up his mug and sipped from it. "My sources have been telling me otherwise, Jasmine."

My mouth gaped as Ethan started laughing.

"You heard we kissed?"

"I heard something like that."

I rubbed my cheeks with my palms, grinning. "I'm writing a complaint to the Kensington Cruises head office. 'To Whom It May Concern. Your staffers are a bunch of creeps!'"

"We're not creeps," Ethan said. "We're bored. Keeping tabs on the passengers is like watching a soap opera. And you and Jake are by far the most interesting plotline."

"Surely, there's *somebody* more interesting than us."

He leaned in. "According to my friend in housekeeping, there may be a throuple staying in one of the penthouses. There are three beds, but only of them has been slept in."

"You're such a gossip." I rolled my eyes. "I hate gossip."

"No, you don't."

"OK. I hate it when I'm the one being gossiped *about*." I tore off another chunk of croissant and dunked it in my coffee. "Let's gossip about *you* for a second, see how you like it." Popping the pastry in my mouth, I said, "Have you and Denise ever hooked up?"

"God, no. I'm much too fragile." Ethan scoffed. "But she's cute. Maybe one day. I wouldn't rule it out."

"Oh." I paused, chewing thoughtfully. "You haven't dated or—you know, done *anything*—since your divorce?"

"I went on *a* date. A few months ago."

"And?"

"I spent three hours mansplaining shared custody laws in the state of Washington and bitching about my wife's lawyer."

Ethan winced.

"My . . . *ex*-wife's lawyer."

Briefly, I set my hand on Ethan's forearm and squeezed. His eyes found mine, and then he nodded.

"Right." Ethan cleared his throat. "Back to Jake."

"Let's not," I sighed.

"Did you know I've been told I give excellent unsolicited advice?"

"Honestly, I'm not very good at taking advice. Even excellent advice." I laughed. "I'm *excellent* at handing it out, though."

"Aren't we all." Ethan stared at his coffee cup as if it were a puzzle, before taking a quick sip. "Well. I could keep telling you about my disastrous divorce, and you can extrapolate if you find anything helpful."

"Interesting . . ." I sat forward in my chair. "We could give it a go. How disastrous are we talking?"

"Emotional Armageddon." Ethan sniffed. "And no, before you ask, neither of us cheated. It was a lot less dramatic than that."

Quietly, Ethan told me the story about how he and his ex had met and fallen in love in medical school, traveled the world, hosted a small wedding at an eco-lodge on Vancouver Island. How, for a while, his life was picture-perfect.

"After we had my son, everything changed," Ethan said tenderly. "Don't get me wrong. We love him more than anything. But neither of us understood we'd have to make sacrifices. We both loved our lifestyles, and our work, and neither of us wanted to do the fifty loads of laundry that comes with having a baby, or get up in the middle of the night with him, or miss out on ski trips with our friends."

I sipped my coffee slowly, watching Ethan. Pain etched into the lines on his forehead.

"We bickered, constantly, and my ex ended up doing most of the work because she's a better person than I am. Which meant she grew to resent me, and that made *me* want to be even more selfish, and . . ."

Ethan nodded, a forced smile on his face. He flicked his gaze upward and met my eye as he shrugged.

"I'm sorry," I said.

"It's OK." Ethan laughed. "Now that I think about it, I'm not sure that story is very applicable to whatever you're going through right now."

I grinned. "Not really, no."

"Maybe if I skipped to the self-realization stage and tell you what I *learned* from my marriage falling apart and two years of therapy?"

I pressed my hands together, smiling. "Sure. Let's do it."

"What I learned is . . ." Ethan continued, his eyes unfocused. "I didn't know what I wanted when I met Sarah. When I got married. When we decided to have a baby.

"I wanted my family to be the answer, and maybe it could have been, but according to Dr. Briggs, I didn't act intentionally in my life. I just floated along and then blamed Sarah when I ended up somewhere I didn't want to be."

I'd been mindlessly tapping my foot on the ground, and I stopped as a sudden force pushed me back in my chair.

"Was that a little bit more applicable?" I heard Ethan ask.

"A little too applicable," I breathed. "I think you just saved me two years' worth of therapy bills."

# Chapter 20

E<small>THAN HAD TO</small> get back to work, something about a passenger who'd indulged too much at the chocolate buffet. I returned to my cabin and lay down on the bed to take a nap, but sleep didn't come. Ethan's loud non-advice kept ringing in my ears.

I'd lucked out with my career. I pursued a passion, and even though I felt intense imposter syndrome every single day at the office, I was thrilled with where I'd somehow managed to land. The possibilities my vocation still had to offer.

But when it came to my family . . . not so much. I'd never been proactive about growing and bettering my relationship with Mom and Dad, because I was too busy *reacting* to them. I thought about how much better my parents and I were getting along on this trip, how just a little effort on my part had helped us start turning over a new leaf. Why hadn't I ever thought to do that before? Yes, my parents were hard on me, but I was so busy being pissed off about their behavior, I never even considered I could still try and improve mine.

I rolled over on the bed, pulling up the covers, wondering if I'd behaved similarly in relationships, too.

Ha. It didn't take a genius to figure that one out. In my late teens and twenties, I was more than happy to go with the flow, drift from guy to guy, because I hadn't wanted to settle down. Fun. Excitement. Drama. Passion. Those were the things that mattered most.

But hadn't that changed by the time I met Brian? Hadn't I started to question whether I was ready for a real partnership? Commitment. Stability. Intimacy. Companionship. My eyes used to glaze over when my friends used those words, but the longer I stayed with Brian, the more I started questioning whether he and I could ever have those things, too.

Brian never wanted to talk about the future; he said he was a man who lived in the present. I went along with it, because that's how I was used to living, too. Never asking myself if I wanted and deserved more than he had to offer. Never asking myself if *I* was truly happy.

I smiled into the pillow, shaking my head in frustration.

Even this morning, all I'd wondered was how *Jake* felt about the kiss, and what it could or couldn't mean. But what did *I* think about it?

What did I really want?

IT FELT LIKE I'd only just drifted off when Uma Auntie gently shook me awake, asking if I'd like to attend the masquerade ball. Groggy, I agreed, and threw on a little black dress and some lipstick. I thought about curling my hair but couldn't be bothered, so I just tied my unwashed hair into a topknot and we were on our way.

The masquerade felt like a bit like a middle school dance. Top 40 music. Black 1920s-style masks that were being handed out at the door. Over-the-top decorations. Last week I might have sneered, but everyone seemed so excited. Today, I thought it was pretty cute.

"It's like an episode of *Gossip Girl* in here," I declared, when we found my parents and several aunties drinking at a high-top table. "Very swish."

"What show is that?" Espresso Auntie asked.

"It's the one with that effervescent blond woman who married Ryan Reynolds," Mom said.

I cocked my head to the side, impressed she was up with the celebrity juice. "Mom. You've seen *Gossip Girl*?"

"Of course." She sipped her martini. "Niki played for me, before she moved out. So much money, these people. You think they would not be so miserable all the time!"

I laughed, and so did everyone else. Mom was giddy and relaxed. Clearly, the massage had done her some good. When she started telling the aunties about Niki's engagement, and how much she wished she hadn't moved to LA, I stiffened, expecting myself to feel jealous. But I didn't. Because we *did* miss Niki. She'd always been a wonderful daughter to them. And if I treated my parents the same way, I knew they'd care about me like that, too.

"Chandni," a voice purred from the side. "You are looking lively tonight."

Mom stopped talking and we all turned to look. Queen B had sashayed over to the table with Ranjit Uncle, her pursed red lips all the more prominent because of the mask she was wearing. Bishan Auntie had chosen the same one as I had—a half mask with gold glitter—and I flicked my eyes down . . . Oh *god*. She was even wearing a similar dress. Black, knee-length, with tulip sleeves. I self-consciously rubbed my arms. Amber had picked out my dress during a post-work shopping spree at Nordstrom the year before, swearing it was fashionable for our age cohort.

Amber was dead to me.

"Thank you, Bishan." Mom smiled. "You are looking well also."

"And *Jasmine*!" the queen said, turning her laser-focus gaze on me. "Did you have a pleasant day?"

"Sure." I nodded, my neck prickling from the attention. I'd gotten used to the queen ignoring me the past few days. "Very pleasant."

"It looked that way," she continued, gesturing at Espresso Auntie. "We saw you this afternoon having coffee."

"Uh-huh . . ."

"Were you on a . . . *date*?"

Oh good god. She saw me with Ethan!

My heart fell into my stomach as the queen batted her eye-lashes at me. For a brown girl, coffee with the opposite sex was never just coffee. It was synonymous for sexual and/or illegal activity. She might as well have witnessed me perform fellatio while nude and worshipping the devil.

"No," I stammered, chancing a look at my parents. Their faces had gone white.

"Very handsome, that man," the queen continued, unable to hide her pleasure in "outing" me. "Much better looking than Brian."

"I . . ." I couldn't breathe. I couldn't find the words.

"So pleased you are moving on so . . . *quickly*."

"That's not . . ." I smiled through the pain, finding my voice, extremely conscious that every auntie and uncle in a ten-foot ra-dius was waiting for me to speak. "That's Ethan."

"*Ethan*," she simpered.

"Dr. Ethan Taylor . . ." I tried again.

Queen B raised her left eyebrow. "Ooh la la. A *doctor*—"

I shook my head. "No ... No ..."

"Yes," said a voice to my left. "Ethan. He's helping us with the dance competition."

I hadn't seen Jake approach, and breathless, I watched as he handed his aunt and father drinks.

"Sorry I was late for our meeting today," Jake continued, avoiding my *What the fuck are you doing?* stare. "Glad you and Ethan got started without me."

"I ..." The queen shook her head. "But ... this Dr. *Ethan* is—"

"One of the cruise ship doctors," Jake said simply. "He's helping us with the music."

The queen continued stuttering, frustrated her disapproval hadn't landed, and when I looked back at my parents, color had returned to their cheeks. Mom caught my eye. I shrugged. She rolled her eyes.

And then we both burst into a fit of laughter.

"What is going on?" the queen huffed. "Chandni? What is the joke?"

"I thought of something funny ..." Mom coughed, though I could tell she was still fighting off laughter. Warmth spread through my belly at the thought that we were sharing a private joke, on the same team. I couldn't remember the last time that happened. Had it ever?

Queen B, vaguely aware that my mother and I had been laughing at her, kept demanding to be let in on the joke. Mom quickly became fed up, and when a new Ariana Grande song started playing, she pretended she knew it (there was no way she knew it) and invited Dad to join her on the dance floor. Several other auntie-uncle pairings peeled off, too, and when Ranjit Uncle even asked Uma Auntie to dance, it was just Jake, Bishan Auntie, and me left at the high-top table.

I couldn't have imagined a more awkward scenario if I tried.

"I'm going to get a drink," I declared. Meaning . . .

*I'm going to get the hell away from both of you.*

"I'll join you," Jake said, stepping in front of me. I was eye level with his chest, but I refused to look up.

"Don't you want to dance with your *bhua*?" I said, to his left pectoral. A tiny piece of lint had settled on the pocket. I resisted the urge to pick it off.

"No."

"I think you should."

"*Bhua*," Jake breathed. I could feel him staring at the top of my head. "Jasmine and I are going to the bar. Would you like another martini?"

"No, no. I am OK. But let me go buy your drink, *beta*," she cooed. "You enjoy the party."

"I am enjoying the party."

Was he still looking at me? Fucker. Go look at your press machine in the gym. Don't bother paying attention to me now.

I stormed off without another word and hightailed it to the bar. I found Denise and flagged her down.

"Jasmine!" She smiled. "How *are* you—"

"Save me!" I whispered frantically. "Please!"

She threw me a bemused look, which quickly transferred to Jake, who had stopped short right next to me. I slid a foot down the bar so our shoulders weren't touching.

"Hey, Denise," Jake said.

"Another martini?"

"A beer, please." He pulled out his wallet, gesturing at me. "And whatever Jasmine's having. How's Billy, by the way? Was it a fracture?"

"A sprain, thank god," Denise sighed, rolling her eyes my way. "My idiot partner fell off the roof. Don't ask me why he was up there in the first place." She grabbed a pint glass, angled it under the beer dispenser. "Jasmine, you want a beer?"

"I . . ." I looked between Jake and Denise, inexplicably furious. "I . . ."

"Wine?"

"The most expensive thing on the menu," I said finally.

She laughed. "Are you sure?"

I turned to Jake, glowering. "Yes."

Two minutes later, Denise returned with a Texas-sized Long Island iced tea, concocted using Grey Goose, Patrón, and some top-shelf rum and gin I'd never even heard of. I thanked her, reminded Jake he needed to tip our new friend generously, and then took a big slurp.

"Can we talk?" I heard Jake ask, after Denise disappeared to help another customer.

"I didn't need your help back there with Bishan Auntie," I replied testily. "I had nothing to hide. There was no reason to lie."

"Yeah, but . . ."

"But you think you need to save me now?" I set my drink down and crossed my arms. "I can handle them on my own. I've *been* handling them."

"Actually, you've spent two decades avoiding them . . ."

Jake trailed off, probably because my face took a turn for the murderous. He smiled, dorkily, and then sidled up closer.

"Anyway. Can we talk? About what happened in the gym today—"

"Can *you* not stand so close to me?" I whined, shimmying another few inches away from. "Your *bhua* is watching."

Jake followed my gaze to where Bishan Auntie was drinking alone at the high-top table and fixated on us like we were breaking news. He nodded stiffly, took a sip of his beer, and then leaned back against the bar.

"I need to talk to you, Jasmine."

"Your needs aren't my concern."

"Look at me," I heard him whisper. "Please?"

I bared my teeth into a smile, turning to him.

"I..."

*You're full of shit.*

*You aren't real.*

"I am so, so sorry for how I treated you this morning," he said finally. "I—"

I put up my hand, cutting him off. "You really don't need to do this."

"Explain myself?"

"Or try to make me feel better."

Jake breathed hard, leaning in closer. "I'm not this guy, Jasmine. I'm not this dick, honestly—"

"Honestly, Jake," I interrupted. "You know what I think?"

He shook his head, frowning.

"I think it doesn't matter who you are."

His eyebrows furrowed.

"There's this side of you who is super . . . macho and vain and *douchey*, and yes, *he* is a dick." I paused, my hand trembling. "And then there's that other guy who shows up sometimes. Who talked to me last night and made me feel *sane*, when I'm so used to feeling crazy all the time. A guy who is sweet"—I poked his bicep—"the guy who your mother raised."

Jake didn't move. His eyes had gone heavy, and it almost looked like he was about to cry.

"But it really doesn't matter which one you are," I said, rushing my words. "If you're an actual dick or a decent guy in a dick costume, when you go back and forth all the time." My voice was shaking, so I took a deep breath. "I'm a big girl, Jake. A kiss can just be a kiss. I didn't come to the gym for a proposal, but for a conversation between *adults*."

Denise returned suddenly and resumed her story about how her partner, Billy, had sprained both his ankles. I wasn't sure why I'd been so jealous of her and Jake at the staff party. It was clear she was this friendly and outgoing with everyone, and I was irritated at myself for letting jealousy get the best of me.

For being jealous in the first place.

A few minutes later, another wave of partygoers arrived, so we said our goodbyes to Denise and edged to the very end of the bar to make room. I sipped my massive drink.

"A decent guy in a dick costume, huh?" Jake said suddenly.

Without meaning to, I burst out laughing. In an instant, the tension in my neck and jaw was released. I was giggling like a toddler.

"I should be a poet," I said.

"You really should." Jake swigged his beer, although his eyes didn't leave me. "You'd be a great poet. A *fantastic* motivational speaker. A—"

"Are we flattering me, or are we working through your bullshit?" I fired.

"We're working through my bullshit." He cleared his throat, suppressing a grin. "Um. So. I guess I'll start by telling you what happened earlier . . ."

"Go for it."

"This is hard."

"Take your time."

Jake ran his hands through his hair, sighing. "Well, let me start by saying that you were right. About everything." He paused. "That first day on board in the coffee shop, and then when we were dancing at the staff party . . . I *was* trying it on with you."

I nodded. I already knew that.

"You're hot." He grinned, and I couldn't help but blush. "You're *really* hot. And hitting on you was just *instinctive*, you know?"

Again, I nodded. My attraction to Jake had been an impulse, too.

"But then after you called me out at the party, and we just talked . . ." Jake's mouth tensed. "Last night, too. We shared some pretty personal stuff . . ."

He edged closer, until I could feel the heat of his body press gently against me.

"I don't talk that way to women I'm just trying to hook up with. I don't talk to anyone like that, Jasmine."

He searched my face, his eyes pulling me toward him.

"When I kissed you last night, I meant it," he said quietly. "It was real."

The music was loud, but the rapid thumping in my chest was all I could hear. Was *this* real? What could I allow myself to believe?

"Then why did you blow me off at the gym?" I said icily. Trembling, I set my cocktail down on the bar so as not to drop it. "You freaked out."

"Yes. But not because of you."

Jake pulled out his phone, set it on the bar, and slid it toward me.

"My bar results were posted early this morning."

"Oh." I was taken aback. "Did you pass?"

"I don't know." He shrugged. "I haven't checked."

"But you were so confident . . ." I trailed off as it hit me. Jake had been checking his phone constantly the whole trip, but maybe it had nothing to do with women. He was waiting for bad news.

"Was the exam really hard?" I asked quietly.

"It was my fault. I got cocky. I partied too much." He scratched his jaw. "My family doesn't know, but I screwed up my grades the last few semesters. That job offer came in early, based on my grades from back when I actually studied."

"Shit . . ."

"No, what's *shit* is that the firm won't hire me if I fail," Jake said. "They won't wait for me to retake the bar. They'll rescind the offer."

I grimaced, feeling terrible for Jake, but also strangely relieved that his behavior this morning was somewhat justifiable.

"Maybe I deserve what's coming," Jake continued. "You're totally right about me. I don't know who I've been the last few years." His voice caught. "I don't feel grounded without my mom."

"Jake," I whispered, resisting the urge to touch him. Hold him. "Losing a parent was never going to be easy."

"As you aptly pointed out when we met, the only thing I have worth being proud of is my résumé, and even that's a lie."

At some point, the music had changed. The party songs had made their way to power ballads. Jake laughed.

"Mom would not be proud of the man I've become."

Slowly, I reached out my hand until my pinkie brushed his. I hooked it through and then tugged him gently.

"So, make her proud," I said softly. "Check those results. Deal with the consequences. And, next time, do a little better."

His face suddenly cracked open. And a smile—so sincere, so utterly adorable—stretched across his face.

"OK." He nodded. "But I can't do it here. I might cry."

"You're so dramatic." I rolled my eyes. "It's only the rest of your life at stake."

I realized I was still holding Jake's hand when he squeezed it.

"Will you come with me?"

I tilted my chin upward until I caught sight of Queen B, who was still perched at the high-top table. Still glowering at me.

"Can't," I answered, letting go of Jake. "We're being supervised."

He followed my gaze, sighing. "*Bhua* really doesn't like you, does she?"

"She thinks I'm going to corrupt you."

"Does she suspect something's going on with us? She acts so weird when you're around."

I tried to keep a straight face but failed miserably.

"What's so funny?"

"OK. *So.*" I put my hand on my hip. "I may have messed with her a little bit."

"You *may* have messed with her," Jake echoed.

"Don't get mad, but . . ." I screwed up my face. "I *may* have told her that you were in love with me."

I nearly died from laughter as I told Jake the story about how I handled the queen's attempt to intimidate me. He was equally amused, said he thought it would be good for her to learn to mind her own business for a change.

"Should we take it up a notch?" Jake said after, puffing out his chest. "I have an idea."

"Go for it."

"Can anyone else see us right now?"

I scanned the room. My parents, Ranjit Uncle, and the others were all across the room on the dance floor, or sitting at tables where the vantage point was obscured by the bar's layout.

"You're in the clear."

Immediately, Jake bent down and retied the laces of his left shoe. I didn't know what he was doing until he let one knee drop to the floor. I gasped.

"Dude. I said I *didn't* want a proposal."

"She doesn't know that." Gently, he clutched my right hand between his palms and stared up at me. "Jasmine Randhawa..."

"Get up," I laughed. "This is so risky—"

"Then we'll be quick." He grinned. "Is she looking?"

I darted my eyes in her direction. The queen's mouth was hanging open.

"Yes," I laughed.

"Keep a straight face," Jake said. "Otherwise, it won't work."

I nodded stiffly, zipping my mouth shut.

"OK. So. In a moment," Jake continued, "when I kiss your knuckles..."

My body shivered.

"... I want you to touch my cheek with your left hand." He paused. "Are you ready?"

I nodded, my heartbeat pounding in my stomach as Jake ever so gently brushed his lips against me. A warm sensation crept up my arm and washed over my whole body, but I forced myself to take a deep breath and follow his instructions. I waited a beat, and then with my free palm, I pressed it against his cheek.

"Now shake your head," Jake said. "Like you're turning me down."

"I'm turning you down," I said slowly, his gaze tearing through me. Our eyes locked, Jake stood up, our bodies in slow motion. My heart...

"Did it work?" he asked suddenly.

It took me a moment to realize he was talking about tricking the queen.

"I don't know," I said quickly, reaching for my drink. "You look."

I took two big gulps, which barely made a dent in the cocktail. Wiping my lips, I turned back around.

"She's fanning herself. That'll teach her."

Jake's mouth twitched as he attempted to conceal a smile. I was suppressing something myself—an odd, searing pain of longing in my chest.

## Chapter 21

≈≈≈

Fifteen minutes later, I knocked on the door to Jake's cabin. He answered immediately, ushered me in, and then quickly closed the door. He'd left the masquerade party first, so we didn't attract even more of the queen's attention.

"You're nervous," Jake said, as he started to pace the room.

I hesitated. "Am I?"

"I'm the one who should be nervous," Jake said, which made me realize he was talking about his bar results. Not the fact that I was standing five feet from his bed. Or that we still hadn't really talked about that freaking kiss.

"Will you check for me?"

"No." I winced. "I can't bear that responsibility. What if you failed? I'd have to tell you."

"So, then you can tell me." He grinned. "After the way I treated you this morning, I thought you'd enjoy being the one to tell me my life is over."

I rolled my eyes, grabbing the phone from where it was lying on the bed. I sat down on the edge. "Your life will not be over, Jake. It will just be more . . . complicated."

Jake sat down next to me, so we were thigh to thigh, and tugged his phone out of my hand. He keyed in the passcode, opened the e-mail app, and then handed the phone back to me before lying flat on his back.

"OK. Do it. Rip the Band-Aid off." He sighed. "I'm ready."

"Actually?"

"Uh-huh," he whimpered.

"If you say so . . ." Tentatively, I clicked on the third e-mail from the top, from the Washington State Bar Association. Behind me, Jake had started humming "Despacito," and I couldn't help but smile.

"You're not taking this seriously," I chided.

Jake stopped humming, and I held my breath as I scrolled past the "Dear Applicant" line and into the body of the text. Scanning the words, I could feel sweat forming at my brow line. The eerie sound of our shared silence.

And then . . .

"Jake," I breathed, relief washing over me. "You *passed*."

He sprung upright, clutching my thigh.

"You passed." I turned to face him fully, grinning so hard my face hurt. "You fucking passed, Jake."

"You're not messing with me?" His voice was so gentle and sweet, and I nearly teared up as I squeezed his face with my palms.

"Jake Marcus Singh Dhillon," I said slowly, repeating his full name as I read it in the e-mail. "I am not messing with you. You're a lawyer. Congratulations!"

His body unclenched as he sighed out and leaned his weight into my hands. "Oh my god."

"Look at you, big shot," I whispered. "Who barely studies and passes the bar?"

Jake laughed, pulling me into a hug.

"Jasmine," he exclaimed. *"Thank you."*

My arms were trapped at my sides as he squeezed me tight and started rocking, cradling me in his warmth, his strength, his scent. Without meaning to, I found myself closing my eyes, letting my head fall lightly against his, wondering what it would be like to be held like this forever. Wondering . . .

*Oh . . . Jasmine.*

*Oh* fuck.

"So!" I cleared my throat, forcing myself to pull away. "How do you want to celebrate?"

"I don't know," Jake replied.

"Let's go back to the discotheque and pop some champagne! Or order everyone a round of forty-five-dollar Long Island iced teas?"

"No . . . I'm not going to tell my family until we get back to Seattle."

"Why? Everyone will be so proud of you."

"Maybe too proud of me?"

I grinned. "I thought you knew this was a Jake-themed cruise?"

"I've gotten enough attention," he said. "I think I'd rather keep a low profile."

"Well, there's a price to pay for my silence," I teased. "I accept Mastercard, Visa, Amex—"

"How about a date?"

My heart stopped beating at the thought of it.

"When we get back to Seattle," he continued. "I'd like to take you out."

I laughed, maybe a little too loud. When I caught myself, Jake was frowning at me. He looked hurt.

"Wait," I said. "You're serious."

"Of course I'm serious." He paused. "There's something here, Jasmine. It's—"

"Even if there is," I interrupted, before he said something I couldn't handle hearing, "I don't think we want the same things."

"Oh yeah?" He bit his bottom lip, and something pulled inside of me. "What do you want?"

Shoving him, I slid over on the bed so there was space between us. "Yes. Fine. I *want* you, too. But . . ."

He reached for my hand, waiting for me to speak. Finally, I turned to him.

"Four years ago, I would have already slept with you."

Jake threw me a wry look.

"Yeah. It's true." I shrugged. "You're hot, and we have chemistry, and I liked to have *fun*. I've dated a lot of guys, Jake. I don't feel bad about that."

"And you shouldn't." Jake nodded.

"But I'm starting to realize that I don't want that kind of fun anymore." I withdrew my hand from his, studying the lines in my palm. "At least, not with just any guy."

I told Jake about how I'd rushed into a relationship with Brian, spent four years of my life going with the flow even though deep down I was ready for more.

"Next time, I know I need to take it slow. I only want to be with someone if I know we could have a future together, that he wants the same things out of life that I do." I paused. "Not that I even know what those 'things' are yet."

Jake was staring at me intently, nodding. I laughed.

"Oh god, I sound so corny right now. I sound just like my *sister*."

"I like corny." Jake slid closer to me on the bed. "And what makes you think I'm not ready for all of that?"

I tilted my chin skeptically. "Really? You're ready to go on a date with an older woman who just said she isn't going to sleep with you right away? Who is looking for a serious relationship?" I gasped, jokingly. "Who might need to figure out pretty quickly if she wants *kids*?"

"Yes."

Goose bumps rushed up my arms, as I shook my head. "I don't think you are . . ."

My voice caught in my throat as I felt Jake's palm on my chin, turning me toward him. My pulse racing, I met his gaze. My knees trembled.

"I like you, Jasmine," he breathed. "A lot."

*Oh, Jasmine . . . Be careful.*

"Even when I'm yelling at you?" I asked.

"Especially when you're yelling at me."

I smiled, leaning into his hand.

"Do you like me?" He chewed on his bottom lip. "The decent guy in a dick costume?"

I breathed out a laugh, suddenly shy. "Is that really you, though?" I asked.

Jake nodded, pulling me ever so gently closer to him. "It's me. I don't know where I went, but I promise you, this is me."

Our foreheads touched, our breaths heavy, and urgent.

"Jasmine," he whispered. "You see the real me."

I'd always made fun of romance, but maybe it was because I wasn't looking for it. Or maybe I was jealous because, despite all my fun, I'd never really experienced it.

But I felt different tonight, sitting here with Jake at the foot of his twin bed, in a cabin that he was sharing with his father. Who knew a seniors' cruise with my parents would have me feeling so romantic, so breathless? That it would have me craving, and yearning, for something so ambiguous, so fantastical, that I'd never even considered it?

"I want to see the real you, too," he said, pulling away. "I don't know if I can yet."

"Are you cold?" I asked, rubbing my arms.

"Are you changing the subject?"

I rolled my eyes as Jake grabbed a hoodie from his suitcase, wrapped it around my shoulders. I sighed with pleasure. It smelled just like him.

"It freaks me out how similar we are," I said finally, finding it strangely easy to share these feelings with him. "You have this front. This bluster." I paused. "I think I do, too."

"Well, I knew that." Jake grinned. "I'm not sure you're as good of an actor as you think if—"

Laughing, I lightly hit him on the arms until he shut up. After, I curled my feet up on the bed, sinking into him as he wrapped his arm around my shoulders. "OK, you're right. It's pretty obvious to anyone who's looking that my 'tough exterior' isn't always so tough."

"What do you need to be so tough about?"

I shrugged. "My heart?"

I could feel Jake tense against me.

"I'm not just talking about Brian."

My head resting in the crux of Jake's arm, my eyes steadfastly on the ground, I told him about how there were days that I felt like my whole life was onstage. Pretending that I didn't care that my parents were distant and worshipped the ground Niki walked on. Pretending to feel like I was excelling at work and deserved the good luck and fortune I'd had to get a job like that in the first place. Pretending that I never doubted the carefree, impulsive, selfish life I'd always lived—even though I found myself questioning everything constantly.

When I told Jake that I'd only signed up to help with the dance competition for the free excursions, and that I was a broke, which I'd never admitted to anyone, I felt the tears threatening to spill again.

"I hate that I did this to myself," I whispered, my voice hollow and parched. "My parents worked so hard to give me opportunities and security, and I just fucking blow it on . . . traveling? Clothes? Box of the month clubs?" I winced. "God. I don't even know where half the money went."

"Pumpkin spice lattes?" tried Jake.

Laughing, I elbowed him in the ribs. "I prefer caramel brûlée lattes."

Jake grinned. "How about avocados?"

"I eat so many avocados. *Organic* avocados." I pointed at my chest. "I'm a stereotype, Jake. I tumbled into all of the millennial pitfalls."

I felt his hand slide up my back, and then his fingers playing with the ends of my hair. "You're not a stereotype," Jake said softly. "You're . . ."

*Impulsive.*

*Ridiculous.*

*About to get way in over my head . . .*

"The brightest light in every room," Jake said.

I scoffed, unsure what to make of the compliment.

"You have this incredible zest for life. It's contagious." Jake shrugged. "I've seen you around the cruise, at the casino with the aunties, playing badminton, at the party tonight. You make everyone laugh. Around you, everybody feels *better.*"

"Except your *bhua*."

"Maybe not her." Jake grinned. "But I'm serious, Jasmine. It's so obvious how deeply you feel, how much you care about the people in your life."

My hands were trembling.

"You see it as it is. You call it as it is. You have this incredible insight about the world, and other people. You're also very self-aware. *Sometimes*."

I felt Jake's fingers brush my chin, tilt my face toward him. Our eyes locked.

"You see your own flaws very clearly," he whispered. "I wish you could see all your strengths, too."

His eyes dropped to my lips and then flicked back up. My muscles went limp.

"Was that a line?" I whispered.

"If you want it to be."

I stayed quiet, pressing my face into the side of his neck. Jake wrapped his arms around me, fastening me to him.

I was lost at sea by his words. The way he was holding me. The heaviness of the connection we shared, like a current pulling me under somewhere never ventured before. Being here with Jake, even considering being with Jake—I knew I was being a little impulsive. I was being Jasmine. But wasn't that OK? Didn't I want to be *me*?

I closed my eyes when I felt Jake's lips brush my jawline. When his mouth dropped to my neck, a moan escaped my lips. Heat pooled at my core, pulsing downward.

I was on fire as our bodies pressed against each other, as Jake's lips brushed a tender spot. I threaded my fingers through his hair and pulled him up to me, kissing him without hesitation.

Without holding anything back.

# Chapter 22

〰〰〰

Niki: Remember I told you one of my friends'
sisters dated Jake? Got the deets . . . You
were right. He's a dud.

Jasmine: yeah, i dunno . . . i think i was wrong
about him . . . . . . he's not so bad
actually . . . . . . . . . . . . . . . . .

Niki: That's a lot of punctuation, Jasmine!

ERE."
Jake glanced down at the small carboard box I'd pulled
out of my purse, his eyes narrowing.

"Open it," I whispered.

I set the box down between our thighs. Carefully, Jake flipped
open the lid. He laughed.

"Cheesecake?"

"Celebratory cheesecake!" I exclaimed. "It's not going to be Cheesecake Factory quality, mind you, but it'll do for now."

"Did you steal this from the buffet this morning?"

Ignoring him, I sectioned off a big chunk with the plastic fork I'd scavenged at breakfast and then popped it in his mouth.

"Any good?"

"It's perfect," Jake said, between mouthfuls. His eyes were shining. "This is the only way I wanted to celebrate passing the bar. You're so sweet, Jasmine."

I blushed. "And *you* are officially a lawyer."

We were in Sitka today, our last stop in Alaska before we'd sail back down the West Coast to Vancouver, and then Seattle. Jake and I had spent the morning with Tess finalizing details for the dancing competition tomorrow and writing our script as MCs, but then she'd shooed us out of her office an hour ago and insisted we make the most of our day.

The sky was clear and the winds were calm, and Jake and I spent the new few minutes devouring the (passable) cheesecake on a park bench while telling each other everything we could think of that we didn't know already, filling in the holes of our respective lives. (Also, discussing how we felt about a certain character being killed off in the fourth season of *Outlander*.)

We both loved green olives, dogs, horror movies, and skiing—downhill, not cross-country. We were both trying and frequently failing to shop ethically and eat more plant-based meals. We both had loyalty cards to and were known by name at our local bookstore, but in reality, we only read about half the books we purchased. We both pretended that we were more confident in ourselves than we actually were.

When I talked about work to anyone else, usually it was to show off a cool campaign I'd been a part of or brag about how our trendy office had a nap room and a kitchen better stocked than any big tech company. But Jake saw through that right away, and I found myself telling him about the imposter syndrome I felt at work. How the only reason I'd made it this far in my career was because my manager was incredibly supportive.

"I didn't deserve how many chances I got," I said. We'd left the bench and had started down a forest trail leading out of the village. "She would spend hours with me after every project, working through every point of feedback. And by hours, I mean *after* hours. She'd stay late all the time to help me."

"She was your mentor," Jake said.

I shrugged. I'd always thought of Rowan as just my manager, but I supposed it was true. Rowan had guided me through much more than just meeting the requirements of my job description.

"Why didn't you deserve her help, exactly?" I heard Jake ask.

"I wasn't well trained when I started, I suppose. I wasn't focused. A lot of people would have given up on me."

"Maybe," he said. "Or maybe Rowan saw your potential and decided to believe in you."

He stopped on the trail, his eyes searching me.

"Maybe you're just not used to that sort of compassion."

I looked up at the trees, my knees shaky, and pointed out a bird we could hear chirping high in the branches. Jake was spot-on. I had never experienced that sort of understanding, especially from my parents. Jake and I hadn't known each other long; how did he already see me so clearly?

"I know we decided to wait until we were back in Seattle," Jake said, after we continued on our walk. "But this feels like a first date."

I nodded. Actually, it felt like much more than a first date. It felt like a sucker punch in the gut.

"Are you going to tell your parents?" Jake teased.

I rolled my eyes. "I thought we were going to take this slow."

"You're just embarrassed of me." Jake pouted.

"*So* embarrassed."

He wrapped his arm around my waist, pulling me closer, and for a brief second, I wondered what it would feel like to tell my parents we were—seeing each other? *Liked* each other? I wasn't ready for a label, and even if I was, there didn't seem to be one that made sense. A label that represented both the intensity of what I was feeling and the pure insanity of the fact that I'd known Jake for little over a week.

My parents would be thrilled if Jake and I got together. He was Punjabi. They knew and liked his family—well, Ranjit Uncle, at least. He would also be the first guy I brought home who didn't turn their nose up at our humble bungalow in the suburbs, or drive a motorcycle, or have personality traits that were borderline sociopathic, or—like that guy I dated when I was twenty-four—deal *drugs*. (To be fair, I didn't know his job in "imports/exports" was code for supplying marijuana and Molly to college students. Well, I had my suspicions, and I dumped him the moment they were confirmed.)

Jake's palm slipped from my waist to my hand, and when he threaded his fingers through mine, he bent down and kissed me on the cheek. I shook my head, thrilled and horrified in equal measure. Wasn't *this* what I wanted? A guy whose touch made my skin shiver with anticipation, but who also understood the real me? A guy who was adventurous, exciting, and kept pace with the way I lived my life, but who I could also bring home to my parents?

I took a deep breath of the fresh mountain air, my hands shaking.

But what if we got together? What if I took him home? And then what if we didn't work out?

My phone buzzed, and I let go of Jake's hand to dig for it in my purse, expecting it to be Niki. It wasn't.

Brian: Mango misses you.

I winced.

Brian had barely crossed my mind the past few days, and the reality that we shared a dog together—and until recently, a life— suddenly dawned on me.

"You OK?" I heard Jake ask, after a moment had passed.

"Yeah," I said sprightly. "All good."

"What is it?" Jake pressed.

I laughed, stalling. We were starting up an incline now, and I steadied my breath, preparing myself for the steep hill ahead.

"Was that Brian?"

I bit my lip, turning to look at Jake. "How did you know?"

He shrugged. "You got quiet all of a sudden."

I paused, unsure what Jake wanted to hear. But more importantly, what I was ready and willing to say.

"It just threw me off," I said slowly. "I'll be fine in a second."

"Do you want to talk about it?"

If Jake had been my friend, or a vacation-time acquaintance from a few days earlier, maybe I would have told him. But now that there was a big question mark hanging over us, I wasn't sure what to say. Did couples or maybe-almost-one-day couples talk about their history, and present complications, with *other* people? I'd never shared anything like that before with Brian or anyone else. Then again, I wasn't sure I'd ever really been in a grown-up relationship.

"I can," I said, stopping in my tracks. We were halfway up the steep hill. I breathed out hard. "Do you think we should?"

"Have the ex chat?" Jake frowned. "Sure."

"I don't know how." I laughed.

"Well," Jake said. "What did the text say?"

My stomach felt squeamish as I showed him. Jake glanced at the phone, nodding stiffly before starting to walk again. I had to jog to catch up.

"He wants to get back together," Jake said, not looking at me.

"No, he doesn't—"

"The dog doesn't miss you, Jasmine. He does."

We didn't say anything for the rest of the climb up the hill, and I tried not to feel annoyed that Jake was acting jealous. Brian and I had been together for years; Jake and I had only known each other a week. But then I thought about how I'd feel if Jake's ex-girlfriend had sent him a text like that. How I *felt* when Denise, a then-stranger at a party, was simply talking to him.

Apparently, Jake and I had something else in common. We both could get a little jealous.

"Whatever that text meant, or didn't mean, it doesn't matter to me," I said quietly, after we reached the top and were admiring the view back down to the harbor. "Brian and I are not getting back together again."

Jake stiffened. "Again?"

I told Jake about how this was the third time Brian and I had broken up this year. The first time lasted five days. I'd only moved half my stuff over to Amber's when Brian had wandered over with a bottle of wine and a bouquet of flowers, told me it was stupid of us not to at least try and work things out. The second time we broke up, we were apart for three weeks, and I had started to feel happy about the decision, but then I bumped into him at a mutual friend's birthday party.

We were on the road to splitsville again by April.

"So, you're still living with Amber," Jake said. "Your neighbor."

"She's more than that now. She's one of my best friends." I nodded. "And she offered to let me move in permanently."

Jake didn't answer, but I could feel him pouting as we continued on our hike.

"I know it seems stupid," I said finally, "but I love Mango so much. I don't want to give her up—"

"Are you sure it's her you don't want to give up?" Jake muttered.

I withdrew my hand from his. "Don't be jealous."

Jake scoffed. "I'm not jealous."

"Yes, you are." I bumped his shoulder with mine. "You're being a baby."

Jake's face cracked a smile, just a small one, and finally, he looked over at me.

"Have you ever had a dog?" I asked.

"Growing up." Jake nodded. "We had a cocker spaniel named Aloo."

"So, you get it, right?" I asked. "I would do anything for Mango. Even live across the hall from my ex-boyfriend."

Jake scowled as he opened his mouth to say something, and I was preparing myself for a lecture, or maybe an argument, when his lips turned into a smile and he leaned forward and kissed me. It caught me off guard, the sudden change of emotion, the too-perfect taste of his lips. I sighed into his mouth, resisting the urge to go further, and finally, we released each other.

"I get it." Jake tucked my hair behind my ears with both hands. "You need to do what you need to do."

"Thank you for saying that," I said, suddenly nervous. "Because it's really over this time."

I thought of Mystery Woman, how decisive it felt to see Brian locking lips with somebody new.

"We've both moved on."

I could practically hear my heartbeat pounding in my chest as Jake brushed hair out of my eyes.

"I finally realized Brian's not what I want."

"What do you want?"

Jake's eyes searched my face. It was too much.

"Are you fishing for a compliment?" I warned.

"Maybe."

I met his gaze. "Too bad you suck at fishing, huh?"

Jake gasped, clutching his heart as I giggled uncontrollably. A group of hikers passed by, amused looks on their faces as they watched Jake tickle me and I tried to break free. I loved that Jake and I could share parts of ourselves we were too vulnerable to share with many people, but also laugh about them. Earlier, he'd been so wounded by Ranjit Uncle's preference for his other sons, his criticism when Jake hadn't caught any salmon. Now, it felt like the funniest thing in the world.

"Your turn," I said, tugging Jake forward. I wasn't paying attention to where I was going and nearly tripped on a fallen branch. "Who do I need to be jealous of?"

Jake laughed. "Nobody."

"That's hard to believe." I paused. "I don't like to gossip, but..."

He raised one eyebrow at me.

"I heard you dated Niki's friend's sister."

Jake frowned. A beat later, he said, "*Oh.* You mean Rupi?"

"Maybe." I shrugged. "I don't know her name."

"Rupi is the only woman I've dated from Seattle, and she has a sister Niki's age, so it must be her." He winced. "Oh god. I don't want to know what you heard about me."

I laughed, although I was nervous. "Did it end that badly?"

"Yes," Jake said dryly. "It did."

We continued on the trail, and Jake told me about how he'd been too busy with competitive swimming to date in high school or college. Then, after his mom passed away, he was too depressed.

"When I moved to Chicago," Jake said, rubbing his hands together, "I told myself I wanted to make up for lost time, and I went a little crazy. I partied a lot. I dated three girls in my class during first semester."

"At the same time?" I gasped, and he shook his head.

"Consecutively, but it still got me a pretty bad reputation at law school."

"Jeez." I bit my lip. "Although, I must say, it's kind of refreshing to see a *guy* get a bad reputation for sleeping around."

"Right?" Jake breathed. "Anyway, after that, it was hard to make close friends, let alone date. Nobody took me seriously, and I don't blame them. I ended up spending my free time with random people I met while partying or on Bumble. Or Instagram." Jake paused. "It was all very . . . superficial."

We stopped briefly at a fork in the trail and took the right path, which looped back to Sitka.

"And what about Rupi?" I asked hesitantly.

"We started dating last summer, while I was back in Seattle." Jake's eyes were on the ground. "We have a lot of mutual friends. We met at a barbecue."

"How long were you together?"

"Four or five months." Jake's nose was running from the cold. "It was good at first, but that's because I was home. I was around my family, my old friends. I was the old me."

My throat closed up, a feeling I recognized as jealousy. I breathed through it.

"But when I went back to Chicago for fall semester . . ."

"You put on your dick costume," I joked.

Jake smiled, sheepishly. "I didn't cheat or anything like that, but I wasn't a good boyfriend."

"How so?"

"Rupi's a nurse. She works really long hours, and her shift work is unpredictable." Jake ran his hands through his hair. "I had the feeling she'd be too busy for long distance and would eventually end it, so . . ."

"You sabotaged yourself."

"I'd wait hours to text her back." He shrugged. "Then I started ignoring her calls, ignoring *her*, until finally, yeah, she dumped me."

"Good for her." I nodded.

"She was a good person. She deserved better from me."

"Do you ever think about asking for a second chance?" My knees felt shaky as we clambered around a rock overhang. "Now that you've moved back to Seattle?"

"Actually," Jake said, his lips moving closer to my ear, "I'm hoping this other woman will give me a chance."

"Which woman is this?" I teased.

He pulled me in tight, his hands dropping to my hips as his eyes told me everything. As I felt pulled in a thousand different directions.

*What the hell are you doing, Jasmine?*

*You're catching feelings, you idiot.*

*You're not ready for—*

"Holy shit," Jake said suddenly, his eyes moving past me. "Jasmine," he whispered. "Turn. Around."

Very slowly, I did as Jake said, unsure of what to expect. Was it a bear? Oh god. Please let it not be a grizzly bear. Anything but a grizzly bear!

I peered around the rock overhang, following Jake's gaze. I blinked, my eyes searching the trail from where we'd come.

My body tensed as I spotted two figures I recognized—their voices and laughter ringing out.

It was Ranjit Uncle, Jake's father, and *Uma Auntie*!

# Chapter 23

≈≈≈≈≈

JAKE AND I ran. And we didn't stop running until we had completed the final mile of the trail and were back in Sitka.

Were Ranjit Uncle and Uma Auntie . . . *dating*? Was there another secret-almost-maybe couple on board?

We were the first of our group to arrive at the pasta bar for dinner, so Jake and I planted ourselves at one of the empty tables and put our heads and the clues together. Neither of us had noticed them spending an unusual amount of time together, except . . . Ranjit Uncle *had* asked Uma Auntie to dance last night. Were there sparks? Had it led to something more?

I wanted to ask Jake how he felt about his father dating, but before I could, the Auntie-Uncle Brigade started to arrive. My parents joined our table, and then the queen, who pointedly looked at my left ring finger, as if she feared I'd changed my mind about her nephew's fake proposal. (LOL!) A few minutes later, Ranjit Uncle and Uma Auntie arrived together. I bit my lip to keep from smiling.

"Hello, Father," Jake said suspiciously, as soon as they sat down with us.

Ranjit Uncle threw him a bemused smile. "Son."

"Where have *you* been?"

"In the village." He nodded. "Beautiful. Just stunning!"

"Who were you with?"

Ranjit Uncle's eyes darted to Uma Auntie, but then he straightened his shoulders and mumbled something about having gone on a solo tour. After, he reached for the menu and started reading it, even though it was upside down. "What's good here, Jake?"

Jake ignored him and turned to Uma Auntie. "What about you, Auntie? Did you have a nice day?"

Jake caught my eye from across the table, his lips twitching into a smile. A waiter had dropped off a basket of garlic bread, and I stuffed my face with a piece to keep from laughing.

"I enjoyed a nature hike," said Uma Auntie brightly.

"Oh yeah?" Jake said. "Jasmine and I did a nature hike, too. Which one did you—"

Jake, who was sitting directly across from me, stopped talking when I kicked him under the table, willing him to leave them alone. He widened his eyes at me. I glared at him in return.

"I forget the name," I heard Uma Auntie say. "The sign was . . . blue?"

"I think all the signs in town are blue, Auntie."

Above the table, the conversation was pleasant. We were pouring water, passing around the bread basket. Below, I could feel Jake's socked foot on my ankle. He'd slipped off his shoe.

"Were you alone, too?" Jake continued. Ever so briefly, his eyes flicked my way. "Uma Auntie, you should have spent the day with my dad."

I reached for my water and chugged, trying not to laugh as Jake needled Uma Auntie and he lightly toed his way up my calf. When he got to my knee, he stopped, traced small circles on the inside of my thigh. Heat surged through me as I struggled to maintain composure.

"The view was spectacular," Uma Auntie answered, seemingly oblivious to Jake's quest to out them. "I wish I remembered the name of the trail."

"Was it a three-mile loop?" I responded, as Jake's toes wandered farther inward. "Maybe we did the same hike, Auntie."

"Maybe," Uma Auntie said simply. "Show me your photos later and we'll compare."

I nodded but couldn't answer. My hands gripped the sides of my chair as Jake's toes reached the plump flesh of my upper thigh. I chanced a look upward. He was sipping water, calmly. Acting as if he was oblivious to the desire he was igniting just beneath the table.

My skin was on fire, my breathing jagged. The conversation resumed around us, but all I could feel was the pressure of Jake's body on mine.

I pushed away my bread, unable to eat or think or even breathe. His gaze smoldered, his eyes asking for permission. My chest tight, I nodded. His toe slid higher, and then . . .

I gasped.

"Jasmine, are you OK?" Dad exclaimed, knocking the wind out of me.

My head spinning, I sat up straight so fast I nearly fell off my chair. The whole side of our table was staring at me. Including Jake, who was unsuccessfully hiding a smile. I took a deep breath and, with every ounce of self-control, looked over at my dad.

"Sorry, yeah." I cleared my throat, as I tried to keep a straight face. "I must be tired. Jake and I went hiking this afternoon."

I scanned the table, waiting for a comment from the queen, a suggestion at impropriety on my part for having spent alone time with Jake, but she was chewing on her thumbnail and stayed quiet.

AFTER DINNER, MOST of us went down to the auditorium to watch a magic show. There weren't enough seats together, and I ended up sitting with my parents on the opposite end of the theater from Jake and his family. Later, in the foyer, the crowd was too large and I couldn't find him to say good night. I couldn't text him, either. The cruise had set sail, and we were far beyond cell service.

Was it crazy that I missed him already? That I just wanted to be *with* him all the time? It was a blessing in disguise that we still had three more nights on the cruise. We needed to take it slow, and I didn't know how I'd behave without hundreds of chaperones around.

"Do you want to watch a movie?" I asked my parents, when we got back to their cabin.

"If you want." Dad yawned. "Although I can't promise I will stay awake."

He peeled off his jacket and outer layers, and Mom sat down at the vanity to take off her jewelry. I flopped down on the bed, watching them.

"Tonight was really fun," I said quietly. "I still haven't figured out that last magic trick with the sword."

"He switched swords," Dad declared. "That's the only way."

"Your father will be up all night working that one out." Mom smiled. She caught my eye in the mirror. "It's been a wonderful vacation, Jasmine."

I nodded, staring at her.

"We're so happy you decided to come."

"Really?" I whispered.

Mom turned around in her chair to face me. Tentatively, she reached out her hand, lightly gripping my chin with her thumb and pointer finger. My stomach churned as her eyes met mine and she kissed the air, her face scrunched in a smile.

Mom's touch. Her gaze. Her attention. It was ... overwhelming. My breath caught and tears formed at the corners of my eyes as I thought of how often she touched Niki like this, how long it had been since she'd shown me this kind of love.

But who was it that my mother could see right now? The good girl who helped out with the dancing competition out of the goodness of her heart, and not because she was selfish and broke? The proper young woman who wasn't sneaking around with yet *another* guy, right beneath her nose? A daughter she could be proud of?

That was Niki. *That* daughter wasn't here.

"Can we talk?" I said suddenly. Mom tilted her chin, studying me, and then withdrew to the vanity.

"Of course."

"I ..."

I cleared my throat, unsure where to begin. I didn't even know what I wanted to say.

*I'm only helping out with the dance competition because I couldn't afford the excursions.*

*The community's golden boy, Jake, and I are ... "hanging out."*

*I wish I'd gone on vacation with you years ago.*

*Mom. Dad. I'm ... sorry?*

"Do you hear that?" Dad said, before I could decide my approach.

"Hear what?"

He beat me to the door, and when we peered outside, there was a stream of passengers rushing by. I caught sight of Margarita Auntie in the crowd and waved at her.

"What's going on?"

"The aurora borealis!" she called, without stopping. *"Chalo!"*

Grinning, I spun on my heels to face my parents. My dad was already getting his coat, although Mom looked confused.

"What did she say?"

"Aurora borealis." I beamed.

"She wants *more* pasta?"

"Mom," I laughed. "It's the northern lights!"

Both of our cabins were on the wrong side of the ship to get a good look, so we followed the crowd up the stairs to one of the viewing decks. There was a buzz of excitement in the air. None of us had ever seen the northern lights before, and hadn't expected to during the trip, either. Usually, it was only visible in the region until the end of April.

The deck was crowded when we arrived. People had stopped short just outside the door, blocking everyone behind, and they were starting to grow frustrated and push. The frigid night air blew in from around them, and I caught Mom shivering. In the rush, she'd forgotten her jacket.

"I can't see," she said quietly. People were pushing from behind now, too. "Can you?"

I shook my head. I wasn't much taller, and neither was Dad.

"Maybe let's try another door?" Dad ventured, and just then it hit me. I knew where to go.

I grabbed my mom's hand, and she took hold of Dad, and I led them back through the crowd to the staircase. They followed me up two more flights of stairs, until we were on the shopping concourse.

"Where are we going?" Mom asked.

I grinned. "Trust me."

I tried not to run as we breezed past the shops and kiosks, all of which were shuttered for the night. When we neared the sitting area beneath the glass atrium, I smiled. Except for a few members of staff, the whole place was totally empty.

"I see this is where the locals hang," I said to the staff as we approached. "Mind if we join?"

"Not at all," said one of the men, who I remembered from the party. "There's plenty of room."

I led Mom and Dad to the couch, the one where Jake and I had first kissed, as it was in the center of the atrium and gave us the best view. The staff had already turned out the lights, and as soon as my butt hit the seat, I let my head fall backward and looked upward.

There wasn't a cloud in sight, the sky an expansive sea of stars backlit in greens and purples and pinks dancing across the horizon. I felt Mom squirm beside me, and I laughed and grabbed her hand.

"Front-row seats," she whispered, squeezing my hand. "Well done, Jasmine."

"I see Jake had the same idea," Dad said, pointing.

We looked up, and my heart surged as I caught sight of Jake wandering over, Ranjit Uncle and Queen B trailing behind.

"Wow," Uncle exclaimed, looking up.

"This is the true magic show." The queen looked dazed, her eyes brimming with tears, as Ranjit Uncle led her over to a neighboring couch.

"Fancy meeting you here," Jake said, stopping short in front me. His eyes were shining.

"Of all the atriums in all the cruise ships in all the world," I said quietly.

Jake smiled at me. "I had to walk into yours."

No one else noticed that we were riffing on *Casablanca*. I hoped they couldn't see the way we were looking at each other, either.

My parents scooted down the couch, making room for Jake. Their attention fixed upward, I chanced a look at him.

"Can I ask you something?" I whispered. Without waiting for him to speak, I pinched the fleecy material of his pants. "Are you wearing *Star Wars* pajamas?"

Jake grinned, glancing down. Darth Vader stared back up at us. "Actually, this is my uniform. It's for *elite* Jedis who protect planet Earth."

I laughed. "Oh yeah?"

"Mhm." Jake pointed up. "Little-known fact about the northern lights. It's not actually caused by the solar wind hitting our magnetic field."

"It's not," I deadpanned.

Jake shook his head, his mouth twitching. "It's the *force*. You see, there are invaders from galaxies far, far away . . ."

We spent the next hour watching the light show, Jake spinning a ridiculous tale about defeating the Death Star, and his mentor and poker buddy Luke Skywalker. Even my parents started listening, laughing along as the story got more elaborate. Turned out, Jake was a bit of a dork. An *adorable* dork. What else would I discover about him? The closer we got, the more I laughed. The more I cared. The stronger my feelings for him grew.

I'd had a lot of fun, and adventures, in my life. I'd gone sky-diving in Australia, motorcycling in Vietnam, and cave diving in

Mexico. I'd dated all sorts of men, and had the pleasure of know-ing fascinating, inspiring, intellectually stimulating people from all over the world. I'd left what I thought to be my small, naive little life behind so many times—only to find myself *here*. On a seniors' cruise. Sitting next to my parents and a guy I technically babysat once at the *gurdwara*. Happier, and more exhilarated, than I'd been in a very long time.

## Chapter 24

⌇⌇⌇

Tʜᴇ ᴅᴀʏ ᴏғ *So You Think You Can Boogie?* had arrived, and nearly every seat in the auditorium was spoken for. We were at sea today, and Jake and I met up early with Tess and a few of her staff to go through protocols and last-minute details, and finalize all the props and music for the performances. Each group was invited to come to practice in the theater throughout the afternoon, too, so Jake and I spent a lot of time running up and down the cruise ship looking for our participants. It was so busy that we didn't get any alone time, only a moment here or there in the elevator, during which he'd quickly squeeze my hand, or my waist. Gestures that weren't only rooted in attraction. Ones that said: *I'm right here.*

*We're in this together.*

I didn't want to compare Jake to Brian anymore, or any of my other ex-boyfriends, but I couldn't help it. The others never felt like partners. They were just the people who took up space in my life, and bed. They were dinner party and traveling companions, roommates, lovers, friends. They were men with whom I'd passed the time, who provided me with a bit of fun while we led separate, parallel lives.

But that wasn't what I wanted anymore. I wanted a partner. I wanted someone who saw the real me, who challenged me. Someone to grow up with, to grow *old* with. It scared the shit out of me, but with every passing hour, I wondered more and more what it would be like if Jake were that partner. What it would be like to bring him home for a family dinner with my parents and Niki and Sam. To find an apartment together and pick out furniture and wake up next to him every day, laughing, while Mango jumped on the bed and licked our faces good morning.

Two hours before showtime, I returned to my cabin and got ready for the evening. I'd already borrowed a bindi and some fake gold jewelry from Mom, which went perfectly with the saffron-colored *lengha* I'd packed in my suitcase just in case. I stood in front of the mirror as I worked up the courage to leave the room, unable to recognize myself. I couldn't remember the last time I'd worn Indian clothes. When I'd even *felt* Indian.

When I was younger, people would stare at our family whenever we dressed up. We'd pass by groups of white people in the parking lot or bus depot or strip mall, on the way to whatever function we were off to, and they'd gawk at us. Niki never minded. She said our outfits were beautiful and they were admiring our culture, but I'd never felt that way. I felt judged and on display and out of place and so angry. Except . . . now I could look back and recognize how I was always angry back then. Angry that I never seemed to fit into our community—not even my own family. But I didn't want to be angry anymore. The past was the past. And today was . . . well, it felt wonderful.

I arrived backstage a half hour before we needed to be there.

Staff must have been on break before the big show, because there wasn't a person around. Except for Jake. He was early, too.

"Wow."

Jake was standing by the curtain, his arms crossed as I approached him. He was wearing a navy blue sherwani with cream embroidery on the cuffs and chest. My cheeks flushed.

I gave him a once-over. "Wow, yourself."

I had spent so long running away from everything. My parents. My community. Maybe with Jake I wouldn't have to run anymore.

I closed the gap until I was standing just inches from Jake. I bit my lip, hoping he'd kiss me, but he didn't. He couldn't tear his eyes away from me.

"Are you finished checking me out?" I joked.

He scratched his jaw. "Not quite."

I raised my eyebrow at him and then sarcastically twirled on the spot. When I was halfway around, I felt him behind me, and I stopped as he pressed into my back. He placed his hands on my wrists, traced his fingers up my arms so tenderly it made me weak in the knees. When he got to my shoulders, he swept my hair over my right side. I held my breath as I felt the weight of his body as he leaned into me, the tickle of his breath.

He kissed me on the nape of neck, and a small sigh escaped my lips as I melted into the floor.

"We can't," I said, unsure if I meant it.

"I know." Jake kissed me again and then wrapped his arms around me in a tight hug. "We have work to do."

Disappointed, I followed Jake to the prop room, tucked in a far corner backstage, as he reminded me that the group dancing the *garba*—spearheaded by Hot Water with Lemon Auntie— had requested last-minute prop changes. I'd totally forgotten.

I was quiet as Jake bustled around the room in search of everything, narrating out loud his thoughts on a few of the details we were still uncertain about. There was a strange rumbling in my stomach as I watched him.

"You OK?" Jake asked afterward. He came over to where I was perching against a bench top. "You went quiet."

"Sorry . . ."

"Don't be sorry," he whispered. "Just tell me what's on your mind."

What was on my mind was the same thing that I was starting to feel, palpably, in my heart. Something I wasn't sure I'd ever be able to articulate.

"Are you nervous?" With his pinkie, Jake fingered the bindi on my forehead.

"Yes." I nodded. "You make me nervous."

"I meant about the show." He scrunched his nose. "Why do *I* make you nervous?"

*Because you make me feel crazy, and not in a bad way.*

*Because I'm falling—*

"Because we're not being careful," I said abruptly. I glanced over at the prop room door, which had closed behind us.

"Let them catch us," I heard Jake say.

"Easy for you to say." I rolled my eyes back at him. "Hey. Speaking of getting *caught*. We never talked about yesterday."

"What about yesterday?"

"That we saw your dad and Uma Auntie together," I said gently. "*And* that you tried to trip them up at dinner."

Jake laughed, tickling my sides.

I hit him. "What if they really are together, Jake? They're clearly not ready to share the news."

"Maybe I want them to." Jake shrugged, but his expression had grown uncertain. "Maybe . . . I want my dad to move on."

"You do?" I touched Jake's hand, stroking his knuckles. "You'd be ready?"

"I just want to see him happy. He's been sad for long enough." Jake laughed. "Last summer, Rupi and I nearly convinced him to sign up for Match.com."

"Mhm . . ." I nodded, my stomach churning at the mention of Rupi's name. "So, what happened?"

"He agreed at first. We were about two pages into the questionnaire setting up his profile, but as soon as the questions became emotional, he freaked out." Jake shrugged. "He changed his mind. Dad's not so great with the emotions."

"A lot of men aren't, especially of that generation."

"It's weird," Jake said. He was staring at the wall behind me, as if he hadn't heard me. "I've spent my whole life feeling more like his daughter than his son, and it just got worse after Mom died."

I squeezed his hand, my thumb tracing small circles on his palm.

"He's old-school. He needs someone to take care of him." Jake shrugged. "Don't get me wrong; *Bhua* helped a lot. But Dad needed his tea brought to him in the morning. His lunch packed. His laundry folded. His dinner served at precisely seven o'clock."

I widened my eyes. "Really?"

"Your dad isn't like that?"

I shook my head, and Jake continued.

"When I moved out again for law school, he finally hired someone to come in a few times a week to cook and clean, but he still looks to me for everything else, not my brothers. Planning his vacations. Filing his tax returns. Buying shaving cream on Amazon so he doesn't run out." Jake laughed. "Everything my mother used to do."

"You're the bearer of your family's domestic and emotional labor." I pressed my hand against Jake's cheek. "That's an impossible, thankless job. I'm sorry."

"Who does that in your family?" Jake asked. "Your mom?"

I nodded. "Niki, too. She's the better daughter."

"That's not true."

"It is true." I leaned backward on the bench. "It used to be me, but then I got fed up and left everything to her."

I told Jake there was a reason I was so desperate to be a normal teenager; I was never allowed to be a normal kid.

"Mom and Dad worked all the time. They were never home when we were young, so I cleaned the house. I did the laundry. I basically raised Niki. But I resented her, too. I hated that her childhood was carefree when mine never was."

"Does she know that?"

I shrugged. "Maybe, although she resented me, too. When I started acting out, living life on my own terms, she saw how much it hurt my parents. She was always the one to pick up the pieces."

"Does Niki still feel that way?" Jake asked. "You seem to have a great relationship now."

"I think she realized she had to stop comparing herself to me." My mouth twitched. I was wishing I could stop using my sister as a measuring stick, too. "She's very mature. Very forgiving. I must have done a good job raising her, huh?" I smiled. "She's perfect."

"*You* are perfect, Jasmine."

"I'm not," I whispered. I didn't know why I was close to tears.

"You're perfect for *me*."

Jake's mouth found mine. His hands cupped my cheeks. His breath tickled my face.

I wasn't perfect, and neither was Jake, but when he held me like this—I almost believed him. That, somehow, two people who were so used to getting it wrong could finally get it right. That, we—Jasmine and Jake—could be perfect together.

I could have stayed in that prop room forever, kissing him. Holding him. Testing the boundaries I'd put in place. Pushing us further. But I pulled away when we heard footsteps in the hallway outside. A beat later, Tess called out our names, and in silent agreement, we scurried around the shelving so we'd be out of sight if she opened the door. There wasn't much room back there. I had Jake up against the shelf, my face buried in his chest. He wrapped his arms around me, his belly rising and falling rapidly in a silent laugh as Tess called our names again and again. I looked up, pressed my palm over his mouth, and shook my head, but I was on the verge of breaking down, too.

His lips brushed against my skin as he mouthed something beneath my hand.

"What did you say?" I whispered.

Jake pressed a kiss onto my palm.

"Come on." I pouted, as Tess's voice and footsteps disappeared. "What did you say?"

His eyes sparkling, Jake clutched my hand and pulled it down from his face. "I'll tell you later. We should go."

We padded through the prop room, and after I pushed open the door, I knocked Jake through the frame with my hip. I tried to close it quickly behind me, but he stopped it with his foot and kissed me on the mouth. I shook my head, laughing as I pushed him off me.

"Get out of here!" I whispered. "I'll follow in a minute."

Grinning, he hung a right and speed walked toward back-stage, and a happy, fluttery feeling rose in my belly as I watched him go. As my mind started racing.

*What has gotten into you?*

*You're out of control.*

*Just like you always used to act . . .*

My heart dropped into my stomach, and on instinct, I reached for my purse. It was still hanging over my shoulder, secure against my hip. But the sudden onset of intense feeling—like I'd mis-placed something—lingered. I shifted my weight between my heels and took a deep breath.

I was letting myself get carried away with Jake. I needed to be more careful.

As the last thought whirred through my brain, the hair on the back of my neck prickled, sending a shiver down my spine. I wiped my lips with the back of my hand, glancing behind me. No. I hadn't forgotten anything. Nothing was wrong. Sighing, I waited another beat, and then I walked through the door and let it fall behind me.

My gaze flicked to the left.

I wasn't alone. Standing there, watching me, was my dad.

# Chapter 25

～～～

S O *YOU THINK You Can Boogie?* went off without a hitch. There were no technical difficulties or Janet Jackson–Justin Timberlake wardrobe controversies or injuries—although Hot Water with Lemon Auntie nearly fell off the stage. (She hadn't wanted to wear her glasses.) An Argentinian couple won the competition with their performance of the tango. Mom's dance troupe came in second, while a group of polka dancers placed third. Jake and I even got a few laughs while we hosted the show. I kept a smile on my face and a lightness to my words, but inside, I was screaming. Luckily, I was good at pretending. Nobody in the auditorium could tell.

Even though Jake and I had planned to join the Auntie-Uncle Brigade at the discotheque afterward for a drink, I disappeared to my cabin as soon as the show was over. Uma Auntie saw me leaving, but I made up an excuse about a headache and kept going. I'd faked it for the performances, but now that it was over, I needed to be alone. I couldn't face Jake right now.

And I definitely couldn't face my parents.

My dad had come backstage to bring my mother her *dupatta*, which she'd forgotten and needed for her dance performance. He'd thrust it into my hand, playing dumb, but I knew he'd seen Jake kiss me. I could always tell when Dad was upset. His fatherly warmth evaporated.

I crawled into bed with my *lengha* still on, my mind whirring in confusion.

What the hell had I been thinking?

I hadn't been thinking. I'd been acting like the same stupid, selfish, impulsive woman I'd always been. The woman my parents were ashamed of.

I wanted to mend the bridge with them, but by now, my dad would have told Mom what he'd seen—and all the progress we'd made would be lost. Sure, they liked Jake, the community's golden boy, but that wasn't enough for them to believe it was OK for *me* to screw around with him.

Because wasn't that what Jake and I were doing? We'd known each other for just over a week. Whatever was going on between us—the fire would burn out. It *always* burned out. Didn't I always throw myself into something else—a crush, a fling, another boyfriend—as soon as the last one was over? Didn't my parents assume the worst of me, because without fail, making the worst possible decision was what I always did?

An hour later, I heard a soft knock on the cabin door. I knew it was Jake and I couldn't bring myself to answer. Around midnight, Uma Auntie slipped into the cabin, and I was awake long after she'd changed, gotten into bed, and her soft snores were filling the room. I barely slept all night, tossing and turning. Around three in the morning, I'd worked myself up into a frenzy and nearly convinced myself I needed to go find Jake, that just being near him would make everything OK. But the feeling passed, and I didn't go. I stayed put.

Around six a.m., I gave up on sleep. I changed and wandered up to a viewing deck, watched the sky turn pink as we cruised around Stanley Park, beneath the Lions Gate Bridge, and then into Vancouver Harbor. As the ship called into port, I realized I'd have service and fished my phone out of my purse. Alongside various texts from Niki and Amber, I had several from Jake time-stamped from the evening before.

> Jake: Where are you?

> Jake: Damnit. You don't have service. I don't know why I texted you.

> Jake: Uma Auntie told me you're sick? Are you OK or are you dumping me lol . . .

> Jake: You must be sleeping. Miss you already. <3 xo

I held my breath as another text came through.

> Jake: Are you awake? Where are you? Just tried knocking again . . . Starting to get worried :P

I knew it would be immature to ignore him, so I swallowed my fears and replied.

Jasmine: just got your texts. i'm on deck 12,
near the swimming pool.

I turned around and sighed deeply, my back arching against the railing as I tried to figure what I was going to say to Jake. But I didn't have any idea, because I didn't know what I wanted from him. I didn't know what I wanted for myself.

A few seconds later, I stood up straight upright when I heard footsteps approaching. There was barely anyone awake at this hour. I blinked, looking for the noise, and then I spotted Ethan coming toward me.

"You're up early." I smiled.

"I just got off night shift." Yawning, Ethan leaned his weight on the railing next to me. "You don't want to know what I had to do last night."

"Well, now I do."

He raised an eyebrow at me. "So. In the human body, when the bowel—"

"OK, OK." I laughed, interrupting him. "I don't want to know."

"Why are you up so early?" Ethan asked. When I didn't immediately reply, he continued, "I'm on my way to grab a coffee. Do you want to come with?"

"No." I shook my head, stalling. Through the floor-to-ceiling window, I scanned the indoor corridor for Jake, but it was empty. "Well, yeah. I do. But . . ."

"But?"

"Jake will be here in a minute."

"*Jake.*" Ethan elbowed me, grinning. "How's that going?"

Facing Ethan, I offered him a big fake smile. He laughed.

"Fine. I won't pry." He paused. "By the way, nice job last night. Tess wouldn't shut up about you two. If you ever want to quit your day job, I think the activities and entertainment department at Kensington Cruises would hire you."

"I'll keep that in mind . . ." I paused. "Were you there last night? I didn't see you."

"I caught the first half hour, but then I got called down to see a patient."

"So, you missed my striptease," I deadpanned.

For the next few minutes, I nearly forgot I was stressed out as Ethan and I chatted and joked around. He was planning to spend his morning off in Vancouver, shopping for his son. With the exchange rate, the toys and books he was looking for were slightly cheaper in Canada. Ethan was in the middle of explaining to me a problematic plotline in his son's favorite fantasy series when I felt like we were being watched.

I looked up. It was Jake, staring at me, like he'd been looking for me his whole life.

"Good morning."

"Hi . . ." My voice came out hesitant. I cleared my throat. "Good morning."

Ethan congratulated Jake on the dance competition and then mumbled an excuse about requiring coffee and disappeared. When we were alone, Jake came to stand beside me against the guardrail. I moved down a few inches so our shoulders wouldn't touch.

"Are you feeling OK?" he asked tenderly.

"I'm fine, yeah."

He studied me. "What happened last night?"

I wanted to tell him. I opened my mouth to explain that my father had caught us kissing, that I hadn't slept a wink and was majorly freaking out about us, but I couldn't find the words. I just shook my head.

"Did I do something wrong?" Jake whispered. I could feel his fingers brush mine, so I pulled my hand away and crossed my arms. There were too many aunties and uncles on this ship, too many prying eyes. Too many people accustomed to watching me fail.

"You're shutting down again," Jake said, after a moment. "Tell me what you're thinking."

"I don't . . ." I shivered. "I . . ."

"Jasmine—"

"I can't do this," I said suddenly, pushing myself off the railing. "That's what I'm thinking."

"You can't do what? Talk to me? *Date* me?"

I nodded, unable to meet his gaze.

"We were going to take this slow. We were going to get to know each other." I was rambling now, pacing the deck. "But what's the point! We would drive each other crazy. We spent the first half of this trip taking turns antagonizing each other, or blowing each other off—"

"What happened last night?" he whispered. "What's this really about?"

I ignored him. "Neither of us are ready for a real relationship. Jake, this will never work."

"That's not true," he whispered, seeming close to tears. "Why are you talking like this?"

"Because it *is* true." I smiled, feeling suddenly at peace. "We're on vacation right now. In the real world, I'm a mess. I'm broke. I'm unreliable and unpredictable and, yes—you were right, I have a few strengths—but there's a lot I need to figure out before I throw myself into another relationship."

"I'll wait."

"And you?" I continued, shaking my head. "You have your own shit to work through. One moment, you're . . ."

*The sweetest, most sensitive, most adorable man I've ever known.*

*Someone I could have a real partnership with.*

*A man who saw the real me.*

"A decent guy." I cleared my throat. "But how do you know the other guy won't come back?" I paused, wondering if he'd interrupt me again, but he didn't. "Jake, you have no idea who you are, either. So how can you be so sure I'm what you want?"

"Jasmine." His voice was low and hoarse as he pressed his palms against my cheeks. "I want you. I know I do—"

"You want me now," I said icily. "But what happens in a few weeks or months from now, when we break up?"

"We're not going to break up. This is *real*."

"We will, and then everyone is going to talk," I said, ignoring him. "But you'll still be perfect little Jake. And I'll be the one with yet another notch on my bedpost."

"Don't throw this away," Jake whispered, his lips trembling. "Just think about this for a minute. You're being impulsive—"

"Impulsive was me throwing myself at you a few weeks after I got out of a four-year relationship. This was just a hookup—"

"Take that back," Jake said. He placed his hands on both my cheeks, staring deeply into my eyes. "We've both had those. This is completely different—"

"Grow up, Jake." I placed my palms on his hands, pushed down until they slid gently off my face. "You were my rebound."

My words were ice-cold, and I shivered as they came out, as Jake's face dropped and shattered on the ground beneath our feet.

I took one last look at Jake, searching his face, for what—I wasn't sure. My feelings the past week, whatever they meant, were just feelings. They would pass, like the changing seasons against my skin. They were fleeting and only focused on the present, on pleasure. They would never, ever lead me to the future that I wanted. I knew I had to ignore how good Jake made me feel to really have any hope of ever changing.

# Chapter 26

~~~~~~~~~

Jasmine: when are you home next?

Niki: End of June. Mom and I are meeting
with the venue for the engagement
party. Why?

Jasmine: that's six weeks away . . . all righty.
miss you, sis.

Niki: Miss you, too.

Niki: Is everything OK?

NEEDED TO FIND my parents.

When I knocked on their cabin door and didn't get a response, I called them, but both their phones went to voice mail.
After, I sent them a message asking where they were and if they
wanted to spend the day in Vancouver together, but neither of

them replied. I shouldn't have been surprised. By now, Dad would have told Mom that he saw me kissing Jake. That, once again, I was fucking around and ruining my reputation. Once again, they wanted nothing to do with me.

After disembarking the cruise ship and going through Canadian customs, I ran into Uma Auntie, Espresso Auntie, and a few others who invited me to join them on their day ashore. None of them knew where my parents were, so reluctantly, I agreed. The morning was overcast, but it cleared slightly by the time we rented bikes and cycled the seawall around Stanley Park, stopping every half mile or so to take photos or have a sip of water or, in my case, see if my parents had texted or called me back. (They hadn't.) After we returned the bikes, we grabbed lunch at a restaurant in Coal Harbour and then made our way up to the shops in Pacific Centre and Robson Street.

Luckily, everyone—even Uma Auntie—was too busy cycling, eating, and then shopping to notice that I wasn't myself. My body was tagging along for the fun, but my head was pounding and my heart didn't feel too great, either. Jake. Mom. Dad. I saw their faces every time I blinked.

We were picking up some clothing for one of the aunties' daughters at Zara when I realized we needed to get back to the ship. It took some coaxing, but finally, I herded the aunties out the door, although we were waylaid several times by a few of them needing to make urgent stops at Sephora and other shops.

Boarding closed at 4:00 p.m., and by 3:15 p.m. I was getting nervous. The aunties were walking slowly, undeterred, and I literally had to link up arms with a few of them to keep them moving along. *Finally*, we reached Canada Place and got in line for US customs. It was 3:35 p.m., but thankfully, there were only a few people in line ahead of us. I hadn't bought anything, and the border guard didn't even look at me while he rifled through my passport and then welcomed me back to the United States of America.

I was about to walk through, when I glanced to the side and realized that Uma Auntie—who had been the first of us to be called up to a border agent—was still at the kiosk next to me. She was being hassled.

I felt sweat on my neck as I glanced at my watch. It was 3:47 p.m. Casually, I leaned against the wall waiting for Uma Auntie, hoping maybe the officer would take the hint and let her through. A minute later, I sighed out in relief when they exited the kiosk and I thought Uma Auntie was finally being allowed through.

Except . . . she wasn't. She was being taken away.

"Uma Auntie!" I called, chasing after them. "The ship is leaving in ten minutes. We have to go."

Uma Auntie, flustered, babbled something I couldn't make out. I turned to the agent.

"Please, the ship is leaving—"

"That's not my problem." She paused. "Are you two together?"

"Yes," I said, at the same time that Uma Auntie said, "No."

"Yes and no," the agent said, looking between us.

"Right." I smiled. "She's my auntie but we're not family. Well, we're sort of family."

"Sure. Got it." She waved me off. "What I need to know is are you coming with us to secondary screening, or are you boarding the ship?"

Uma Auntie gestured for me to go on without her, but I could tell she was nervous, and I couldn't leave her. I took her by the arm, and we followed the agent to a windowless back room with nothing but a metal table. She instructed Uma Auntie to place her belongings on it and then, after donning rubber gloves, started going through her shopping bags.

"No cell phones," the guard barked, when my phone started buzzing. It was Mom, finally calling me back, and reluctantly I pushed decline.

"Sorry." I paused. "Is this going to take long?" It was already 3:52.

"It's going to take as long as it takes."

The guard finished up with the shopping bags, and then turned to Uma Auntie's purse. I could feel my foot shaking as I watched her. We still had a few minutes. We could do this.

"What is this?" the guard asked, as she pulled out a ziplock bag containing a brass candleholder, tea lights, a cigarette lighter, and a small tin drum with *vibhuti*.

"It's for my puja," Uma Auntie said, her voice shaking.

"For *what*?"

"It's religious," I said impatiently. "She's Hindu."

The guard opened the *vibhuti*, smelled it. "And what is this?"

"Ash," I said. "Sacred ash. Right, Auntie?"

Uma Auntie nodded as the guard inspected the rest of the contents in the bag and then set it aside. Next, she pulled out a small baggie of uncooked rice.

"For the puja?" she asked sarcastically.

"Yes," I said, annoyed by her cultural insensitivity. I flicked my eyes at Uma Auntie, remembering her elaborate puja setup back in the room. "Did you bring everything with you?" I asked gently.

Eyes wide, she nodded. "I never travel anywhere without it."

"You should have really left this . . . stuff . . . on the ship, ma'am," the guard said.

"Why should I!" Auntie snapped. "Is God not allowed into *Canada*? I thought this was supposed to be a welcoming country!"

After that, the guard went even slower, and my stomach sank to the floor as I realized there was no way we were going to make the ship. The guard was scrupulous in her inspection, going over every object in Uma Auntie's purse—which to her looked like trinkets, or junk, but to Uma Auntie were priceless and personal beyond anyone's imagination. At 3:59, when the guard pulled out another ziplock bag of dried flower petals mixed with what definitely looked like a Schedule I drug of the Controlled Substances Act, it occurred to me that we weren't just not making the cruise ship. We were going to be stuck in this room for a long, *long* time.

"You do realize," the guard said slowly, "that despite the legalization of cannabis in both Canada and the state of Washington, smuggling the substance into the country is prohibited under federal law?"

"I know," I said, clutching Uma Auntie's hand. "*We* know. But that is *not* marijuana."

"What is it?" the guard asked icily. I looked at Uma Auntie.

"I . . . I don't know what it is."

"Uma Auntie," I whispered harshly. "Help me out here."

"It's a flower!" she said abruptly. "I pressed it after my friend Manjula's daughter's wedding, you see. From the *jai mala*. The flower—"

"Is it a cannabis flower?" the guard asked.

"No," I snapped, losing my cool. "Does she look like a drug smuggler?"

"You'd be surprised." The guard walked over to the door, banged loudly twice, and then stood with her back against it as she crossed her arms and smiled. "Now I hope you ladies don't have anywhere to be."

TWO HOURS LATER, after tertiary screening, during which police dogs sniffed through both our belongings and body parts, and where we were grilled by at least three other customs officers, Uma Auntie and I were released into an empty cruise ship terminal.

"Jasmine," Uma Auntie whimpered. "I'm so sorry, *beti*."

"Don't be." I smiled, leading her to a bench. "These things happen."

"You should have gone ahead."

I gasped. "And miss out on all that *fun*?"

Tears welling, Auntie clutched my wrists and tugged me close. "You're a good girl, Jasmine. Thank you for staying."

I held Uma Auntie in a big hug as I waited for her to regain her composure. She was clearly shaken up—and I didn't blame her. Her privacy had been violated.

"Now let's not waste another moment," she said, after rifling through her purse for a tissue. "I'll get us a hotel room and then train tickets back to Seattle in the morning. This was my fiasco."

I waved her off. "Really, Auntie. It's not like we're missing much. Vancouver is so close to Seattle, we're practically home. Don't worry—"

"But our cabin!" Uma Auntie gasped. "I suppose we could ask your parents to pack up our suitcases and bring them to Seattle?"

Suddenly, I remembered my mother's missed call, everything that had unfolded over the last twenty-four hours. Nodding, I pulled out my phone to call her. She answered on the first ring.

"Jasmine?"

"Mom." I paused. "Hey."

"I am returning your call."

It wasn't a question, and her tone was so terse I could tell she had heard about Jake and me. I nearly dropped my phone as my hand started trembling.

"Your father and I went to Gastown for lunch," Mom continued. "Just the two of us."

"Great, yeah. That's actually not why I called." I paused nervously, looking at Uma Auntie. I didn't want to pass the blame.

"Funny story . . ." I laughed. "I'm still at the terminal. We missed the boat—"

"You *missed* the boat?"

"Mom . . . it's not what you think—"

"*Bus,*" she snapped. "I don't want any of your excuses. I have held my tongue for too long."

"But, Mom," I whispered, "I'm with—"

"You and Jake are having too much fun to watch the time, *hah*?" Mom laughed, the sound full of pain and hurt and spite. "When will you grow up, Jasmine? When are you going to *behave*? You think you can go around being kissy-kissy with anyone you want? Brian? Then Jake? Do you think your actions will not have any consequences?"

"*Mom,*" I tried, but I couldn't find the words. I couldn't speak.

She raged on and on, and at some point, I felt Uma Auntie's hand on mine, squeezing me, bringing me back to the present. I wiped my face with the sleeve of my jacket, snot and tears staining the sleeve. I put the phone down on my knee, Mom's voice yelling and spewing the same awful words she'd been saying since I was fifteen. Words that stung more deeply now that, on some level, I no longer believed they were true.

A minute later, Mom came up for air and the phone went

silent. I took a deep breath in and out, but before I could say anything, Uma Auntie grabbed the phone from my knee.

"Chandni," she said sternly.

"*Uma*?" Mom exclaimed.

"I had a customs issue, and your wonderful daughter very graciously stayed behind to help."

Gently, Uma Auntie brushed a stray hair from my forehead, while I strained to hear what my mother would say.

"I think you owe Jasmine an apology."

# Chapter 27

〰〰〰

Jasmine: long story, but i got stranded in
vancouver. i'd love to stay friends so don't be
a stranger! i know you have your son during
your weeks off, but message me anytime
you're in seattle and free to hang? i'll make it
work!

Ethan: Stranded!! Oh BABY, that story's
going to be a good one. Yes absolutely, there
will be no getting rid of me. I'm pretty clingy.

Jasmine: perf! love me a clinger.

UMA AUNTIE AND I didn't talk about Mom's behavior on the
phone while we grabbed dinner downtown and then checked
into a hotel by the waterfront. We spent the evening reading by
the hotel pool, and later, watched reruns of *Seinfeld* while eating

minibar Pringles in bed. I didn't feel sad or angry anymore. I felt numb.

"Can I ask you something, Auntie?" I heard myself say, a few minutes after we'd turned out the lights.

I heard her roll over in bed. "Anything."

I pulled the plush duvet up to my chin. "Are you and Ranjit Uncle dating?"

Even though it was dark and I was staring at the ceiling, I could practically hear her smile.

"You thought I was going to talk to you about Mom.".

"Yes, well." Uma Auntie cleared her throat. "I was waiting for you to bring her up, but sure, we can talk about Ranjit."

"Jake and I saw you two together." I paused. "We were ahead of you on the trail in Sitka."

"Ah." Uma Auntie snorted. "So, that's why Jake was acting so odd at the pasta night."

"You don't have to tell me." I rolled over to face her bed and could only just make out her profile from the faint city light gleaming through the curtains. "I know it's not my business. I was just curious."

"It is human nature to be curious about everyone else's business," Uma Auntie said. "But to answer your question, no, we are not together. Your Ranjit Uncle is very lonely. He needs to talk. He needs a friend. The man needs some damn *perspective*."

I nodded, but I didn't say anything as I curled my knees into my chest.

"You know," she continued, "some people say I am a good listener, Jasmine."

I grinned. "Oh, do they really?"

"Some people." Uma Auntie demurred. "Your mother, for example."

My jaw tensed.

"I was planning on staying in the cabin alone. Chandni asked me to join up with you."

"What?" I cried. "Why would Mom do that?"

"Why do you think, *beti*?" Uma Auntie said plainly. "She's worried about you. She has a tough exterior, much like you, young lady, but she cares about you very much."

"Mom doesn't care about me. She cares about what people *think* about me."

"Hush. She is your mother. How can you honestly believe such things? Regardless of what she might say. Or *not* say." Uma Auntie paused. "You recently ended a long-term relationship, Jasmine. Someone you shared a life with. Chandni is worried—"

"If she's so worried," I snapped, "why doesn't Mom try and talk to me herself?"

Uma Auntie didn't answer, but a beat later, I felt her presence next to me. I closed my eyes as she sat down on the edge of the bed, stroked my hair, the way Mom used to when I was little.

"I don't get it," I said, as Auntie's calm presence washed over me. "She accepts *you*. And you were never a 'good Indian girl.'" I paused. "I mean that as a compliment, Auntie."

"I know. And I take it as such." She paused. "I don't have children, but I imagine people act differently with their sons and daughters than they do with their peers and friends." Her hand moved to my ear as she tucked my hair away from my face. "May I ask you something now, Jasmine? Are your mother's accusations correct? Are you and Jake . . . 'kissy-kissy'?"

I laughed, remembering how Mom had phrased it. Uma Auntie giggled, too.

"Yes." I paused. "Well, we were. We had started seeing each other. It's over now."

"Why is that?"

This was always the part of a conversation where I shut down. Niki, or one of my friends, would push me to talk about my feelings—but I'd derail their efforts by changing the subject, or cracking a joke, or even getting pissed off.

Because what if you told everyone who you really were, and what you wanted, and how you felt deep, deep down—but they didn't care? Or even worse, they *did* care—but then stopped? What if they looked you in the eye, grounded you, sent you to your room, and told you that how you felt didn't matter, because you, *Jasmine*, weren't good enough for them?

It was hard to pinpoint exactly why I opened myself up that night to Uma Auntie. Maybe she really was a good listener. Maybe it was because I felt safe with her, the same way I'd felt with Jake. Or maybe I was just tired of pretending all the time.

"Jake and I are too similar to be together," I said, after I told her about how I'd ended things with Jake that morning. Uma Auntie had since turned on the light, and we'd ripped open the second can of Pringles in the minibar. "We'd kill each other. *Besides*, it's way too soon. I need to sort out my shit before I jump into another relationship."

Auntie popped a chip into her mouth, nodding. I turned my gaze toward her.

"Right?"

"Sure." She shrugged. "That sounds like a responsible idea."

"But am I right?" I whispered.

Maybe she knew what I was asking. Maybe she could tell I wanted her to say I was *wrong*. Jake wasn't a rebound. Two wrongs sometimes could make a right. By walking away from Jake, throwing away whatever we had, I had made a mistake.

"In my experience," Auntie said, wiping Pringle crumbs off

the bedspread, "there is never a right or wrong answer. And as far as 'sorting out your s-h-i-t,' that project will never end. It takes a whole lifetime. The trick is finding a partner where you can both work on yourselves side by side and support each other." Uma Auntie laughed, softly. "That's a trick your mother taught me. She and your father have come so far over the years."

My lips trembled as Uma Auntie's words cut through my chest. From the outside looking in, it was clear that my parents had a good marriage, but I had always assumed it was luck. True love. Because they were from a different generation and felt they had no choice but to make it work.

I swallowed hard, suddenly furious at Mom. Why couldn't she have *talked* to me about relationships, like her own, instead of yelling her disapproval and freezing me out? Why wouldn't she ever explain to me what she'd been telling Uma Auntie all these years, and try and meet me halfway? Warn me that Brian wasn't a good choice based on her own life experience, rather than simply hammering over and over about how he was "no good"? Yes, I was stubborn. And back then, there was a good chance I wouldn't have listened, but she could have tried. That was the one thing that hurt the most. She never even tried.

I closed my eyes, imagining a different universe in which Dad hadn't caught us sneaking around and ruined all the progress I'd made with my parents. A universe where, maybe, Jake and I . . .

"Do you . . ." I started, and then shook my head when Uma Auntie caught my eye.

"You want to know what I think about you and Jake, *nah*?" Uma Auntie placed her hand on my cheek, smiling. "Let me give you some advice, coming from a woman whose business is everyone's curiosity." She paused. "It doesn't matter what I think, or even what your mother thinks. What matters, Jasmine, is what *you* think. Only once you accept yourself will there be any hope of others accepting you, too."

I always obsessed too much, or didn't think at all. I rolled closer to Uma Auntie, sighing deeply. Still, maybe she was right. Whatever happened next didn't depend on Mom or Jake or Brian or anyone else. It depended on me.

# Chapter 28

~~~~~~~~

Amber: Jasmine! Guess who handed in her
brief and doesn't have to work over this
weekend? Meeeeeeeee

Jake: I don't even know what to say. I don't
know what just happened. Call me. Please? I
miss you.

Niki: You got left behind in Vancouver with
Uma Auntie?? Everything OK? Mom sounded
weird on the phone . . .

Brian: Hey . . . you home yet?

Rowan: You stopped posting pictures halfway
through your vacation! I'm in the office
tomorrow, let's grab coffee and catch up?
Also, there's a new TikTok trend and I'm too

embarrassed to ask anyone else to explain it
to me . . .

T HE FOLLOWING MORNING, I joined Uma Auntie on the floor
of our hotel room for a guided meditation. It was hard. My
mind wandered constantly and there was no way I was doing it
right, but I showed up. I sat on the floor for twenty minutes, and
I tried. For beginners, Uma Auntie said, that's all you could do.

Back in Seattle, Amber picked me up from King Street Station.
She wanted to maximize her Saturday off and drove us straight
to the Arboretum for a drizzly walk through the Botanic Gar-
dens. She'd been so busy with work that we hadn't spent quality
time together most of the time we'd been roommates. Amber
updated me on how her boss had strongly hinted that her promotion was about to be approved by the company's board, and I
filled her in on what had happened with my parents and Jake on
the cruise. I also told her about how strapped I was financially. I
thought I would feel embarrassed revealing my failures to her,
someone who was so successful and even owned her own condo,
but I wasn't. Actually, I was surprised by how easily everything
came off my chest, how much I wanted to share with her—a
wonderful friend who, I realized now, I had always kept at arm's
length.

I felt refreshed by the time we got back to the condo. Amber
and I streamed a chill playlist onto her Bluetooth speaker and
chopped vegetables for a stir-fry while debating whether or not I
should reach out to my mom and to make amends. (I hadn't
heard from my parents, other than a quick note in the family
group chat that said they'd arrived home safely.) I was thinking
about texting Brian back to see if I could have Mango that evening, when I heard her barking in the hallway.

"Mango!" I squealed, throwing open the door. Her ears perked up at the sound of my voice, and before I knew it, she was leaping through the air and hurling her fifty-pound self into my arms. I recoiled back at the weight, hitting the wall and sliding down as she licked my face and whimpered in excitement. I buried my face into her fur, breathing in her scent.

"I missed you," I whispered, before pulling away. Tears welling in my eyes, I flicked my gaze upward. Brian was smiling down at me.

"You're back."

"I am." With some difficulty, as Mango was still jumping on me, I pushed myself to standing. "How are you?"

"Good." Brian shrugged. "Can't complain. You?"

Instead of answering, I leaned down and gave Mango another hug, my insides twisting as I realized what I needed to do.

"Can we talk?" I said quickly, before I lost my nerve. "Can I come in?"

"Yeah. Of course. I'd love—"

"I don't want to get back together," I interrupted. "Just so we're clear."

Brian looked as if he was about to say something, and my pulse raced as I wondered if he and I weren't on the same page. Had Jake been right? Had his *Mango misses you* text really meant that *Brian* missed me, that he wanted to give it another go? Did—

I bit my lip, shaking my head before my thoughts could run away, and I remembered it didn't matter what Brian's text had meant, or what *he* wanted.

What mattered was what I wanted.

Mango and I followed Brian into the condo. It looked exactly the same as when I moved out, except cleaner, because none of my clothes, books, and magazines were strewn around the furniture like they used to be. I sat down on the edge of the couch, which I'd always found a little too trendy and not all that comfortable, and Brian took the opposite side. Mango leaped up, too, and wedged herself between us.

"How was she this week?" I started, looking at the gas fireplace instead of at Brian.

"Good. Having a dog sitter helped." He paused. "Is Mango what you wanted to talk about?"

I was chewing the inside of my lip. Stopping, I flicked my eyes toward Brian. "Yes. And that I'm going to be moving out of the building, soon."

Reluctantly, I told Brian what had occurred to me while I was hanging out with Amber this afternoon. Although I was welcome to stay with her as long as I liked, and loved sharing a space with her, being her roommate wasn't a good idea.

I'd been stubborn, and when anyone had hinted at this earlier, I didn't want to hear it. But now I knew for sure. I needed to move out of the downtown core and save money for a while instead of paying exorbitant rent. I needed to live more than twenty feet away from my ex-boyfriend, someone with whom I shared a complicated history and would—at some point or another—be tempted by. Most of all, I needed a fresh start.

"I don't have the money, or anywhere to live, and I know the responsible thing would be to let you have Mango," I said afterward, my voice shaking. "But I don't want to give her up, Brian."

"Me, neither," he said quietly. "So, what do we do? Flip a coin?"

"No." I swallowed hard, smiling at him. "I think we should share custody."

"She's not a child—"

"She is, in a way." I shrugged. "We both love her, and she loves us both. Why can't we co-parent? People do it all the time."

"Yeah, but for a dog?"

We were both petting Mango. My hand was on the top of her head, which was nestled in my lap, and Brian's palm was on her belly. Mango had already fallen asleep. She was a dog, yes, but she was *our* dog. She took up a big piece of our heart, and our life.

"So, how would it work?" Brian asked me. He must have been thinking the same thing. "Week on, week off?"

"Something like that." I shrugged. "I was thinking she could stay here until I get settled. I can come over in the afternoon, before you're home from the office. But once I get my life together, I would like to move back downtown and keep her half the time. We could work out the details then?"

Brian nodded, his eyes on Mango. Her paws were twitching, as if she were running away in a dream.

"So, this is really it," Brian said, after a moment. "The end of an era."

"Yep." I smiled. "We had a good run."

Brian slid his palm up to my hand, clutching it. I squeezed back.

"I'm sorry for my part," I said quietly, turning my gaze toward him. "I blamed you for everything, but I wasn't easy to live with."

"You were great, Jas." Brian smiled. "I'm the one who's sorry."

He trailed off, his eyebrows furrowing. Maybe Brian felt just as lost. His friends had moved on to a different phase of life, he wasn't close to his family, and the only reason he liked his job was because of the salary. Still, we never talked about his emotional reactions to any of it. We'd taken our own problems out on each other, instead of being there for each other for support.

Over the years, I'd grown to resent Brian so much for not being the partner I hadn't realized I needed him to be. And despite his flaws and incompatible values and character traits that drove me nuts, he had *some* good qualities, at least enough to make me fall for him. He was a blast to hang out with. He was funny, and great at parties, and could make the daily humdrum of life feel exciting. He was generous, and always bought the first round of drinks. He loved animals. He spoiled Mango rotten.

"You know, if we're going to be co-parents," I said slowly, "it might be easier if we're friends, too."

"Really?" he said skeptically.

"Eventually." I laughed. "Not yet."

"No, not yet," Brian said. "I'm not sure I could handle seeing you with some other guy."

I must have made a face, because Brian cocked his head to the side, smiling.

"What is it?"

I winced.

"Jas . . ."

"I saw your coworker leaving here a few weeks ago."

"Oh god."

"She seems nice," I offered.

"Did you talk to her?"

I grimaced. "We shared the elevator. She thought I was Amber . . ."

Brian let go of my hand and scratched his jaw. "I'm really sorry you saw that. I . . . I wasn't trying to make you jealous—"

"I know."

He looked back at me. "It doesn't mean anything. It's casual—"

"I don't care," I interrupted, and even though I meant it, I didn't want the details, either. "Just . . ." I paused. "Don't be a dick to her, OK?"

Brian smiled. "I'll try my best."

# Chapter 29

≈≈≈

Jake: It's me again. I'd love to talk. When
you're ready ... I'm here.

A FEW DAYS LATER, I found myself in the boardroom alone
with Rowan. She'd invited me to hang back after a staff
meeting so she could catch me up on a big campaign our biz dev
team had reeled in while I was on vacation. We'd have our hands
full that summer. The client had a tight timeline.

"I really appreciate this," I said afterward. Rowan had started
gathering her tablet and papers but stopped when she saw my
face.

"I don't know if I've ever properly thanked you, Rowan."

"For?"

I laughed. "For ... giving me so many chances to step up. For
all the feedback and late nights and extra meetings." I paused.
"For everything."

"Of course ..." She tilted her chin to the side. "Jasmine, I
think of you as my protégé."

"You do?"

She pulled her chair closer to mine. "You remind me of me, when I was younger. I know, I *know*. Day one of diversity and inclusion training tells us that's affinity bias." She rolled her eyes. "But mediocre white men have been hiring their mini-me's for centuries, so I'm not going to feel that badly about paying special attention to you."

I shook my head, still not understanding. "I'm not like you ... You're ..."

*Accomplished.*

*Competent.*

*Creative.*

"You're the best, Rowan."

"I am now." She lowered her glasses, eyeing me. "But I had to learn a lot of things the hard way. You are extremely talented, but you were very young when you joined us. I didn't want you to suffer as much as I did."

"Oh." I smiled, suddenly feeling emotional as I thought of what Jake had said to me on the cruise about my imposter syndrome. I wasn't used to people believing in me. *Seeing* me, and being OK with my imperfections.

"Thank you," I said again. "You've been an incredible mentor to me. I'm so lucky—"

"You stop that right now." Rowan smirked. "You'll make me blush."

"I'm serious, Rowan. I wish everyone ..."

I paused, an idea taking shape.

"Wouldn't it be great if all junior staff had someone like you?" I said slowly.

Rowan frowned. "How do you mean?"

"The company's grown so much the last few years. We have so many new hires straight out of college, and they all—"

"Look like toddlers?"

I grinned, rolling my eyes. "*That*, and they would probably benefit from some wisdom. What if we started, like, a *buddy* system? Matched people up?"

Rowan reclined in her chair, smiling at me. "A mentorship program. One that pairs new hires with more senior staff."

"Yeah . . . Anyway, it's just an idea—"

"It's a great idea." She slapped her hands against the table, nodding to herself. "We've been thinking about how to better integrate the newbies, and this is *perfect*. Although . . ."

My stomach churned, waiting for the drop.

"I don't have the bandwidth to take this on. Can I tell management you'll spearhead the initiative?"

"Really? *Me*?"

"You're the only senior staff member on TikTok, and you're cool enough to connect with our coworkers who were born in the 2000s." Rowan raised an eyebrow. "Plus, when you're enthusiastic about a project, it's infectious. I think you'd be perfect."

I straightened my shoulders, grinning.

"I think I'd be perfect, too."


"HE BLOCKED ME." I gasped and looked up at Mango, who had been belly up on Amber's couch since we got back from our run. "I can't believe it!"

Without moving, Mango opened one eye and then shut it again.

"You're right." I returned to my phone and switched from

Instagram to my messages app. "He could have deleted his account. You're *so* smart, Mango."

> Jasmine: hey, can you do me a favor? i can't find jake's ig … did he block me or delete his account?

I set my phone down and returned to meal prepping. Two minutes later, Niki replied.

> Niki: It's gone!

Then she texted again.

> Niki: Maybe this is good, Jasmine. Now you can't creep him ;)

I rolled my eyes, smiling. Niki was right. I had been obsessively checking Jake's profile the last few days, even though he hadn't posted anything since before the cruise. And although I was curious about why Jake had taken down his social media profile, I was a little bummed. Cyberstalking was the only way I still had contact with him.

After a long, long FaceTime with Niki, I'd come to the realization that I wasn't ready to text him back, or talk to him; I didn't know what to say. Regardless of how I felt, or thought I'd felt when we were on vacation, my head and my heart felt too full to make sense of those feelings. I had a full slate on at work, and Mission Find a Cheap But Not Creepy Apartment was going nowhere, not to mention the fact that I'd been single just over a month. I needed to give myself some space.

A knock on the door snapped me out of my thoughts. Mango barked once but then decided she was too tired to investigate and went back to sleep. What a formidable guard dog. I wiped my hands on my jeans and walked to the door, expecting it to be Brian to pick up Mango for the evening. But when I glanced through the peephole, I realized it wasn't him. It was Mom.

"I was hoping you would be home." She smiled limply as I opened the door. She looked tired and was still in her work clothes. I hadn't heard from her or Dad since she yelled at me on the phone.

"Hi…"

Mom sighed nervously. "I don't want to intrude if you and Amber are busy…"

"She's still at work." I stepped to the side. "Do you want to come in?"

Mom followed me inside and, after petting Mango hello, sat down on the couch. "Smells tasty. What are you cooking?"

"Eggplant lasagna. Amber's vegetarian." I gestured to the tray of noodles I'd been in the process of assembling. "And spicy lentil soup with carrots and spinach."

"Spicy *lentil* soup?" Mom teased. "Isn't that dal?"

I glanced at the recipe open on my laptop, cringing when I realized the food blogger had essentially ripped off the traditional South Asian dish I'd eaten every day growing up.

"Yeah…" I grinned. "I guess I'm cooking dal."

"Well, I'm glad you learned how to make," Mom said. "Even if I wasn't the one to teach you."

We didn't speak for a moment, studying each other. Easily, I could imagine us never addressing what happened on the cruise ship again. We could slip back into the state in which we'd habituated the last four years, coexisting on the fringes of each other's worlds. But she was here. For the first time, she'd come to *me*. Maybe she didn't want that, either.

"Do you want a drink?" I asked, going over to the fridge. "Tea? Water? That's all we have, except beer—"

"I'll have a beer."

I whipped around. "You like beer?"

"Sure." Mom shrugged. "I could drink a beer."

Nodding, I opened a tallboy of pale ale, poured it into two glasses, and then joined her on the couch.

"Amber has decorated *so* nicely," Mom said, rubbing her hands against the brocade texture of the cushions. "Is she an interior designer?"

"She works in the oil industry." I paused. "Mom, let's just cut to the chase, OK? Tell me what you came to say."

She sipped her beer, slowly, and I smiled as she pursed her lips at the taste and then set the glass down on the side table.

"Do you want me to start?" I asked.

"No. I'll go." Mom cleared her throat, her eyes on the wall, the floor. Anywhere but me.

"I lost my temper with you," she said finally. "Your Uma Auntie had words with me again when we got back to Seattle. You were so generously helping her with the customs agent and . . ."

Mom had started tearing up, and instinctively, I reached out my hand. She took it.

"I think I've been very hard on you, Jasmine."

I nodded, tears welling in my eyes, too.

"Sometimes, I think about that retirement party when you were young." She sniffed, squeezing my hand. "And what happened afterward . . . How everything changed . . ."

"Mom," I whispered. "I never wanted to embarrass our family. I was just being a dumb kid. I was fifteen. That guy was in

*college*. That's weird, Mom. But all you cared about was that people saw us. You didn't stand up for me. You didn't ask me why I
went along with it or how I was doing or if he pressured me or
hurt me—"

"Did he?" Mom gasped.

"Not at all." I shook my head. "What I mean is, my friends
used to talk to their moms about that kind of stuff, but I never
could."

"I should have been there for you, *beti*. All this time." She slid
closer to me on the couch. "You know, your father and I had no
family here. Our parents were far away. We had no guidance, no
idea if what we were doing was right or wrong. The community
was all we had. They were who we looked to for everything . . ."

Her lips trembled as she took a deep breath.

"We wanted what was best for you. And at the time, for a
daughter . . ."

Mom crumpled into my arms, holding me close. Holding me
like she hadn't since I was a little girl. No, she hadn't been there
for me, but had I ever tried to see her side? Could I have not
thrown my choices and my rage in their face at any opportunity,
and instead, given them a chance to change with the times?

"I'm sorry," she cried into my hair, and I realized it was the
first time my mother had ever apologized to me.

"I'm sorry, too," I said quietly. "I'm sorry we're not close."

I laughed, pulling away from her.

"Do you know I actually miss the days when you yelled at me
all the time? But when I moved in with Brian . . ."

"I know." She swallowed. "Niki told me I had to support you.
I had to keep my mouth shut. Otherwise, I would lose you."

"Niki always knows what to say, what to do . . ." I paused. "It's
funny. I started getting along with you and Dad on the cruise

when I started trying to act like her. I felt like . . . if I want to have a good relationship with you, then I have to hide who I am."

"That's not true—"

"I know that now." I smiled. "And I know I've made my life, and yours, harder than it should have been, but I need to be clear about something. I don't regret any of the choices I made." I grinned. "Not even that 'no-good' Brian."

Mom laughed with her eyes.

"They all led me . . . *here*. To me. I like me."

"I like you, too, Jasmine," Mom declared. "And I love you even more."

Mom slid closer to me on the couch, and when she lightly squeezed my chin with her thumb and pointer finger, I felt myself melting into her, and the couch, as she wrapped me in her arms and held me like she hadn't since I was a little girl. My gut twisted thinking about how much time we'd wasted, how much time we'd spent apart. But I didn't want to live in regret. What mattered was that we were here now.

# Chapter 30

≈≈≈≈

Jasmine: hey, so i changed my mind. is it too late to join the group dance at Niki's engagement? be warned. i am a terrible dancer and am only doing this to make niki smile.

Diya: IT'S NEVER TOO LATE! She will be SO happy. I recorded myself doing the moves and will e-mail you the video when I get home from the office. You have the whole summer to practice!

ARE YOU SURE about this?" Mom asked. I nodded just as I felt Dad squeeze my hand in support.

"Yep." I smiled at my parents. "I'm ready."

"OK." Mom shrugged. "Then here we go!"

Sighing, I pulled my *dupatta* over my head and we walked into the *gurdwara*. It had been renovated since I was last here eighteen years ago, but I couldn't put my finger on what had exactly changed. I followed my parents up to the front altar, and quickly, we bent down and touched our heads to the floor in respect. After we slipped a few notes into the donation box, Dad found a seat on the left side of the room, and I followed Mom to the right.

We sat down on the floor cross-legged, and as Mom and I nodded silent hellos to the women seated nearby, I tried not to focus on all the things that made me angry, like the fact that men and women customarily sat separately, or that our *granthi*—who was leading a prayer at the front altar—was always a man, or that later downstairs in the *langar*, our meals would be cooked and served by women.

I took a deep calming breath, the kind I'd been attempting ever since Uma Auntie convinced me to start meditating regularly, and instead decided to focus on the things that made me happy. Our community and certain cultural traditions were not perfect, but wasn't there a lot to be proud of? One of the things I admired most about the Sikh faith I'd grown up in was how generous and selfless it encouraged people to be. Anyone around the world could walk into a *gurdwara*, and no matter who they were or what they believed, they would be fed a hot meal at the *langar*. How incredible was that?

I scanned the room, smiling at the aunties and uncles I recognized, at Mom, and then at my dad. I'd painted everyone in the older generation with the same brush, convinced they were stuck in the past, but times were changing. Many of them, like my parents, were changing, too. One month ago, who would have thought that I would be moving back into my parents' house under my own volition, and that living together again was actually going *well*.

I smiled, thinking about how last week I'd come home late after a work event and joined my parents on the couch for a *Selling Sunset* marathon. All three of us had had a few drinks, and we ordered Domino's at midnight—the first time my parents had ever done something like that—and we stayed up so late that we were all exhausted for work the next day.

We didn't just watch TV that night. I ended up telling my parents the truth about my dismal finances and admitted that I'd only helped out with the dance competition to score the free excursions. They didn't shut down or pass judgment on me. Mom joked about how she would have signed up to help, too, if it meant saving money, and Dad ended up telling me all about the financial mistakes he had made as a young man. He told me I shouldn't be too hard on myself, that everyone messed up sometimes and I should use the experience as a learning opportunity. It was nice to hear him say that, to really *talk* to him, and feel like I could have a relationship with him separate from the one with my mother. I told him as much. He said he thought us spending more one-on-one time together was a good idea, too.

Over the next hour, the *gurdwara* started filling up as more people joined the religious service. There were so many faces I recognized from my youth or the cruise, and I wasn't surprised when Bishan Auntie waltzed through the door. However, I did not expect to see the next person who entered right behind her.

Jake.

I slouched as he and the queen made their way up through the central aisle to the altar, my eyes following from behind my *dupatta*. He was wearing jeans and a white collared shirt, and he'd tied a red kerchief around his head in the same way many Sikh men without turbans covered their hair. After he touched his head to the floor, he scanned the crowd, as if he were looking for someone, but eventually he frowned and took a seat with the other men.

My heartbeat quickened as I willed myself not to look over. During one of our long conversations on the cruise, Jake had mentioned he rarely went to *gurdwara* anymore, so I hadn't expected him to be here. And there was no way he was looking for me just now; he knew I hadn't been in decades. I only joined today because my parents were going, and I thought it might be nice to see what I'd pushed aside all these years.

More than three weeks had passed since we got back from the cruise, and I still hadn't replied to Jake's text asking me if we could talk. Every night before I fell asleep, I crafted a response in my head that I never ended up sending—still not sure what I was going to say, or what it would mean. Sometimes it was an apology, an admission that I had ended things so abruptly because I'd projected my insecurity about my parents' approval onto him. Other times, it was a rambling, incoherent string of words about how I was working on myself and trying to prioritize my family and was both ready and not yet ready to explore a romantic relationship. But always, *always*, the draft message ended with the same feeling I so palpably felt right now watching him praying twenty feet away.

*I miss you.*

*I miss us.*

Downstairs, the *langar* was packed. I got split up from my parents while waiting in line for lunch and ended up bumping into Bishan Auntie. Well, I didn't exactly bump into her. She spotted me from across the room, waved, and walked directly toward me.

The queen seemed genuinely pleased to see me, which made

me suspicious enough to look around the room for hidden cameras. But it turned out she hadn't come over to put me down or call me out or tell me I was on a revival episode of *Punk'd* or *Jackass*. She told me she'd heard I'd stayed behind with Uma Auntie during her customs issue.

She called me "thoughtful."

A compliment from the queen? A *real* compliment? It felt both good and icky, and as we made pleasantries, I tried not to think of her as a caricature of the Wicked Witch of the Pacific Northwest. I tried to remember that she was human. There was no excuse for how she treated me and my family when I was younger, but there was an explanation. That's how she'd been raised. The patriarchy was propped up by women, too.

But did that mean she couldn't change? From what Jake had told me, Bishan Auntie was on a difficult journey of her own, one full of hardships and obstacles that might challenge her worldview. Maybe Bishan Auntie's backward thinking would evolve, and the next time a young girl in our community did something "bad," she wouldn't be ostracized. Maybe the queen, too, would grow tired of pretending all the time.

Later on, I found myself standing alone in the corner, watching people eat and talk and laugh. I scanned the room for Jake, wondering what I would do and say when I finally found the courage to face the big question confronting us. I found him near the kitchen at a table full of uncles. I waved, but he was far away and didn't see me, his eyes down on his plate as he chewed thoughtfully on his food. I smiled, watching as he used his right hand to gracefully tear off chunks of puri before dunking it into the bowl of *chole*, and then popped everything into his mouth.

I took a few steps to the side so I'd be in his eyeline when he looked up, and I played with the bangles on my wrist as I watched him eat. Call me crazy, but I felt lighter, somehow, just looking at him. Being in the same room as him. And just as this overwhelming surge of . . . *something* . . . crashed over me, Jake stood up.

His mouth curling into a smile, he turned around.

And then he wrapped his arms around another woman.

"DID YOU HAVE a nice time?" Dad asked from the driver's seat. I looked up from my phone and smiled at him in the rearview mirror.

"I did. I caught up with Sweetie."

"Sweetie!" Mom exclaimed. "I remember her. How is she?"

"Great. About to pop out baby number two."

After I bolted from the *langar*, I'd gone outside and run into Sweetie, her husband, and their toddler walking to their car. I told my parents about how we exchanged numbers, and that she, Daljit, and Krisha were still close friends. Sweetie was going to organize brunch.

Although I was excited at the prospect of being reunited with my old crew, it wasn't enough to revive my spirits after having seen Jake hug another woman right in front of me. After Sweetie and her family left, it had taken me exactly three minutes of Instagram stalking to confirm that Jake's mystery woman wasn't a mystery at all.

She was Rupi Sachdeva.

Jake's ex-girlfriend.

Rupi was a nurse, twenty-seven, and based on the number of photos she'd posted featuring homemade tortes and cakes, she was an enthusiastic baker. On the drive home, I scrolled through her feed. When I clicked on the same photo for the third time, I scolded myself and tucked my phone beneath my thigh. A second later, it buzzed. It was Niki, replying to my earlier text about me having seen Jake and Rupi together.

> Niki: OK, so . . . I did some digging.

> Jasmine: and?

> Niki: Are you sure you want me to tell you?

> Jasmine: niki. spill.

> Niki: Fine. Last week, Jake called Rupi out of
> the blue and asked her out for dinner. That's
> all I know, but reading between the lines . . .

> Jasmine: they're back together.

> Niki: Are you OK? You should have said hello,
> Jasmine. Did he even see you?

I glanced out the window, squinting as the warm June sun streamed through the glass. He hadn't noticed me today, but in a very real way, Jake had seen me with better clarity than anyone I'd ever met. And hadn't I seen him, too? Didn't our time together mean something to him, too? But now . . .

"Is there something on your mind?" Dad said suddenly. I tucked my phone into my purse and wrung my hands together.

*Yes. I missed my chance with Jake.*

"I have a lot on my mind, to be honest," I laughed.

We were at a red light, and Dad turned around to face me.

"We noticed Jake was there today." His eyes darted to Mom for a moment. She patted his forearm reassuringly, as if signaling to him to keep going. Dad cleared his throat. "Did you speak with him?"

I shook my head.

"I see."

Dad opened his mouth but then closed it again before turning back around. Although my parents and I were making progress, we all understood that talking about my love life was a step too far. There were certain things that would make them uncomfortable, that they just didn't know how understand.

"Well, we are here if you need us," Dad continued jovially. "If you would like to tattoo your whole face or sell sunsets or . . ."

He cleared his throat as Mom and I both suppressed a laugh.

"We just want you to be happy, *beti*," Dad said. "Whatever that means to you."

The news about Jake getting back together with Rupi was literally breaking my heart, but right then, the pain subsided—just a little bit. My parents finally realized they didn't need to understand all of my decisions to support me. I breathed in, warmth spreading over my chest, my neck, flushing my cheeks.

"I know."

"And we are here for you, *beti*. No matter what."

Jesus Christ. Did he want to make me cry?

"Thanks, Dad." I playfully rolled my eyes. "I know that, too."

# Chapter 31

～～～

Niki: OMG. Thank you SO much for convincing Mom to use Google Drive to track everything for the engagement party. She was sending me pictures of her Post-it Notes!!

Jasmine: hahah i know. she's nuts. i love it.

Niki: So she's not driving you crazy? I really appreciate you helping out so much . . .

Jasmine: don't stress. it's really fun! and it turns out i have strong opinions about table skirts . . .

D RINKS TONIGHT?" ROWAN asked.

I swiveled my chair to face her. "It's Monday."

"Yeah, so?" She crossed her arms. "It's easier to get a babysitter on Monday nights."

"Who's all going?"

"I'm about to send an e-mail blast to the whole office. I'm thinking it'll be a nice informal kick start to your mentorship program."

I grinned. I'd e-mailed out the information early this morning, and by lunchtime, more than ninety percent of staff had signed up to be either mentor or mentee. I was trying my best to focus on the part of my life that made me happy, not heartbroken, and feeling like I could make a difference here at the office definitely made me happy.

"Count me in," I said. "But you know I'm on a budget right now, so I'm only staying for one."

"Jasmine," Rowan sighed. "Tonight's on the company."

"Oh!" I shimmied on my chair. "Well, then I guess I'm staying for three."

Now that I was commuting downtown, I worked more regular hours—although I still frequently left early to hang out with Mango or take her on runs. I texted my parents that I would be home late—not because I had to check in with them, but because I wanted to—and then took out my headphones so I could finish up my work by end of day. I was replying to an e-mail I'd been putting off when I felt a tap on my shoulder. I looked up from my screen. It was Jake.

"What the . . ."

I pulled off my headphones, speechless. During this morning's three-minute meditation (that's all I had time for today), his face had appeared against my will more than once. Had I manifested him? What sort of witchery had Uma Auntie been teaching me?

"Sorry to barge in on you like this . . ." He played nervously with the cuff link on his left wrist. "Your receptionist said I could just walk in."

"Yeah," I breathed. I was not mentally prepared for this interaction. "It's fine. Our office is pretty chill."

He leaned down, as if he was about to give me a hug, but then hesitated and kept his arms by his side. The space was open-plan, and suddenly, I could feel my coworkers' eyes on us.

"Do you want to sit?" I gestured to the empty desk next to me, pushing past my nerves. "My seatmate is out sick out today."

"Sure."

"Want a coffee or something?"

"No. Thanks." Jake lowered himself into the chair. "I've been drinking way too much coffee again. And I only have a minute. I have to get back to the office."

"Ah. How's the new job?" I asked brightly. I knew my voice sounded fake. Oh well. Presently, I was faking being a normal human person. "Killing it, I presume?"

"Nope." Jake chuckled. "Law school may teach us about the law, but no actual life skills. I spent forty minutes yesterday working up the courage to call a client on the phone—and I had *good* news for her."

I laughed.

"Most days I feel like a fraud."

"It's a steep learning curve." I shrugged. "You'll get there. And I'm sure you're doing better than you think."

"Thank you. I love my cases. I respect my colleagues. So I hope you're right."

My heart raced as Jake tilted his head and smiled at me.

"You were at *gurdwara* yesterday," he continued. "*Bhua* told me later she talked to you. Why didn't you come say hi?"

"Uh . . ." I picked up a pen and stared spinning it in my fingers. "Well . . ."

"It was packed . . . I wish I'd seen you."

"It's fine!" I squirmed, dropping the pen on the floor. "Don't worry about . . ."

Jake and I leaned over to pick up the pen at the same time, and our foreheads brushed on the way up. Shaking, I sat back in my seat as he drank me in, in a way that made all the blood rush south. He wanted me to say hello? He wanted us to be friendly?

No. I could never be friends with Jake. I could never meet up casually at the *gurdwara* or the office and not want to share every single thought that popped into my head—or hear what was going on in his brain in real time, too. I could never be at a party or in a crowded room and not want to seek him out, stand by his side, or have him whisper something into my ear.

I could never look deeply into his eyes—like I was right now— and not want to hold his hand. Kiss him. Rest my head in the crook of his arm, look up, and tell him how much he meant to me. How much I'd fallen for him.

Because I did. Fucking hell, I had really fallen for him.

My eyes stung as I forced a smile on my face and stuck out my hand. Jake flicked his gaze down, seemingly bemused. I waved my palm around, gesturing for him to take it. Finally, he did.

"Thanks for stopping by," I said briskly. "I should get back to work."

"You want me to go?"

I nodded, our hands still gripped together.

"OK." He lowered his voice. "If you're not ready to talk yet, I respect that. I'll wait."

"You'll wait?" I whispered. "What's there to talk about anymore?"

"Jasmine . . ."

I tried to withdraw my hand, but Jake held tight. He shook my hand slowly, his eyes moving to my lips. I shivered.

"Jake, you should really go." I pulled away from him and crossed my arms. "This is . . . weird."

"What's weird?"

"You being here." I cleared my throat with resolve. "It's inappropriate. You're with Rupi—"

"Rupi?" A flash of horror crossed Jake's face. "We're not together."

"Yes, you are." My gut twisted, confusion rising in my belly. "*Yes*, you are."

"*No*, we're not."

"You must be," I stammered. "I heard you asked her out for dinner."

"To *apologize*." Jake's mouth twitched. "To apologize for how I behaved during our relationship. For being a douchebag?"

I'd been holding my breath. And when I released it, heat pooled into my core and there was no hiding the stupid, shit-eating grin spreading across my face.

"Oh."

Jake smiled. "Yeah."

"So, you and Rupi are *not* back together."

"No." Jake paused. "We had dinner, just the one time. We ended things on a better note. Yesterday, we even had a nice chat at the *gurdwara*."

"So, that means you're . . ." I breathed out. "*Single*."

"Extremely."

"Interesting," I squawked.

"You know, for someone who resents the gossipy auntie culture, you sure make some quick judgments of your own."

I shoved him, and he caught my hand with his fingers and then tugged me gently so my chair rolled closer to him. I knew my colleagues were watching now, but I couldn't bring myself to care. I couldn't take my eyes off Jake.

"I've missed you," he whispered. "A lot."

Oh good gracious. I was literally swooning in my chair.

"I sit at a desk all day, *every* day," he continued, his face pained. "I'm supposed to be working hard and motivated and stressed out and so excited about this new amazing job I have. But I get so distracted because all I can think about is you, Jasmine. All I care about—"

I pressed my palm over his mouth and shook my head, smiling.

"Stop."

Jake blinked.

"We're not in an episode of *Outlander*, Jake," I chided. "Don't make some big speech full of promises you can't make yet."

"Right," he said as I dropped my hand. "Of course. We were going to take this slow."

"Slow," I repeated.

Jake grinned naughtily.

"I'm worth the wait," he teased.

"Yes, you are." I bit my lip, nervous, yet confident we were on the right track. "And I'm worth the wait, too."

# Chapter 32

～～～

Brian: I'm going to be traveling mid-July. Are you able to take care of Mango?

Jasmine: i just asked my parents if she can stay here, and they're cool with it! absolutely.

Brian: Sweet, thanks. What's it like living at home again lol?

Jasmine: it's great, brian. really, really great.

ON FRIDAY NIGHT, Jake and I met up at the Cheesecake Factory for our first official date, and that same weekend, we hiked the Summerland Trail in Mount Rainier National Park. On our third date, the following Saturday, Jake made a reservation at a trendy tapas restaurant near Chinatown his coworker had recommended. Afterward, Jake walked me to my car and kissed me for the first time since the cruise. I was bursting with anticipation. He pressed me against the car door and kissed me goodbye, his lips gentle yet passionate. As his fingers played with the strands of my ponytail, I nearly caved and pushed him into the back seat. My attraction for him had only grown, and I wanted him so much.

But I didn't cave. Despite the fact that being in his presence made me want to do things to him that quite frankly were still illegal in some parts of the world, we both needed to take this slow. I knew myself—my strengths and my weaknesses—and if Jake and I had any chance of working out long term, I had to proceed slowly.

As the new associate at his firm, Jake's hours were long and his workload grueling. Over the next month, we only saw each other during the week for the occasional coffee or lunch date downtown when his schedule allowed. But we had the weekends—well, at least the ones Jake wasn't called in to work. Many of our dates were outdoors because I was following a strict budget, and we took Mango on long walks and hikes, swam, or went paddleboarding at the beach. We even joined Ethan and his son, Landon, for a picnic in the park. As the summer wore on, I started introducing Jake to my friends. He won over all of my high school girlfriends at wine night, and got along with Amber so well at brunch I kind of felt like a third wheel. We also joined Niki and Sam for a double date the weekend they were in town. Niki and I initiated the guys into our sister ritual of watching rom-coms, taking them to an old theater downtown to watch *Sleepless in Seattle*. (Sam was the only one who hadn't seen it; Jake, who admitted he'd seen it at least five times, still cried at the end.)

It made me overwhelmingly happy to see how well Jake fitted in with those closest to me, but I was nervous about whether or not Jake would feel the same way when I met his group for the first time. The weekend he moved out of his dad's house and into an apartment downtown, I showed up in my gym clothes with a case of beer and a Bluetooth speaker for a day of bonding and unpacking. Jake's school friends were already there, helping him build his new IKEA furniture. Within an hour, my nerves and half the beer were gone. Jake's friends were just like him, sweet and silly and with a killer sense of humor. We spent most of the day teasing Jake about his extensive *Warhammer* collection.

"So, what did you think of my friends?" Jake asked, after everyone had left. He stopped hand steaming the curtains we'd just hung in the living room and looked over to the kitchen, where I was polishing off another slice of pizza.

"Douchebags?" he pondered.

"Totally," I said, my mouth full. "Even bigger ones than you."

"They think you're really cool." Jake nodded. "And funny. And down-to-earth. *And* good for me."

"They said that?" I swallowed my food and bit my lip, suddenly feeling shy.

Jake nodded.

"Well, I like them, too," I deadpanned. "A little *too* much, honestly. Is Zack single, or . . ."

Jake aimed the steamer at me and pretended to shoot. I cackled in return.

After we'd finished up the curtains, taken out the recycling, and vacuumed the debris all over the floors, Jake flopped down on the couch he'd found on Facebook Marketplace the day before. His khaki shorts rode up his thighs, and when he yawned and stretched his back like a cat, his Maggie Simpson T-shirt rode up, exposing a few inches of his core. My mouth began salivating more than I cared to admit, while I briefly allowed my gaze to drift up to his chest, his shoulders . . .

"Are you checking me out?" Jake asked suddenly.

"No!" I blushed.

He pulled down his T-shirt, grinning. "Well, don't. I haven't had time to go the gym in . . ." He sighed. "Weeks, honestly."

"You're a busy man."

"I'm going soft."

"I don't mind soft," I said quietly. "Do you?"

Over the two months Jake and I had been seeing each other, we'd had many long conversations about the journeys we were each on—and a big part of his was how he cared too deeply about how people perceived him physically. Mostly women. Also his sports-obsessed father and brothers. He'd deleted his social media indefinitely—which he said only heighted his vanity and insecurities—but was still getting used to the idea that he didn't have the time or energy anymore to work out five times a week. To maintain what, in his mind, was a perfect athletic physique.

"I don't mind," Jake said, his eyes searching my face. "As long you're still attracted to me."

"I don't think there is anything you could do to yourself that would make me not attracted to you."

Jake's mouth parted as his gaze locked onto mine. My pulse quickened. I was provocative and flirty with Jake all the time, but we were always in public, or around other people. I'd meant those words as a joke, but now that we were alone, it didn't feel all that funny.

"It's only nine o'clock," Jake said after a minute. "Do you want to watch Netflix?"

"And chill?" I chided, suddenly worried he'd viewed my remark as an invitation, that he'd grown tired of the minimal physical contact I'd insisted on.

"Just Netflix." He patted the empty seat next to him on the couch. "But we could go for a walk if you'd prefer."

"No, I'm a little tired." I'd been holding my breath, and I let it out with a sigh. "Netflix sounds good."

Jake smiled.

"But I'm not going to sleep over."

"When you pass out later and beg me to let you stay, I'm going to carry you to your car like a gentleman."

I rolled my eyes, padded over to Jake, and flopped down next to him. He reached for the remote control and then spread his right arm on the couch behind me, his face fixated on the screen. I hadn't been alone with Jake, properly alone, we-could-do-whatever-we-wanted-as-*loud*-as-we-wanted alone, since . . . well, ever. So even though we were exhausted and covered in dust and sweat, just sitting here on a secondhand couch watching television felt somehow . . . *titillating*. Was that the right word to describe the way my skin tingled, just being near him, at the mere thought of him touching me? I'd read that word in a romance novel the week before. I hoped I was using it right.

I leaned until my back pressed against him and then let my chin fall to the side. Jake was squinting at the television—he vehemently denied he needed prescription glasses—flicking through that week's top ten movies. His mouth was pursed, and his body felt stiff next to me, as if he were uncomfortable, or more likely, just trying to be respectful. I bit my lip, heat coursing through me as our bare knees knocked together and my mind raced.

*I can't wait a moment longer. Let's finally bang!*

*Whenever I'm with you, I feel like I'm home.*

*Jake, I'm scared.*

"Don't," he said quietly to the television. My stomach pulsed as he turned to look at me.

"You don't have to say or do anything. I can tell you're not ready."

No, I wasn't ready. But I wanted to be. I could feel myself nearly there, at the edge, and if Jake pushed me—even nudged me just a little—I knew I would fall off.

But he knew I couldn't be pushed. I had to take the leap myself.

"No speeches, either." Jake grinned naughtily. "We're not in an episode of *Outlander*, remember?"

"No, we are not. We have modern medicine and women can vote."

"Central heating and cooling."

"Condoms," I added thoughtfully. "Historical fiction would not be nearly as interesting if they'd had condoms."

Jake cleared his throat as I shifted next to him, moving closer. His fingers played lazily with my hair as I closed my eyes and rested my forehead against his chest. I breathed in hard through my nose, his scent rendering me dizzy. My hands slipped up around his neck, and I stroked the hair on the back of his head.

"Can I kiss you?" I whispered.

"Jasmine . . ." His voice was raspy. "Do you really have to ask?"

"Yes, because it's going to be a pretty amazing kiss, and then I'm going to stop."

Chuckling, Jake pulled away, but only for a moment. The next thing I knew, his lips were on mine, and I felt weightless in his arms as we melted into a kiss, deeper and more surreal than I'd ever had before. Was this what it felt like? To allow yourself to fall, naturally, slowly, like a feather floating in the wind? The two of us together—was it inevitable?

"Let's stop," Jake grunted.

I blinked out of my daze. His eyes were going cross-eyed, and I giggled.

"Maybe just one more—"

He interrupted me with his mouth, kissing me harder, faster. As his hands fell to my waist, I sat up and wrapped one leg around his hip, straddling him, our lips and bodies pressed feverishly together.

"I really just wanted to watch Netflix," he whispered into my hair.

"Mhm."

Smiling, a moan escaped my lips as he dragged his lips down the soft part of my neck, kissed the hollow of my collarbone. I writhed against him, my body—on a low simmer all summer— sparking a flame. I ran my hands over his arms, his shoulders, gripping hard as he pulled away, and stared deeply into his eyes.

"Jasmine . . ."

He was breathing hard, but from the intensity of his gaze, I knew this wasn't about sex.

"Yeah?"

"I . . ."

A rapid knock on the door sent us both reeling. I climbed off Jake as quickly as I could as he composed himself and tugged down his T-shirt.

"Zack, buddy?" Jake called. "You miss me already?"

"*Beta*, it's me!"

My mouth gaped at the sound of Ranjit Uncle's voice.

"Jake, your Bishan Auntie and I are here to drop off a house-warming gift!"

The queen was here, too?

Oh shit.

I raced across the room, grabbed my purse, and bolted into Jake's bedroom. I was breathing hard, wondering what to do and where to hide, when I felt Jake's hands on the back of my arms.

"It's fine, Jasmine," he whispered.

I shook my head, trembling. "I'm going to hide. Closet, or under the bed?"

"Come on . . ." Jake said to me, just as Ranjit Uncle called out again.

"One second, Dad! I'm in the—uh—bathroom!"

Slowly, Jake turned me around and then used his pointer finger to tilt my chin upward.

"I'm pretty sure my dad knows about us, Jasmine." He screwed up his face. "*Bhua*, too."

"Well, *my* parents have no idea." My eyes frantically darted to the bed. Was there enough room for me to crawl under? "I don't want them to know."

"Why?"

*Because my parents and I are in a really good place and I don't want to jeopardize that?*

*Because I'm worried they will judge me for dating again, so soon after a long-term relationship?*

*Because what if I bring home a guy they actually like and respect and who makes me really happy, but then . . . what if it doesn't work out?*

I crossed my arms and took a step backward. Jake was studying me with a gentle expression.

"I'm not ready," I said, my tone final.

"OK. You're not ready."

I tried to ignore the sadness in his voice as he kissed me on the cheek. A beat later he nodded toward the closet.

"Go hide in there, then. You'll have more room."

# Chapter 33

~~~~~~~~~

Tanya: Thank you so much for lunch, Jasmine.
I learned A LOT. As soon as we got back to
the office I wrote down everything you said
haha.

Jasmine: i'm glad our chat was helpful!

Tanya: I already have a few more questions
about how to manage my supervisor's
expectations while I'm on temporary
assignment later this year. But I'll save that
for our next lunch...

Jasmine: no need to wait, fire away! i'm your
mentor...this kind of thing is what i'm here
for. ☺

D ON'T BE A quitter!" I cheered. "You're almost there!"

He tripped, nearly stumbling onto Mango as we jogged the last quarter mile of our run.

"Come on, you slacker. Get it together!"

"God," Jake mumbled, sucking air. "You're worse than my old coach."

It was a sweltering evening in late August, and Jake and I were drenched by the time we collapsed on the lawn in front of my old condo building. Watching Mango lap up water from the communal doggy bowl, I stretched back on the grass and stared up at the sky. "Nice work!"

Jake dropped down next to me, still breathing hard. "Thanks."

"Glad you skipped the gym to come running with me?"

He winked and then jokingly dropped his gaze to my ass. "This workout *does* have a better view."

I gave him the eyes, laughing as our heads fell back on the lawn. The senior partner Jake worked for directly was on vacation this week, so he'd been able to cut out of work earlier than usual. It was only Thursday, and this was our third night in a row hanging out.

After we cooled down and stretched, Jake and I dropped off Mango at Brian's. Chelsea—*Un*mysterious Woman—was over, and the four of us engaged in the obligatory small talk required of two exes on good terms and their dates. The first few encounters had been weird, especially when I had to explain to Chelsea that I'd let her believe I was someone else that first time we met in the elevator. But that was in the past. Things with Jake and me were going well—*really* well—and Brian seemed happier than he'd been in years. Although he'd initially seemed lukewarm about Chelsea, it was clear that his affection for her had grown.

Jake had evolved over the last few months, grown into a better version of himself. I had, too. Who knew? Maybe Brian could as well.

Using my old key, we slipped into Amber's condo across the hall. She'd finally gotten that big promotion, and I'd been charged with keeping her plants alive while she and Danica were on a monthlong celebratory vacation in Europe.

"Why does she have so many plants?" Jake asked, as I showed him the detailed, color-coded instructions she'd left me.

"She got really into plants after I moved out." I shrugged. "I don't know. She calls them her *babies*."

"Do she and Danica plan on having kids?"

I shook my head. "Amber is adamant plants are all she can handle. She doesn't even want a cat."

"Interesting." Jake pulled out a stool at the kitchen island while I poured us tall glasses of water from the tap. "What about you?"

"What about me?" I smiled.

"Do you think you want kids?"

I passed him his water and stalled by draining half my glass. I wiped my mouth with the back of my hand.

"I think I do," I said finally. "I know I'd be happy if it didn't end up happening, but yeah." I bit my lip. "I could see myself as a parent."

"Interesting."

"You find this topic very *interesting*, Jake." I grinned. "What about you? Do you want kids?"

"I do, yeah." He stretched his arms above his head. "Maybe just one, though. My brothers were so competitive when we were young. I think I'd prefer to have one kid, and I'd make sure they knew they were perfect, and exactly who they were supposed to be, and the only person they needed to compete with was themselves."

I smiled, his reasons resonating with me. "One child actually seems like a pretty good idea. Not to mention, it's environmentally friendly."

I refilled our water glasses, weirdly nervous. Jake and I had talked about everything from the climate crisis to our childhood traumas to the plot points of the original *Star Wars* movies, but we'd never talked about the future.

"Anyway." Jake cleared his throat, kissing my forehead as he stood up from the stool. "Do you think Amber would mind if I showered?"

"Go ahead." I scanned the room. "I bathe Mango here all the time."

"Really?" He scrunched up his nose. "Does Amber know?"

"No." I paused. "So how can she disapprove?"

I heard Jake hop in the shower while I tackled the succulents in the bedrooms, the herb garden on the balcony, the jade plants by the television, and then the Chinese money plant in the kitchen. There was bamboo in the bathroom, which I'd forgot to attend to earlier in the week, and Jake had left the door ajar, so I knocked it open with my hip and closed my eyes.

"Can I come in? Are you decent?"

"Very indecent!" he called out.

I opened one eye. The shower curtain was pulled all the way closed, so I walked in.

"Don't mind me."

"This soap smells *amazing*," Jake called out, as I watered the bamboo. "I feel like I'm in a five-star hotel or something."

"She uses Dove bodywash, Jake."

Jake pulled the curtain back a few inches and popped his face out. "It's delicious!"

My heart soared at the sudden realization that Jake was butt naked with nothing but a plastic shower curtain standing between us. We'd avoided being alone together after Ranjit Uncle and Bishan Auntie nearly caught us making out a few weeks earlier. I'd ended up hiding in Jake's bedroom closet for thirty-five minutes while he tried to get rid of them and the queen rearranged his cupboards. Talk about a mojo killer.

"How's the bamboo doing?" Jake asked.

"Clark Gable is alive and well." I nodded.

"Oh my god. She *names* them?"

"After Old Hollywood actors, yes. Judy Garland is the big one near the fridge."

"You need any help?" Grinning, Jake splashed water at the plant, but most of it hit me in the face. I guffawed.

"Don't you dare."

He splashed me again, and squealing, I set down the watering can.

Jake blew me a cheeky kiss, and I laughed. He could be such a dork sometimes. And silly. And sweet. And *fun*. And suddenly, I was overwhelmed by the simple idea of what it would be like to share a bathroom with Jake. To care for plants together, or Mango, or a child.

To share a life together.

"You OK?" I heard him ask. I had zoned out, and I blinked until I was back in the room. He searched my face.

"I'm perfect," I whispered. "*You* are perfect."

Jake opened his mouth to speak, but he seemed to realize I

wasn't making a joke and closed it again. I placed my watch on the windowsill, inching forward until our noses were nearly touching.

I felt a weight on my chest—three little words—that felt like both a burden and blessing, heaven and hell. When had I started feeling like this? It came on so gradually, but now there was no denying it. I licked my lips, staring into Jake's eyes. I wanted to scream those words out loud. I wanted to run. I wanted . . .

Without warning, I threw my arms around Jake's neck and kissed him, viciously, stepping into the shower with my clothes still on. He didn't miss a beat, catching my weight as I stumbled over the lip of the bathtub. He pressed me up against the wall, taking charge, kissing me with tender ferocity. He was soaking wet, and my hands slid over his body as he tore off my T-shirt. I laughed against his mouth as his fingers caught beneath the elastic of my sports bra, tight against my ribs. He wrestled it from my torso, and I sighed as I broke free and his fingers explored my breasts, then my stomach.

"Are you sure?" he grunted, pulling away from me to check. Nodding, I tugged down my shorts. They fell in a pool by my feet and I stepped out of them. Jake's eyes dropped.

"Are *you* sure?" I teased. "I thought you were a gentleman."

He slid his hands up my body, gently stroked my face. His thumb dropped, catching on my bottom lip. I grew limp as his eyes smoldered.

"Do you want me to be a gentleman?"

I shook my head, slowly, as I sucked his thumb.

"What do you want?"

I wanted to be with Jake. I wanted all of him, in every possible way. He knew my mind. He had my heart. I was ready for him to have this part of me, too.

"You."

Grinning, he pushed me against the wall, hoisting me up until I wrapped my legs around his waist. He moved against me, and I closed my eyes and tipped my head back, water streaming down on my face.

This felt good. This felt *right*.

Jake and I were one hundred percent worth the wait. It was the best sex I'd ever had.

"ARE YOU GOING to tell Amber about this?" Jake asked. We were still wet from the shower, naked, cuddling beneath the throw blanket she kept on the couch.

"Obviously."

Jake winced. "Do you have to?"

"Don't be embarrassed. She'll think it's hilarious."

"I wouldn't call what we just did *hilarious*." Jake pouted.

I rolled my eyes. "Men and their egos."

"You've always known about my ego."

"That's true." I brushed his lips with a kiss. "I can't say I wasn't warned."

Somewhere across the room, Jake's phone buzzed. We stayed still, basking in the afterglow, but when it vibrated again a minute later, he reluctantly unwrapped himself from me and padded over to it.

"Oh. It's not work. It's Dad." Jake smiled as he studied the screen. "And he's got a date!"

"Really?" I grinned.

"Yeah. They're going to the beach tomorrow."

Jake flopped back down next to me and showed me the text. He'd been helping his dad create an online dating profile, and just last week, Ranjit Uncle had started messaging with a woman his age who'd also lost her spouse in recent years. Apparently, Ranjit Uncle had also been opening up a bit more emotionally ever since developing a friendship with Uma Auntie. He'd started talking more with Jake about love and grief, and even knew about Jake's plan to enroll in a hip-hop dance class this fall. He still didn't think dancing was a sport, but according to Jake, not laughing in his face over the idea showed real growth.

"How are your parents doing?" Jake asked me, after we joked about whether he'd give his dad "the sex talk" before the big date. "They're going to miss you when you move out."

"They are." I nodded. "I'll miss them, too."

Although I talked openly with my parents about the eventuality, I wasn't leaving just yet. I wanted to pay off my debts and save a bit more first. My goal was to get my own apartment by the end of the year.

"Is everything ready for the engagement party next weekend?"

"Mostly." I shrugged. "But they're still stressed. The venue has a hard capacity limit of five hundred people. There are five hundred eleven people who RSVP'd yes."

"I'm sure a few people will have to cancel," Jake said, and I nodded in agreement. I'd been telling my parents the same thing. "By the way," he continued, "does that five hundred eleven count include me?"

I tilted my chin toward Jake. Niki's engagement party fell on Labor Day weekend, the same time as Jake's annual camping trip with his brothers. "No. You're going to be away."

"Well," Jake said slowly, "I don't have to be."

I smiled wryly. "Oh?"

"Yeah," Jake said. "I called my brothers last week and asked them if we could go a few days earlier if, hypothetically, I needed to be home for Labor Day."

"You don't *need* to be there, Jake. This camping trip is important to you."

"You are more important to me," he said quietly. "Your sister's engagement is important."

I sank into the couch, moving my weight off Jake as I imagined what it would be like to have him at my side at the party. I wasn't sure why, but the certainty I'd felt right before I'd jumped him in the shower had wavered. Jake must have been a mind reader, because a beat later, he sat up on the couch and cupped my cheeks with his palms.

"Jasmine," he said, waiting for me to meet his gaze. "My dad definitely knows about us. *Bhua*, too, I think. They're happy for us."

My heart raced. "But . . ." I stammered. "But—"

Jake cut me off. "There's no way your parents haven't figured it out, either. I know they respect your boundaries, but come on." He smiled. "They must know. Where do they think you are right now?"

"They don't know," I insisted. "They just assume I'm out with friends."

Jake cocked his head to the side. He didn't believe me.

"What are you afraid of? It's not the community. I know you don't actually care what the aunties think." He pressed his fingers over my lips before I could speak. "And don't say your parents, either. They just want you to be happy. They told you that."

I licked my lips, casting my eyes downward. Suddenly, my whole body felt heavy.

"Don't I make you happy?"

Happy didn't even begin to describe how I was feeling. The connection we'd developed over the last few months had only intensified the raw sexual attraction I'd felt for Jake from the very beginning. And now that we'd had sex, I felt closer to him emotionally, too. The weight on my chest felt more solid, heavier. I nearly couldn't breathe.

"Jasmine?"

I nodded in response, unable to look at him. "You'd also make my parents happy. *Too* happy."

"So . . ."

"So, what if we break up? They'd be so disappointed. I don't want to disappoint them again—"

"Who says we're breaking up?" Jake interrupted.

"Have you ever been with someone and *not* broken up?"

"That's not a valid argument, Jasmine—"

"Don't lawyer me, *Jake*."

He stopped mid-sentence, and when he smiled a beat later, the tension dissolved. He wrapped his arm around me tighter, squeezing. I smiled.

"What I'm trying to say is," I whispered, "I've broken my parents' hearts many, many times before. And I don't want to risk doing that again, not unless you and I are . . ."

"Serious," Jake finished.

I nodded.

"You know that I'm serious about you, right?"

I burrowed my head into the crux of his neck instead of responding. I did know.

And it scared the shit out of me.

# Chapter 34

~~~~~~

Jasmine: do you have bear spray?

Jake: Two cans ... lol. Don't worry. I'll be
coming back in one piece.

Jasmine: good. otherwise you're useless
to me.

Jake: You're so romantic.

Jake: Apparently the backcountry site we
chose has no cell service ... Sorry. I just found
out. I'm going to be out of touch for a few
days. ☹

Jasmine: oh ... really?

Jake: We're on the highway again, so I gotta
go ... Have a great time at the party, OK?

Jake: I miss you.

Jasmine: i miss you, too

[Not delivered]

I TOOK A FEW days of vacation the week leading up to Niki's engagement party. I was so looking forward to the big day that I wasn't able to concentrate at the office, and besides, there were loads of last-minute tasks, errands, and airport pickups. Sam's parents had both flown in, as had his brother, sister, and their respective spouses and children. The night before the party, Mom and Dad had them all over for dinner, and with fifteen people all together, it was the first time one of our family dinners didn't fit at the kitchen table. Because that's what the Mukerjis were now— Niki and Sam were getting married, and our families were becoming one. It would never again just be Mom, Dad, Niki, and me opening Christmas presents together in the living room or having a lively discussion (slash fight) while preparing a Thanksgiving feast or celebrating a milestone, or a big win or loss. Everything was about to change.

I was strangely teary as we all crowded together around the kitchen island to toast Niki and Sam. I'd bought two bottles of Moët—because it was my little sister's engagement, and damnit, I'd been saving plenty that summer—and Sam and I poured it into champagne flutes, and when we ran out, wineglasses.

I raised my glass, catching Niki's eye as Mom and Dad turned on the waterworks and toasted the happy couple. Niki smiled and then asked me the million-dollar question with her gaze. My hands trembled, just the slightest, and I threw her a look that said, *Stop it—this is your day, not mine!* Sisters didn't need words to communicate. She furrowed her brows, shaking her head ever so slightly.

*It's your day,* I repeated telepathically. *Now pay attention to Mom's speech. She's bawling over there.*

My parents and I had prepared a Punjabi feast for dinner—*matar paneer, dal, baingan bharta,* and *saag.* It was gorgeous outside, so everyone took their plates to the backyard. I ran upstairs to grab my Bluetooth speaker—Sam had a party playlist in mind for the evening—but I got distracted by my phone, which I'd left on the bed. Even though Jake had no cell service, I'd been obsessively checking my phone the four days he'd been gone. I'd grown used to seeing him all the time, or at least hearing from him. A *good morning, sleepy,* which he'd send me as soon he woke up every day. A side-eye or flower emoji when he was stuck in a long meeting. An essay sent via text about the book he'd just read and thought I'd might enjoy. A voice mail. A voice note. A signal that always told me I was on his mind.

I scrolled through our old texts and eventually landed back on the last one I'd sent. It was still undelivered.

My nose ran as I lay back on the bed and pulled up my knees. Did Jake know I missed him? Did he know he was on my mind, too?

I swallowed hard, overwhelmed and breathless as I finally admitted the truth to myself.

I loved him. I loved him so fucking much. Did Jake know how deeply my feelings ran?

"Jasmine?" Dad hollered suddenly from the bottom of the stairs. "Are you coming?"

"Just a second!" I called back.

My parents had been through more than I could have ever imagined. They were poor, traditional immigrants who'd worked hard to make it in America, who'd had to adapt to a different culture and set of values. If Jake and I ended up breaking up . . . yes, they'd be disappointed. But they would be fine.

It would be *me* who was left heartbroken.

I took a deep breath in, and then out, and then heaved myself upright. For someone who prided myself on being adventurous and bold and brave, I sure could be a real coward. Jake should have been here tonight, next to me and my family. He should be there tomorrow.

I lowered my thumbs to the keypad on my touch screen, summoning all the confidence I could muster.

> Jasmine: i'm sorry, jake. i wish i'd asked you
> to stay this weekend. i want you here next
> to me. i . . .
>
> [Not delivered]

I held my breath.

> Jasmine: . . . screw it. jake, i love you, all right?
> i LOVE you. and i can't wait for you to come
> home.
>
> [Not delivered]

I was so used to playing it safe, keeping my guard up, but that hadn't worked, had it? Being honest and vulnerable and opening oneself up to the possibility of heartbreak—this was bravery.

And whatever happened, even if Jake and I were to shatter into a million pieces, I would still have my family and my friends and my passions.

I would still be me.

"MINTS?"

Niki nodded.

"Lipstick?"

"Check."

"Phone."

She patted her sparkly clutch. "Check."

"Speech?"

"It's on my phone."

I glanced up from my tablet, narrowing my eyes. "What if your phone dies?"

"It won't. It's fully charged."

"But what if it does?" I put my hand on my hip. "And you can't read from your phone up there. That's so amateur hour."

Niki sighed. "Fine. I'll go print my speech."

"What a *good* girl." I bobbled my head side to side and imitated my parents' accent. "And very beautiful! You should wear makeup more often."

"Rude . . ."

"Seriously," I deadpanned. "I don't think anyone is going to recognize you."

Niki came after me with her mascara wand, but then she hugged me, and then we both started crying (gross) and ended up having to fix both her hair and makeup.

Afterward, Niki and I took a selfie and I posted it on Instagram. At some point over the summer, I'd started posting pictures of myself—rather than just of other people, nature, or scenery. I never did tell Niki how I felt that, despite how great a sister she was to me, it hurt that she always took my parents' side over mine. That she tried to handle me like I was a bomb that could explode at any time, and from which she needed to protect our parents. I was opening myself up more to her, but this I kept to myself. Niki already had enough guilt about moving to LA, and I didn't want to burden her. Besides, I didn't blame her. My parents showed their devastation, and their pain, whenever I acted out. They showed Niki how much they needed her. I never did. I wouldn't make that mistake again.

We'd set up the venue the day before, so we only arrived a few minutes before the party started. The banquet hall was tastefully decorated—thanks to a certain someone in the family with an art degree!—and the food smelled *delicious*. I joined my parents at the bar for an aperitif as we watched the first guests trickle in, the anticipation for the evening fizzing delightfully. After a minute, I felt Mom's hand on my forearm. She pointed and I followed her gaze.

"Do you see that man Niki and Sam are talking to?"

"Yeah." I squinted. "What about him?"

"Do you think he's handsome?"

Frowning, I studied his features. They were standing halfway across the hall, so I couldn't see him all that well.

"Sure. I guess."

"How handsome?" Dad pondered.

"I dunno." I shrugged. "It's hard to tell from here—"

"I like his beard. What do you think, Chandni?"

Mom nodded. "Very, *very* sexy! But what matters is what Jasmine thinks."

"Why would it ma . . ." I trailed off, turning to look at my parents. My stomach dropped. "Wow . . . Are you trying to set me up with him?"

Mom batted her eyelashes innocently. "He is Sam's friend from Mumbai, Jasmine. Single—"

*"Mom!"* I breathed.

"And engineer!" Dad proclaimed. "He is the perfect match for you, *beti.*"

"Why, because he's brown and *employed*?"

"You must not be so picky, *hah*?" Mom swatted me on the arm. "It's high time you settle down."

"*High* time." Dad wobbled his head in agreement. "We have arranged for his parents to come meet you tomorrow morning. Nine a.m. *sharp.*"

"I . . . I . . ." I couldn't speak I was so stunned. "Dad, that's—"

"And you must wear a *salwar kameez,*" Mom interrupted. "His family prefers traditional girls. Those crop tops you wear are too modern."

My jaw was on the floor as my eyes flitted between my parents. What the actual fuck? After all the progress we'd made this summer, suddenly, they decided I needed to find a husband? That *they* were going to be the ones to pick him out? I blew air out through my nose, trying to keep calm. Employ some of those real-world mindfulness techniques I'd read up on and had yet to try out in the real world.

"Mom." I smiled through gritted teeth. *"Dad."*

"Yes, *beti*?"

"I . . ."

*I am taking a deep breath.*

*I am* not *going to overreact.*

Mom's lips twitched first, and a beat later Dad's face split into a grin.

*I am being messed with!*

"Oh my *god*," I whined. "You're joking." I threw my hands in the air. "Thank god, you're joking!"

"It was your father's idea," Mom giggled. "He wanted to hire a paid actor to come to the house."

"Did we convince you?" Dad grinned.

"*Yes!* You guys were scarily convincing." Laughing, I turned back to Niki, Sam, and the mystery man talking to them. "Who even is that guy?"

"Diya's husband, Mihir."

I nodded in recognition. Niki and Sam had first met at their wedding.

"Anyway," Dad added a moment later, "maybe you will meet someone else at the party."

Smiling, I glanced back at my parents. "Oh really?"

"Maybe," Dad said quietly, and a knowing look passed between him and Mom.

"What's going on?" I laughed.

Mom shrugged innocently.

"What . . ." I trailed off as I felt a presence next to me, someone warm and familiar. Slowly, I turned to face him.

"Hi." Jake smiled over at me, his eyes full of wonder.

"Wha . . ." He'd taken my breath away, and I stood there stammering, unable to form words.

"It's good to see you, too." He grinned. "You look beautiful."

"You look"—I shook my head—"like you're not at Cape Lookout. What are you doing here?"

He sidestepped the question, glancing quickly at my parents and then back to me.

"I know I didn't RSVP. Is there room for me at a table?"

I still couldn't believe he was here, and I nodded, starry-eyed, as Jake greeted my parents. They seemed to know he'd been on a camping trip and kept saying how pleased they were to see him, that he'd decided to join last minute.

Jake was *here*. He'd come home. I wanted to tell him in person how much I loved him. I wanted to tell him how ready I was to take a leap of faith with him. I wanted to hold his hand, I wanted . . .

A smile spread on my lips as Jake caught my eye, and I nodded. Why couldn't I hold his hand? We were together.

"Mom," I said, during a lull in their conversation. *"Dad."*

They looked over at me expectantly.

"I have something to tell you."

I stepped to the side until I was right next to Jake, and then I interlaced my fingers with his. I blew air out through my nostrils as I gathered my courage.

"Jake . . ."

God, this was hard. I cleared my throat.

"Jake and I . . ."

"We know," Dad interrupted. "You and Jake are an *item*."

My mouth dropped.

"You *know*?" I exclaimed, just as Jake laughed and mumbled, "I told you so," into my ear.

"Of course." Mom elbowed Jake in the ribs. "We have been taking bets on when you would finally tell us."

I laughed. "No . . ."

"Ranjit and Bishan are in on it, too." Dad nodded. "I believe Bishan guessed you would make the big reveal tonight?"

"She did indeed." Mom squinted over my shoulder. "Ah. She is here! *Chalo*. Let's go pay up!"

The rest of the evening flew by, a little too quickly, actually. After the cocktail hour came dinner, and then the speeches, and then the dance performances. For the first time in my life, I performed a choreographed Bollywood dance—rather poorly, despite the practice—in front of a room full of aunties and uncles. But I didn't feel judged or embarrassed or shy. I was imperfect, sure, but I felt like me.

After, the houselights went down, and the DJ invited everyone out to the dance floor. I joined Niki and her friends in the middle as the speakers blared "Jalebi Baby," and a few minutes later, Jake found us. My stomach did flip-flops as he drew closer.

"How did I do?" I shouted over the music.

"You were great!"

"You're lying, but thank you. And thank you for helping me practice."

He didn't hear me—the speakers were too loud—so I shimmied closer and repeated it into his ear. His hands found the dip in my waist as we started dancing, following the rhythm, and I briefly let my forehead fall to his chest.

"Everyone's watching," Jake whispered into my hair.

"Let them watch." I bit my lip and scanned the room, taking note of my parents, Ranjit Uncle, and Bishan Auntie. Uma Auntie, too. "Oh my god. They really are watching. Your dad is even *pointing* at us."

"He's disappointed he lost the bet by one day. Apparently, he thought we'd confess to the relationship tomorrow."

"Too bad." I giggled. "Hey. You never answered my question before."

"What question?" Jake said, after he'd spun me in a twirl and I was safely back in his arms.

"What are you doing here?" I studied his face, the DJ's strobe lights flashing it to life. "You weren't supposed to come home for a few more days."

Jake tucked a loose strand of hair behind my ear and smiled.

"What changed your mind?"

"You changed my mind, Jasmine."

"Me?"

Jake nodded. "Early this morning we were hiking up a hill, and then all of a sudden, our phones started buzzing."

"You got my texts . . ."

"It was blind luck." Jake squeezed me tighter as we swayed to the beat. "And cell service only lasted for a minute, but yeah. I got your texts."

My chest tightened.

"And?"

"*And* telling me you love me for the first time in a text, which also contained the words 'screw it,' was probably the most romantic thing I've ever seen."

I cringed, shoving him playfully. "Sorry about that . . ."

"Don't be sorry." Jake rested his forehead against mine, breathing hard. "I love you, too, Jasmine. I've loved you since . . ."

"That first day I yelled at you on the cruise?"

He grinned.

"Since I scared you at the gym?"

Jake paused, his fingers tickling my bare skin between the top and skirt of my *lengha*.

"Do you remember when we were hiding in the prop room?" I closed my eyes and nodded, recalling how I'd covered his lips with my palm, and he'd whispered against my skin.

"I took me a little longer to figure it out," I said finally.

"But we're here now."

I swallowed hard, nodding.

"And I'm not going anywhere."

"You better not," I teased.

"I promise." Jake brushed his lips against my cheek. "Jasmine, you are the most important thing in my life."

Blood rushed to my head as the music changed to Beyoncé's latest single, and my life became seriously at risk of being worthy of its own *Outlander*-style romance.

"I love you so, so much," Jake continued. "You make me feel . . ."

Laughing, I pressed my palm against his mouth and shook my head.

"You love me. I love you. Et cetera, et cetera." I sighed playfully. "I get it, Jake."

He laughed so hard his body crashed into mine as we swayed.

"The thing is . . ." I was suddenly conscious of how good it felt to be in his arms. How much I wanted him. "I'm more of a *show me how you feel* kind of woman."

Jake leaned back, his mouth parting.

"You want me to show you . . . right *now*?"

I bit my bottom lip, nodding.

*"Here?"* Jake cleared his throat, as I felt his body stiffen against me. "What do you suggest?"

"Well," I demurred. "I may or may not have the key to the coat check."

Jake cocked his head to the side, shaking it at me. "The coat check," he repeated.

"All the gifts are being stored there," I said, giving him my best sexy eyes, "and being the sister of the bride, well, some idiot trusted me with the key."

"You mean Niki?"

I laughed, flicking my eyes to my little sister, who was danc-ing with Sam five feet away and would not stop gawking at Jake and me.

"Yep." I turned back to Jake. "So, are you game? Or are you too much of a good Indian boy to be corrupted?"

Jake released me from his grip, scratching his jaw. "You know I'm game."

"Great." I did a quick scan of the room. "I'll go first."

"I'll grab a drink—"

"And meet me there in five?"

Grinning, Jake kissed me on the lips—yes, he kissed me, albeit chastely, with the Auntie-Uncle Brigade and both of our families watching—and made a beeline for the bar.

I exhaled and looked around me, the reality of what was hap-pening shaking me to my core. I could be in love with a sensitive, smart, successful, dorky, funny, wonderful guy who I would be proud to bring home to my parents, and also still be me. The woman who took chances and lived life without regrets. Who was brave and artistic and *cool* and liked to have fun . . .

The woman who was about to get lucky in the coat check. The woman who had a brand-new adventure ahead of her.

# Acknowledgments

I had a lot of fun writing Jasmine and Jake's story, and I am hugely thankful to my editor, Kerry Donovan, for giving me the opportunity. And thank you to everyone at Berkley for bringing this book out into the world, especially Dache' Rogers, Elisha Katz, Mary Baker, Christine Legon, Stacy Edwards, Stephanie Singleton, and Victoria Chu.

As always, a big thanks to my rock star agent, Martha Webb, and her brilliant colleagues at CookeMcDermid. I am eternally grateful. Thank you as well to Stephanie Caruso at Paste Creative for your support.

Finally, thank you to my family and friends for always being my champions; my husband, Simon, for all the little things; and our mini goldendoodle, Joey, for the unconditional love.

Keep reading for an excerpt from
Sonya Lalli's previous novel, featuring Niki . . .

A HOLLY JOLLY DIWALI

*Available in paperback from Berkley!*

W E NEED TO talk."

I paused the television just as Matthew McConaughey pressed his palm against Jennifer Lopez's flawless cheek. Mom and Dad stood at the bottom of the stairs dressed up for the party I'd already thought they'd left for. Their faces were stone, and when Dad put his arm protectively around Mom's shoulder, my stomach bottomed out as I imagined the reasons for said "talk."

1. They were getting a divorce.

I sank farther into the couch, mentally shaking my head. This was unlikely. Most Indian couples their age, however miserable and fluent in English, refused to learn the d-word. Besides, my parents' marriage seemed to be a happy one. Trust me. My bedroom was just down the hall from theirs, and sometimes I could hear how *happy* they still made each other. Ugh.

2.   One of them was sick.

My hands trembled just thinking about this scenario, but then I remembered they'd both had physicals the month before, and their doctors had said everything was just fine. I should know. I drove them both to and from their appointments so they didn't have to pay for parking.

3.   Jasmine.

Yes. *Jasmine.* My whole body relaxed when I realized the most likely scenario was that my older sister was up to something again. On the verge of a scandal. Had broken up with her deadweight boyfriend du jour. (Oh god. Let it be that!) Or maybe she was just being a run-of-the-mill *pain* yet again, and my parents wanted to vent about it before they ran off to whatever function was on that evening.

"Yes?" I asked, satisfied I was ready to hear the answer.

Silently, they trundled toward me, but instead of taking one of the many seats in our living room, they chose to stand directly in front of the TV.

"What is up?" Dad asked cheerfully. "Busy?"

"Very." I laughed. "What is *up* with you?"

He glanced at my mom, who was clearly about to do the heavy lifting. I blinked at her, and although I was curious what it was Jasmine had done to upset them again, I was ready to get back to *The Wedding Planner.*

"We are worried about you, Niki."

I scrunched up my face. Hold on a second. They were worried about *me*?

"You are?"

A knowing glance passed between them.

"Care to elaborate?" I asked.

"Niki, it's Saturday night," Mom said. There was a tinge of annoyance in her voice, like when I didn't rinse my plate before putting it in the dishwasher. "Why are you home?"

"What is *that* supposed to mean?" I scoffed, oblivious to the point she was trying to make. "Mom, I—"

"Enough is enough." She held up her hand like a conductor, waving me off. "Niki, you are very ... very ..."

"Successful?" I volunteered. "Obedient? *Lovely*—"

"Single," she interrupted.

Wow. Mom burn.

Yes, I was single and had been for a while, but I didn't know how the "very" played into that.

I tucked my legs under me. "What's your point?"

"You know," Dad continued, "there are apps for dating. Have you heard?"

"No," I deadpanned. "What's a dating app?"

*"Well,"* Dad started, but then Mom cut him off.

"She knows very well what a dating app is. Niki, are you on the Tinder? The Bumble? The Hinger?"

I smiled, even though I was irritated. Clearly, they'd done their research before the big talk.

"I am not," I said flatly. "TBH, I don't like the idea of meeting people online."

"TBH?" Mom echoed.

"To be honest," I explained.

*"Ah,* so you would prefer to meet people in person?" Dad gestured at Matthew McConaughey. "I see you are meeting so many good candidates."

Mom grinned, and even I had to laugh at that one.

Dad burn. Very nice.

"Niki, we are not upset with you—" Mom started pacing, she always enjoyed theatrics. "We are *so* proud. But we have been thinking you should be . . . putting yourself out there. You understand?"

"Like, I need to start dating."

"*Hah.*"

"Maybe I'm already dating. How do you know I don't have a secret boyfriend?" I crossed my arms. "Or girlfriend, for that matter? Maybe I have several. *Maybe* I'm a total player."

Mom narrowed her gaze at me. "And when do you see all these boyfriends and girlfriends? On the bus home from work? Do you sneak them into your *parents'* house after you come straight home every day?"

I groaned, burrowing my face into the pillow. Another mom burn. But this one stung.

You see, they weren't totally wrong. My friends *constantly* told me that I would never meet anybody if all I did was work, (occasionally) go to the gym, and socialize with the same group of people—which these days was usually in someone's living room rather than out at bars. Diya, who was one of my best friends from college and lived on the other side of the world in Mumbai, was particularly hard on me during our weekly video chats. Her glamorous Indian wedding was just a few weeks away, and before I'd declined the invite because I couldn't get the time off work, she'd even threatened to fix me up with one of her cousins or friends.

But what happened to the good old-fashioned meet-cute? Maybe in the produce section of my local grocery store, or if I were to drop a pile of papers in front of the office hottie, regardless of the fact that my office was, uh, paperless.

Now I was twenty-nine years old and getting zinged by my

parents, the same parents who used to stomp their feet whenever Jasmine flitted in and out with a new guy. The same mom and dad who, up until today, seemed *thrilled* that I still lived at home, that I wasn't in a relationship they needed to worry about.

I sighed, glancing up at them. I was annoyed but not surprised, as far too many of my South Asian friends were starting to sink in an all-too-similar boat. One day we're practically barricaded inside with our textbooks, "boys" not only not a subject worth discussing but, more often than not, entirely off limits.

And then?

And then, as if overnight, we're of marriageable age. Suddenly, we're not girls in need of protection but women, and being *very single* was our very own fault.

"I'll make more of an effort," I said finally, because I did want to get married one day, and there was no point in fighting the inevitable. "But I don't like the apps."

"Fair." Dad nodded. "Thank you."

I grabbed the remote, ready for the conversation to be over, but they didn't budge. Oh great. The talk wasn't yet over.

"Yes?"

I was looking at Mom because she was the one who clearly had more to say. Her mouth was weirdly tense, and she was playing with the buttons on her cardigan as if they were puzzle pieces.

"*Beti,*" she said affectionately, which was strange, because her love language was sass. "Do you . . ."

"Mom, please. Just out with it, OK?"

She nodded primly. "OK? OK. I am *outing* with it. I am . . ."

"*Mom!*"

"Do you want us to set you up?"

My jaw dropped. Like, to the *floor.* I could practically hear it land on the hardwood, my jaw shattering every which way.

"But . . ." I sputtered. "*You* didn't even have an arranged marriage!"

Mom and Dad snuck a look at each other, sly and knowing and with so much intimacy they really shouldn't have expressed in front of their own child. They were both in their early twenties when they moved to the US, and their (very) old-fashioned meet-cute took place at the local *gurdwara*. They weren't introduced by family or friends, so it was technically a love marriage, but from the stories I heard, they matched so well they might as well have been arranged. They were both raised in the Sikh faith. Tick. They both valued their Punjabi heritage and family values. Tick tick. So within five months of first laying eyes on each other over plates of *aloo paratha* in the *langar* hall below the prayer room, they were married.

Triple tick.

"We didn't have an arranged marriage, no," Dad said, looking back at me. "And we are not suggesting this for you."

"Exactly." Mom cleared her throat. "We are just saying *if* you were to be interested in meeting someone, outside of the apps, then maybe we know somebody." She paused, searching my face. "Maybe you could go for coffee, and if you like each other, you can—"

"Bang?"

Dad blushed, while Mom pretended not to hear me.

"Niki, you can date *normally*. We will not interfere. We don't even know the boy." Mom sighed. "He is nephew of our friends. Apparently, very sweet. *Modern*. A doctor—"

"Wow, a doctor? Sign me up!"

"We do not approach you with this lightly," Mom continued, ignoring me. Her voice was suddenly small and weak, and it made me feel terrible. Like a terrible daughter who, despite every effort to the contrary, had somehow still managed to disappoint them.

"You know"—she turned to Dad and placed her hand tenderly on his beard—"we were Niki's age when we were married."

Their body language mirrored the romantic cheek hold going on in the background between Matthew and Jennifer, and for the first time in a long time, I *felt* very single.

Were my parents trying to make me feel worse than I already did?

No. They weren't cruel. They were a little cheeky, intrusive, and condescending at times, but they were good parents. The best, actually.

And I, being the good daughter that I was, told them to give their friend's nephew my phone number.

**Sonya Lalli** is a romance and women's fiction author of Punjabi and Bengali heritage. Her debut novel, *The Matchmaker's List*, was a Target Diverse Book Club Pick, and Sonya's books have been featured in *Entertainment Weekly*, *USA Today*, NPR, *The Washington Post*, *Glamour*, and more. She also writes psychological thrillers as S. C. Lalli. Sonya lives in Vancouver with her husband and their mini goldendoodle, Joey.

Ready to find
your next great read?

Let us help.

**Visit prh.com/nextread**